THE FORGOTTEN CHASE

Also by Cap Daniels

THE
FORGOTTEN CHASE

CHASE FULTON NOVEL #9

CAP DANIELS

ANCHOR WATCH
PUBLISHING
** USA **

The Forgotten Chase
Chase Fulton Novel #9
Cap Daniels

This is a work of fiction. Names, characters, places, historical events, and incidents are the product of the author's imagination or have been used fictitiously. Although many locations such as marinas, airports, hotels, restaurants, etc. used in this work actually exist, they are used fictitiously and may have been relocated, exaggerated, or otherwise modified by creative license for the purpose of this work. Although many characters are based on personalities, physical attributes, skills, or intellect of actual individuals, all of the characters in this work are products of the author's imagination.

Published by:

ANCHOR WATCH
PUBLISHING
** USA **

13 Digit ISBN: 978-1-951021-01-6
Library of Congress Control Number: 2020931339
Copyright © 2020 Cap Daniels—All Rights Reserved

Cover Design: German Creative

Printed in the United States of America

Dedication

This book is dedicated to . . .

My beloved sister Teri.

My sister was sixteen years old when I was born fifty years ago on a snow-covered January day in East Tennessee. She was a stranger to the cold, blowing snow of the Appalachian Mountains, having spent the bulk of her young life in the golden sunshine on the beaches of Florida where our father served aboard seagoing Naval vessels. To say the least, East Tennessee was not paradise for a sixteen-year-old Florida girl.

Naturally, I have no memory of that day, but Teri says that ugly little newborn baby boy was the only thing that made life so far away from the beach remotely tolerable. I grew to be a terrible thorn in her side, but I blame her for that. She spoiled me as if I were her own beloved child. She is THE reason I reached adulthood expecting the world to give me everything I wanted—because that's exactly what she gave me every day of my childhood.

I'll never possess the wealth to repay her, nor will I ever have the words to adequately thank her for the love without limits she's shown me every moment since the day I entered the world. She is a remark-

able woman of enormous character, brilliance, and compassion. I would not be the man I am, nor would I have the self-confidence to create these novels without the foundation of love, faith, and limitless potential my sister built for me as I grew from a helpless child into the man I've become.

To my sister Teri, I wish to say:

I love, respect, admire, and treasure you beyond the boundaries of life itself. Thank you for the countless sacrifices you've made for me and for the love you've shown and taught me for half a century.

Special Thanks To:

My Remarkable Editor:
Sarah Flores—Write Down the Line, LLC
www.WriteDowntheLine.com

Sarah has become such an integral part of the creation of this series that it is impossible to determine where my creation ends and hers begins. She continues to be the greatest teacher I've ever known and a magnificent friend. Five times a year, she turns my error-filled stories into books that are enjoyed by thousands of readers all over the world. I treasure her involvement in the creation of this series and pray that I never see the day when I have to do this without her.

My friend:
MSgt Todd M. Wilbanks, USMC Retired

Todd signed on to be a beta reader between books two and three, and since then, he and I have formed a friendship based in mutual respect and shared history. Although never simultaneously, Todd and I have left boot prints in the same sand ten thousand miles from home and lost friends we loved in those desolate, godforsaken places. I am grateful for both Todd's friendship and his selfless service to the greatest country on the Earth. Semper fi.

The Forgotten Chase
CAP DANIELS

Chapter 1
Spy School

"Welcome aboard. I'm Commander Jenkins, and this is Dr. Sims, our medical officer."

I offered my hand. "I'm Chase Fulton. Thanks for picking us up, commander. It was getting a little hard to breathe out there."

Having never been aboard an American nuclear submarine, I found myself at a significant disadvantage. Until recently, my partner, Stone Hunter, had been chief of security at the Kings Bay Naval Submarine Base near Saint Marys, Georgia. My other traveling companion for the trip was former Russian SVR officer and assassin, Anastasia "Anya" Burinkova. I doubted if she'd been given a peek inside an American sub, but after all I'd been through with her, nothing would surprise me.

The most recent adventure that landed the three of us aboard the sub, prowling the depths of the Black Sea off the Russian coast, was perhaps my most daring to date. I'd discovered the Russian Intelligence Service wanted to have me drawn and quartered on the steps of the Kremlin, so I hatched an ingenious plan to give them exactly what they wanted . . . almost. With the help of the good ol' American Navy, we let the Russians watch as Anya torched *Aegis*, my fifty-foot sailing catamaran, sending it, and all hands aboard, to the bottom of the Black Sea a couple dozen miles off the coast of Sochi. Fortunately for me, what the Russians believed to be *Aegis* was actually the shell of a boat built to look identical to mine and designed to sink quickly and convincingly. By all indications, it had worked perfectly, and Hunter, Anya, and I escaped into the welcoming arms of Commander Jenkins aboard the nuclear submarine U.S.S. *Tennessee*.

Commander Jenkins stared at Anya, but not the way most men do. Instead of desire, his eyes were full of what I perceived as dread. "We need to get you wrapped up and tucked away, ma'am. I've got a hundred forty-four sailors on this boat who've not seen a woman in seven weeks, and probably haven't seen a woman like you their whole lives."

"I will try to look not pretty," Anya said in her heavily Russian-accented English.

When I met her nearly six years before, I'd fallen head over heels in love with everything I thought I knew about the striking Russian. The way she looked was only the tip of the iceberg. Her accent back then wasn't as strong since she'd been practicing English for a decade for the sole purpose of seducing, interrogating, and flipping an American operative. I was that lucky operative. Our romantic relationship was relatively brief but agonizing. Most importantly, though, it was over.

Jenkins chuckled. "Ma'am, I'm afraid you're going to have a tough time pulling that one off, especially in the eyes of my crew."

The commander turned to Hunter. "Let me guess. It's your job to keep these two out of trouble."

My partner shook the commander's hand. "No, sir. Even I can't pull that one off. I'm just here to keep 'em alive. I'm Stone Hunter."

"Nice to meet you, Stone. Welcome aboard the U.S.S. *Tennessee*, SSBN-734, an old Ohio class, ballistic missile sub that was built . . ." He paused and shot Anya a look. "Well, she was built to keep *her* comrades in check."

Anya raised a dripping-wet eyebrow. "*Former* comrades. I am now with new comrades who have much better manners."

"Okay, then," the commander said. "To keep her *former* comrades in check." He turned to the medical officer. "Give them a quick once-over, and I'll rustle up something to throw over her head until we can get them tucked away."

By the time Commander Jenkins returned, the doctor had shined his penlight in our eyes, taken our blood pressure, and counted heartbeats. "They're just fine, skipper."

"Thanks, doc. I've got Staff Sergeant Bell on the way up to escort them to sick bay."

The commander handed each of us a towel and a stack of dry clothes. "Get these on, and pull that hood over your head, ma'am. It won't be possible to parade the three of you through my boat without at least some of the crew getting a look at you. We're in the business of keeping secrets, but this one isn't our normal variety. It's not every day we pluck three spies out of the Black Sea."

In what must've appeared to be practiced unison, Hunter and I said, "We're not spies." Anya, on the other hand, didn't say a word.

Our saltwater-soaked clothes hit the deck, and we dried ourselves with the sandpaper the Navy called towels. Hunter was struggling to keep his eyes in his head with Anya only inches away and wearing nothing but goosebumps. We dressed in sweatpants and shirts with *Navy* stenciled across the chests. Anya's sweatshirt was big enough for all three of us to wear at the same time.

A disembodied voice filled the compartment. "Are you ready to go, sir?"

I turned, expecting to see our escort, but no one was there. "Uh, yeah, we're ready."

A hatch opened, and through it came the head of a young Marine. "I'm Staff Sergeant Bell, and this is Sergeant Washington. We're from the Marine Detachment, US Embassy, Romania.

We've been assigned to the U.S.S. *Tennessee* specifically for this mission. Sir, if you'll follow me, we'll escort you to sick bay. Mr. Fulton in front, and Mr. Hunter in the rear, please."

Their presence and mission were underscored by the Monadnock PR 24s on their left hips and the Beretta M9s on their right. They executed their strides with determined purpose.

At six-foot-four and two hundred twenty pounds, I made a fine shield to hide Anya, but Hunter, being only a couple of inches taller than her, would've provided little concealment. Not being particularly concerned with anyone noticing the baggy sweatpants and shirt from behind, we followed Staff Sergeant Bell's instructions and formed a single-file line.

Having the chief of naval operations order a detachment of Marines aboard especially for our mission felt like overkill, but who was I to question decisions made at that level? Beyond my confusion over such a decision, I was secretly glad they were on board.

"Make a hole! Coming through!" the sergeant ordered as we traversed the interior of the massive sub.

At my size, the hatches proved to be a bit of a challenge, but Anya and Hunter ducked through them, barely breaking stride. Sailors clad in navy-blue uniforms scampered about the boat doing whatever submariners do. Life aboard *Aegis* was relaxing and comfortable. Life aboard the U.S.S. *Tennessee* was going to be neither.

"Make a hole!" he ordered again as we met a group of four sailors staring at a panel of gauges, valves, and electronics more complex than anything aboard my boat. The four men pressed themselves against the bulkhead, making room for us to pass. As we stepped through the hatch behind the sailors, Anya quietly gasped.

Instinctually, I turned. "What is it?"

She shook her head in a crisp movement and shoved me forward, her face invisible beneath the bulky hood of the Navy sweatshirt. Hunter noticed our exchange and spun on his heel, apparently trying to find what had caught Anya's attention. Sergeant Washington put his hand on Hunter's shoulder, encouraging him to continue down the corridor, and my partner knocked the man's hand from his shoulder with one swift, decisive motion.

When we reached sick bay, we found the outer hatches manned by two Marine corporals at parade rest. They promptly snapped to and opened the hatches for the five of us to squeeze inside. The compartment held four cots and a large light suspended from an arm, reminding me of something I'd seen in a hospital operating room.

Bell and Washington deposited us inside and turned to leave, but Hunter was still steaming over the hand-on-the-shoulder stunt Washington pulled in the corridor.

Hunter grabbed the sergeant by the arm. "Listen to me, Marine. If you ever put your hands on me again . . ."

Washington leaned in, his eyes narrowed, and I was afraid I was about to witness my partner deck a U.S. Marine in a tiny compartment aboard an American nuclear submarine.

Washington said, "Stone Hunter? Is that you?"

My partner formed a tight fist with his right hand, but paused, staring back at the young Marine. "Jimmy Washington? What are you doing on a sub in the Black Sea?"

Hunter unclenched his fist, and Washington smiled. "After I left Kings Bay, I got picked up for embassy duty, thanks mostly to that letter you wrote for me. I owe you one, chief."

Hunter turned to me. "This kid worked for me at Kings Bay for eight months, but he was a lowly little lance corporal back then. Look at him now, all grown up with his sergeant stripes."

The two men shook hands, and Hunter pulled him in for a brief man hug.

Hunter withdrew and stuck his finger back in Washington's face. "Old friends or not, if you ever put your hands on me again, you're going to find out how a size ten boot feels in your ass."

Washington looked down and laughed. "Ha. Those are clearly size nines, and if you try it, you'll draw back a nub . . . sir."

Bell and Washington disappeared through the hatch and into the corridor.

Anya pulled the hood from her head, exposing an amused smile. "I know why you like him, Chasechka. He is just like Clark."

Hunter pointed toward Anya. "I'm gonna take that as a compliment, little lady."

"It is compliment," she said, "but I know why Marine put hands on you."

The hatch reopened, and Dr. Sims came into the room. "Okay, welcome to Sick Bay Two. This'll be your home for the duration of the cruise. I've not been briefed on how long you'll be aboard, but we can't exactly let you roam around a ballistic missile sub."

"I need to get a transmission off, letting somebody know we're alive," I said, interrupting the doctor.

"That's already been done. Our orders for this mission came straight from the chief of naval operations, so we floated the commo buoy and sent a coded message as soon as the three of you were safely aboard."

"Thank you for that, but there are some other people who will be worrying about us if we don't let them know we're okay."

"I'm sorry, Mr. Fulton, but we're running deep, and we won't be surfacing anytime soon."

Thoughts of my wife, Penny, wondering where I was and if I was still alive poured through my mind. I had to find a way to let her know I was alive and well.

The doctor continued his briefing. "Your meals will be brought to you here"—he pointed toward a door in the corner of the cramped space—"and there's a head and shower through that hatch. Does everyone feel all right? No headaches, blurred vision, dizziness, signs of decompression sickness?"

The three of us shook our heads.

"Okay, then. There will be a Marine on the hatch around the clock. If you need anything, let him know. One of my corpsmen or I will check on you regularly. In the meantime, make yourselves at home, and try not to make a lot of noise."

"So, we're stuck in here?" I asked.

"Until the skipper says differently," the doctor said, "I'm afraid so."

"Tell him I'd like to speak with him when he has a moment."

The doctor nodded and closed the hatch as he moved down the corridor and away from Sick Bay 2, our new home away from home.

Hunter sat on the cot beside Anya. "What were you saying about why Washington tried to shove me around out there?"

She looked up at me. "I can say to him anything, yes?"

"Yeah, but I wouldn't recommend grabbing his shoulder. He seems to be a little touchy about that."

"There was man in corridor. His uniform says Smith, but his name is not Smith. Is Gregory Sidorov."

Anya had our attention.

I said, "How can you be so sure? You saw him for less than a second."

"He has scar below left ear in shape of crescent moon. I gave to him this scar when I was girl of only thirteen. I was in state school with Gregory."

Hunter held up a finger. "Wait a minute. Are you telling us a Russian you went to spy school with is on this sub?"

"It was not spy school. It was fighting school. This is where I learn fighting with knife, and yes, Gregory Sidorov was in same school with me."

I closed my eyes, trying to calculate the unimaginable odds of Anya seeing someone she knew on an American nuclear submarine. "Did he see you?"

"I think he did not because of hood."

The implications of what Anya was suggesting were impossible to imagine, but I had no choice in what I had to do next. I turned the latch to open the door into the corridor, but found it wouldn't budge, so I sent my fist into the metal hatch several times. "Guard!"

Seconds later, it opened a few inches, and a Marine stuck his head into the space. "What is it, sir?"

"I need to see the captain immediately."

Chapter 2
That Dog Can Hunt

Apparently, when an American covert operative who recently sunk a sailboat and is trunked aboard a submarine in the Black Sea asks to see the captain, everything else can wait. Commander Jenkins knocked on the door of Sick Bay 2 before I could question Anya any further about the man she believed to be Gregory Sidorov.

"The Marines seem to think you need to talk with me," the skipper said as he squeezed into the compartment.

"Thanks for coming so quickly. It's actually Anya who needs to speak with you. She made a discovery I think you're going to want to hear."

The seasoned sub commander raised his eyebrows and turned to Anya. "Okay, let's hear this discovery of yours, ma'am. I've got a boat to run, so I'd like to keep this as brief as possible."

Anya licked her lips and glanced at me as if asking permission to speak. I nodded, and she started talking. "When Staff Sergeant Bell brought us through submarine, I saw man in uniform."

Jenkins glanced at his watch. "We've got a hundred and forty-five men in uniform on this boat, including me. Please tell me this story is going somewhere meaningful."

Anya's tone turned sharp. "Is going someplace deadly, commander. You should listen to me."

Commander Jenkins let out a long, impatient breath, and Anya continued. "This man was wearing uniform of petty officer first class electronic technician nuclear, and name on his uniform was Smith."

With impatience peppering every syllable, Jenkins said, "Yes, Petty Officer Greg Smith is one of the finest nuclear reactor operators in the sub service. I handpicked him for my crew, and I'm lucky to have him."

"His name is not Greg Smith, commander. Is Gregory Sidorov, and he is agent of Russian government."

Commander Jenkins pulled his glasses from his face and pointed the stem at Anya. "Now you listen to me, lady. You're a guest on my boat, and Greg Smith is one of the finest sailors in the Navy, on the fast track to chief, as a matter of fact. He knows as much or more about this submarine as I do. If you're going to accuse one of my sailors—"

Anya narrowed her eyes. "How did he get scar below left ear?"

Jenkins shook his head. "What?"

"He has scar below left ear. How did he get this scar?"

"I don't know. You spend enough time on boats, you're going to get hurt."

Barely above a whisper, Anya said, "I gave to him this scar when I was teenage girl in state school near Moscow. Before I defect, I was Russian SVR officer, and Gregory Sidorov is same."

Jenkins turned sharply to me. "How much of this can you confirm?"

I shot a quick glance toward Anya and then back at Jenkins. "I can't vouch for the time she and Sidorov spent at the state school, but she was definitely a Russian SVR operative. I've got the scars to prove it."

Jenkins closed his eyes and let two contemplative breaths make their way through his chest. When he reopened his eyes, they were laser-focused on Anya. "Do not leave this compartment. I'll be back in five minutes." With that, he rose and secured the hatch behind him as he paced down the corridor.

Hunter picked at his teeth with a toothpick he'd magically acquired from someplace. "Well, that was interesting, Red Sonja. It looks like you really know how to shake things up on a Navy sub."

Anya ignored him and glared at me. "Is him, Chase. I know this."

It was me she was trying to convince. I'd made no effort to hide my distrust, and I doubted if there was anything she could ever do to regain the confidence I once had in her.

Faith is a delicate and fickle psychological phenomenon. The innocence of youth places little value on faith. We tend to trust those around us until the day inevitably comes when someone betrays an unspoken pact—shreds a contract we hadn't realized existed. That is often the first hammerblow to chip away at the naiveté of the young. That's the day trust becomes more than a word, more than an unspoken expectation—the day we begin to tighten our circle and start to understand the difference between friendship and acquaintance, between telling the truth and not lying.

"I've seen what you can become, Anya. I've watched you change like a chameleon to serve your masters and to save yourself when the situation demanded, so you'll understand if I'm hesitant to take you at your word. Honestly, I'm running scenarios through my head, trying to determine how you could be manipulating the captain of a U.S. Navy submarine to benefit yourself."

It may've been the acting skill she'd developed in training, but on any other face, the look in her eyes would've been genuinely pained disappointment.

"I have not always worked only to save myself." She turned her back to me as she pulled the baggy sweatshirt over her head, revealing the nine-millimeter entry wound scar near her shoulder blade.

She earned that scar saving my life and the life of the woman I considered to be my sister, my operational analyst, Elizabeth "Skipper" Woodley.

Before I could react, the compartment door burst open, and Commander Jenkins pushed through the space. Anya lowered her sweatshirt, and Jenkins threw a blue file folder, bound with a thick rubber band, onto the cot between her and Hunter. "He had the scar when he joined the Navy. According to his personnel record"—he pointed toward the file—"he told the doctor at MEPS it was from a bicycle accident when he was thirteen."

Hunter lifted the file and removed its rubber band. I'd never seen a Navy personnel file, so I didn't know if it was thicker or thinner than it should've been, but he thumbed through the pages as if he were a career personnel clerk. After embarking on another mining endeavor with his toothpick, he said, "How many kids do you know who grew up in downtown Chicago and owned a bicycle?"

Anya cocked her head. "Gregory Sidorov was born in Moscow, not Chicago."

Hunter waved the file. "His jacket says he was born and raised in the Windy City."

"Is sometimes windy in Moscow."

Commander Jenkins lifted a handset from the bulkhead. "This is the captain. Detain Petty Officer Greg Smith, and inform the XO it was done on my order. I'm on my way to the con." He deposited the handset back into its cradle, snatched the file from Hunter, and even more quickly than before, he was gone.

"It looks like you convinced the skipper," I said.

Anya frowned. "I am confused. Skipper is analyst and sister to you, but also Commander Jenkins is skipper, no?"

"Yeah," I said, "it's one of those bizarre English things. I call Skipper that name because she used to skip when she walked. Anyway, the men on the sub call Commander Jenkins *skipper* as an informal term for captain of the ship."

"So, two kinds of skipper, yes?"

"Yes, exactly. So, back to the issue at hand. It looks like Jenkins believes you."

Hunter sucked air through his teeth. "Actually, I'm not convinced he believes you yet. It looks to me like he's erring on the side of caution until he can get things figured out. If Anya's right about Smith being Sidorov, that's too big a chance for Jenkins to take without looking into it. If she's wrong, he'll apologize to Smith, and it'll be business as usual."

Anya looked up at me. "Chasechka—"

I held up a hand. "Let's just go with Chase from now on, okay? No more Chasechka."

She blinked and pretended to smile. "Okay, Chase. I know you do not trust me now, and maybe never, but I have no reason to lie to you. You save my life two times, and now I am going to America forever. There is for me no gain to lie."

"I'm afraid there's too much water under that bridge, Anya."

The look on her face said she'd never understand that phrase, but perhaps out of some sense of misplaced anger, I made no effort to clear it up for her.

* * *

Exhaustion outweighed our curiosity over what might be happening outside our door, and soon, the three of us were sound asleep.

When my body had sufficiently recharged, I opened my eyes to see Hunter sitting on a stool, watching Anya sleep. "Don't get those thoughts in your head, partner. She looks like that on the outside, but it's only skin deep. She's a scorpion. I know first-hand."

The corners of his mouth turned downward. "No, it's not like that. I was just thinking what her life must've been like, you know?"

I sat up on my cot. "It wasn't great. I'll tell you that. Her mother was murdered when she was four or five, and she spent the next twenty years training to snare me. Well, not *me* specifically, but someone like me. I just happened to be the first trail she sniffed, and when that girl trees you, you know you've been caught."

He nodded. "Yeah, I get it, but don't you think you're being a little tough on her?"

I let my eyes drift across her beautiful, peaceful form as she slept like a child. "I don't have a choice. If I don't shove her away, I'll end up right back at the top of that tree where she keeps her honeypot. I'm not letting that girl bag me again."

Chapter 3
Fight Like a Girl

Time aboard a submarine is measured in hours and minutes, just like on the surface, but submerged, the hour hand has little meaning. There's no difference between 3:00 a.m. and noon aboard a sub. My watch was the only device in Sick Bay 2 that gave me any connection to the dry world hundreds of feet above our heads.

Two sharp raps came on the hatch before Jenkins and another slightly younger, but equally commanding man entered our space.

"Good afternoon," Jenkins began. "I'm sorry we have to keep you tucked away in here, but I'm sure you understand." He turned to the man who'd entered the compartment with him. "This is Lieutenant Commander Mitchem, my executive officer."

We rose and shook Commander Mitchem's hand. He shook our hands out of courtesy but ignored almost everyone except Anya. "So, you're the one."

Anya met his gaze. "You are asking or telling?"

Mitchem squinted. "I'm not sure yet, but we need to talk."

"We *are* talking," Anya replied.

Mitchem took a seat and pulled out a small spiral-bound pad. "I was a Naval Intelligence officer before being promoted to serve as Commander Jenkins's XO on this boat, so this situation with Petty Officer Smith has become my little freak show."

Anya said, "I do not know this word, freak show, but his name is not Smith. Is Gregory Sidorov."

Mitchem crossed his legs. "That's what I hear, but so far, he denies that accusation, and I'm having second thoughts about questioning the loyalty of a sailor who's building an exemplary career in the Navy, when all I've got to go on is the word of a former Russian spy who spotted him from beneath a hood for part of a second in a dark corridor. I'm sure you're starting to understand my hesitation, Ms. Burinkova."

"Is Fulton, not Burinkova, and give to me paper and pencil."

Mitchem reluctantly handed his pad and pen to Anya, then she scribbled several lines of Cyrillic script. "Give to him this, and watch pinky finger on left hand."

He took the pad from her and stared down at the page. "What does it say?"

"You would not believe me if I tell you. Give to linguist or ask Chase."

He turned sharply to me. "You read Cyrillic?"

"Some," I said.

He tossed the pad to me. "Translate that on the next page."

I caught the pad and studied the Cyrillic script. I couldn't suppress my smile as I reached for Mitchem's pen.

I wrote, *Major Kochenkov says the girl will continue to defeat you until you stop perceiving her as a girl and start seeing her as a fighter.*

Mitchem opened the hatch and spoke to the Marine outside. "Find Lieutenant Warren, and get him in here double-quick."

"Yes, sir," came the Marine's obedient reply.

The XO read my translation and then stared at Anya. I wasn't enjoying confinement on Commander Jenkins's submarine, and

I was starting to enjoy the XO's interrogation even less. A rap came on the door, and Mitchem stepped into the corridor.

Seconds later, he returned with what I assumed was Lieutenant Warren's translation of Anya's Cyrillic. "All right, Ms. Burinkova, I'm going to read you two English translations, and you're going to tell me which one is closer to what you wrote."

He read mine first and then unfolded Lieutenant Warren's. "Major Kochenkov said the bitch will kill you if you don't look at her like a fighter instead of a schoolgirl."

Anya smiled. "Is Fulton, not Burinkova. I told you this already. Intelligence officer should remember such things. Russian does not translate perfectly into English, but second is more accurate than first."

Mitchem wadded the two translations into tight paper balls and tossed them into a can in the corner of the space. "So, what am I going to see Petty Officer Smith's left pinky finger do when he reads your little note?"

"Every officer has nervous reaction outside of their control. Mine is twitch in nose. Sidorov cannot stop left small finger curling when caught in lie." She pointed toward the script she'd written. "When I gave to him scar below ear, this is what commandant of school said to him."

Forty-five minutes later, Lieutenant Commander Mitchem, Navy Intelligence officer turned second-in-command of the U.S.S. *Tennessee*, was back in Sick Bay 2 with one hundred forty-two pictures of sailors serving aboard the sub. The only three missing were the skipper, Mitchem, and Gregory Sidorov.

"Do you recognize any other members of my crew, Ms. Fulton?"

Anya smiled. "Gregory's finger twitched, no?"

"Just look at the pictures, please."

After nearly an hour of carefully examining every picture, she said, "I do not think I have ever seen any of these men before."

The XO gathered his pictures and turned to me. "We're floating the commo buoy, and the skipper says you have a message you'd like to get off."

"I sure do."

He glanced at his watch and then slid a black satchel toward me with his foot. "There's a pair of clippers and a razor in there, along with a uniform. Have one of these two do something with the mop on your head, and get rid of that beard. You've got thirty minutes to look like a naval officer. We'll have someone escort you to the con when you're ready."

Penny Fulton would lose her mind if she thought Anya was cutting my hair, so the task fell to Hunter, who made great sport of the endeavor. Twenty minutes later, I could've passed for a Naval Academy grad . . . almost.

"You look good in uniform, Chasechka. Is where true heart is."

I didn't understand exactly what she meant, but I said, "Thanks, but no more Chasechka."

Hunter laughed. "You can wear that lieutenant junior grade bar all you want, but I ain't never gonna salute you or call you sir."

I scowled down at him. "You'd better stand at attention when you talk to me, *Sergeant* Hunter."

He gave me the single-finger salute I expected. "I wish Clark could see this crap."

* * *

"Diving officer, take us to periscope depth if you please." Commander Jenkins's orders weren't barked as I'd seen on TV. He was soft-spoken but undoubtedly in charge.

"Periscope depth, aye, sir."

"Welcome to the con, Lieutenant"—Jenkins squinted at the name tape on my chest—"Jones. Rumor has it you'd like to pull an E.T. and phone home. It's lunchtime on the East Coast, so somebody will probably pick up when the phone rings."

"Thank you, skipper. I appreciate that."

He shot me a quick wink and turned back toward the bow— at least I assumed the bow was that direction.

Jenkins ordered, "Float the buoy."

"Float the buoy, aye, sir."

Jenkins leaned in and pointed toward a sailor sitting in front of a massive array of electronics. "Tell him the number you want to call."

I gave the sailor Penny's number, and Jenkins continued calling out instructions to his crew. "Comms, send the packet."

"Send the packet, aye, sir."

Several seconds passed, and the communications officer reported, "Packet sent and receipt acknowledged, sir."

"Thank you, comms. Now, let's dial that number for Lieutenant Jones."

"Aye, sir."

Jenkins removed a handset from a cradle overhead and handed it to me. "Thirty seconds, Lieutenant."

I nodded. "Thirty seconds, aye, sir."

He grinned.

I listened through cracks, scratches, and beeps until Penny's electronic voice filled the earpiece.

"Hello?"

"Hello, Mrs. Fulton. I thought you might like to know I'm alive and well."

I had to pull the handset away from my ear as she squealed in delight.

"I've only got a few seconds, but I want to let you know we're safe and dry, and tell Maebelle to fix three plates. We'll be home soon. I love you."

Jenkins reached for the handset and returned it to its cradle. "I'm sorry, but that's it. XO has the con."

Lieutenant Commander Mitchem replied, "I have the con."

Jenkins led me to his cabin and secured the door behind us. "Chase, it looks like your girl was right. We'll be turning Smith —or Sidorov—over to the CIA tomorrow morning off the coast of Greece in the Southern Aegean. You and your team will see the sun the day after tomorrow in Sicily."

"She's not my girl, skipper, but I'm glad to hear she wasn't playing games."

"No, son, she wasn't, and she did America quite a favor picking Sidorov out like that. I don't know what's in store for her, but if what she did here is any indication, I think she's going to be a fine addition to the American intelligence community."

"I'm glad to hear all of that, skipper, but I've got to tell you, part of me was hoping Anya was wrong about Sidorov. The thought of the Russians being able to put an agent on board an American nuclear sub scares the hell out of me."

Jenkins took two more of his trademark deep breaths. "All of me was hoping she was wrong. This is far from over. Sidorov isn't the only one, and I'm sure of that. The Navy is going to have one hell of a time sniffing them out. Something tells me they'll be calling your traveling companion for a little help."

"We all need a hobby, and picking out Russians sounds like one she's pretty good at."

Jenkins patted my shoulder. "Go share the good news with your team, and keep the uniform. From what I hear, you've earned the privilege."

* * *

Surprised that I was allowed to roam about the sub unescorted, I returned to my compartment. "They're handing Sidorov to the

CIA tomorrow before we leave the Aegean for the Med, and then we'll be getting off the next day in Sicily."

Hunter beamed. "That's great news. I've got nothing against subs in general, but I'll be glad to get off this tub and see the sky again."

"What will your CIA do to Sidorov?" Anya asked.

I shrugged. "I don't know. That's not my world, but he'll be given an opportunity to cooperate. I'm sure of that. And it's not only *my* CIA, by the way. Now it's yours, too."

"He will not cooperate. He will find way to kill himself."

"Maybe you're right," I said, "but they'll keep a close eye on him."

"They will torture him, no?"

"No, that's not what we do. Not at first, anyway."

"Yes, I am sure he will kill himself," she said again.

I let my eyes meet hers. "You didn't try to kill yourself when the CIA had you in custody."

Her mischievous smile appeared. "That is because I am not like Gregory Sidorov. I fight like girl."

Chapter 4
I Should've Known

Commander Jenkins's timetable wasn't as accurate as I'd expected. Instead of spending just two more nights in captivity, we endured three, but the food was good, and surprisingly, we caught up on some much-needed sleep.

Jenkins knocked once and stuck his head into our compartment. "Ma'am, we're going to need you incognito again, so break out the hoodie. You two can wear whatever you want. It's eighty-five degrees and sunny over the Med this morning. Your ride will be here in ten minutes."

"And what's our ride?" I asked.

The commander grinned. "You'll see."

Right on time, a pair of Marines showed up to escort us from what had been our home sweet home for far too long.

"I think I'm going to miss the *Tennessee*," I said as I ducked through the hatch.

Anya rolled her eyes. "I think you will not. You have beautiful wife and honeymoon to finish."

Just as we'd been lined up when we came aboard, I followed the lead Marine with Hunter in the rear and Anya sandwiched between us. Thankfully, we didn't encounter anymore Russians masquerading as American sailors.

I'd never seen the sky look more beautiful. Even though I'd been aboard the sub for less than a week, I felt like a man just released from prison when I climbed through the hatch and onto the exterior deck of the *Tennessee*.

I should've known disembarking would be almost as much of an adventure as coming aboard. Hovering forty feet overhead was an SH-60 Seahawk helicopter.

"So, I guess that's our ride, huh?"

Commander Jenkins shielded his eyes against the bright morning sun. "Yep, that'd be her. It was a pleasure having you and your team aboard, Chase. You're welcome back anytime."

I shook his hand. "Thanks for everything, skipper, and I appreciate the offer, but I'll be honest—I'm much happier up here than down there."

He scanned the horizon. "Not me. Down there is where I belong. Sailors should be on ships, and ships should be at sea. Land is but a hazard to navigation and a place to birth new sailors."

Hunter said, "We sure appreciate what you did for us, commander."

"I'm the one who should be thanking the three of you. Especially you, ma'am. Who knows what might've happened if you hadn't discovered Sidorov on my boat. The free world owes you a debt of gratitude."

Anya peered from beneath the hood. "There are more."

Jenkins nodded. "Yeah, I'm sure you're right, and you'll no doubt be involved in plucking them out."

"I will do what is asked of me."

"Me, too, ma'am," Jenkins said, looking skyward. "Here comes the elevator. It's time for me to head back inside. Enjoy the ride, and keep fighting the good fight." He gave a crisp salute and made his way back inside his tin-can home.

A member of the helicopter crew descended from the hovering Seahawk on a thin cable. The man handed a pair of harnesses to Hunter and me and then helped the hooded Anya into hers. Over the sound of the rotors above and the swirling wind, the man threw his hands into the air. "Whoa! You're not a dude."

Anya pulled the hood from her head and laughed. "No, I am not dude, but is okay for you to finish with harness. I will not bite you."

He looked up at me, and I shrugged. "I wouldn't trust her if I were you," I said. "She's definitely a biter."

A moment later, Anya and the crewman were ascending to the waiting helicopter.

When the three of us were safely aboard, the pilots lowered the nose and turned to the north. Before we'd flown a mile, the sub was, once again, submerged and silently prowling the depths.

The crewman stowed the hoist cable and removed his harness. "Welcome aboard. I'm Petty Officer Clinton. Would any of you like a water or Gatorade?"

"Nice to meet you, Clinton. I'm Chase, and this is Hunter and Anya."

He stared at the Russian. "I wasn't expecting . . ."

"Is okay, Petty Officer. I was not expecting to ride on cable to helicopter, either. I would like to have water, please."

"Ma'am, you can have anything you want."

She shot a glance toward me. "This is not true. I cannot have *everything* I want."

Clinton wiped his brow. "You can from me, ma'am."

We drank our bottled water and watched the Mediterranean Sea drift beneath us at 140 knots until a coastline came into view to the northwest.

I tapped Clinton on the knee with my water bottle. "Where are we?"

He leaned toward the door and scanned the horizon. "That's Sicily over there, and we're approaching the boot of Italy off the nose. We've got a little over an hour before we'll be back on deck."

"On the deck of what?" I asked.

"NSA Naples," he said. "Best food in the world."

"Better than submarine chow?" Hunter asked.

Clinton chuckled. "Well, maybe not quite as good as sub rations, but close."

"I didn't realize we had a naval air station in Naples," I said.

Clinton shook his head. "No, sir. It's Naval Support Activity Naples. NSA, not NAS."

I was suddenly glad I hadn't worn the uniform. That would've been a dumb question from a naval officer.

Hunter scratched his chin. "If my memory serves, NSA Naples is on the International Airport."

I checked my watch. "That'll come in handy. If all goes well, we'll be feet dry in Georgia in less than forty-eight hours."

Anya leaned in. "That is Georgia in United States, no?"

I chuckled. "Yep. From now on, that's the only Georgia there is for you."

She smiled. "I can go to baseball match again there and have chilidog, yes?"

I took Anya to her first, and only, baseball game several years before in Athens where I'd once caught a few thousand fastballs crouched behind home plate at Foley Field. A perfectly timed foul ball, driven into the backstop net fifty feet in front of us, startled Anya, and she spilled her first chili dog all over herself. That felt as if it'd been another lifetime, and in many ways, it was.

"It's a baseball *game*, not a *match*," I said, "but yes, you can go to all the games you want and eat all the chili dogs your heart desires. I can probably even get you season tickets at UGA."

At that moment, I knew exactly what I'd do with Anya once the State Department and every other alphabet soup agency finished debriefing her.

We landed at NSA Naples and headed for base operations, where I could, as Commander Jenkins put it, pull an E.T. and phone home.

"Skipper, it's Chase."

"It's about time you called. We've been worried to death. Where are you?"

"We finished our cruise, and now we're in Naples. Do you think you can get us home?"

She huffed. "Ha! What kind of question is that? Of course I can get you home. I got you a submarine, didn't I? Compared to that, an airplane's a snap."

"Actually," I said, "I don't think you got us the submarine. I think that was a gift from the chief of naval operations."

"Minor details," she said. "Okay, you're booked on the four eighteen flight this afternoon. There aren't any non-stop flights, so you'll change planes in Paris and land in Atlanta twelve hours later. And before you say it, I know, I know . . . I'm the best."

"Yes, you are, Skipper. We'll see you in a couple of days. Now, I'd kind of like to hear my wife's voice if she's not too busy."

"She's on the phone, but you're never going to believe with whom."

"Let's hear it," I said.

"She's talking to somebody about her screenplay. I'll let her tell you the details, but it's exciting."

Skipper's tone made it clear she was almost bursting at the seams to spill the beans, but I didn't want her stealing Penny's thunder. "That's great news. Tell her I'll call before we get on the airplane this afternoon."

"I will, and I'll see you in a couple days."

* * *

Surprisingly, our passports survived the ordeal of sinking the dunker. The attaché from the U.S. Embassy made the required entries, including purple stamps, and Hunter, Anya, and I were officially and legally authorized to make the flight to Atlanta's Hartsfield International Airport. Although it was the end of a mission, the trip felt more like the beginning of a new assignment. Perhaps that's what my life had become: one long series of missions strung together by brief intermissions in the action.

Something would have to be done with Anya when we made it back to the U.S., but the State Department would be handling that. She wouldn't be joining my team anytime soon, if ever. Having her skillset on the team would be an enormous benefit, but it came with a truckload of baggage I neither wanted nor needed. Penny's insistence on bringing her back to the States was enough trouble in itself. Incorporating her into American operations was not a mission I was interested in taking on.

The officers and sailors of NSA Naples made us feel right at home, although the curious, and sometimes suspicious glances were impossible to ignore.

What are these spies doing in our midst? had to be the thought running through most of their heads, but fortunately, the time came to catch our flight before too many questions could be hurled our way.

To no one's surprise, Anya garnered more than her share of attention from the sailors. The bevy of dark-haired, olive-skinned Italian girls didn't stand a chance against the leggy blonde Russian. She made a show of touching arms and flashing her seductive smile, knowing all the while she could tear any one of their hearts out—both literally and figuratively.

The more I watched Anya work her magic, the more immune I became to her charm. It was all an act, ultimately devoid of sincerity and emotion. She had to be the valedictorian of her graduating class at State School 4, where cute Russian girls were trans-formed into seductive, irresistible Russian women.

Unlike my passport, my satellite phone hadn't survived the sinking. The man from the embassy was kind enough to issue me a new one straight from the cultural attaché's locker. I hope those guys know they're not fooling anyone; the whole world knows they're spies, even though they'd deny it as vehemently as I do.

"Is that you, Chase?" Penny asked seconds after I pushed the send button on my new sat-phone.

"It is. How are things in Georgia?"

"Things are amazing. I've got so much to tell you."

"I don't have a lot of time right now. Our flight is boarding, so let's hear the top two, and you can tell me the rest when we land."

"Okay, so first," she began, "remember the company who wanted an option on my screenplay?"

"Sure, I do."

"Well, they found a producer who wants to create a pilot episode for a potential miniseries, or maybe a prime-time series. Isn't that incredible?"

I couldn't hold back my smile. "No, Penny, that's not incredi-ble. It's exactly what I expected. That's great news. I'm so proud of you."

"Thank you. I love the way you support me when I have crazy ideas."

"There's nothing crazy about wanting to be a screenwriter. You're amazing, and I'll always support whatever you want to do."

Her tone turned somber. "The next thing I have to tell you isn't so great."

"What is it?"

"It's Clark. He's not doing well. They think he's got some kind of infection in his back. He's on his way to Emory Hospital now. Skipper and I are driving up."

"It must be serious if they're taking him to Emory," I said.

"It is, Chase. It's real serious."

"Okay. I'll be home tomorrow afternoon. Skipper has the flight information. Does she know what they're going to do with Anya when we get to Atlanta?"

"I don't know," she said, her voice softening. "She's on the phone with somebody about that right now. Call me from your layover, and I'll let you know what she finds out. Is she okay? I mean, are she and Hunter okay?"

"Yeah, they're fine. She was a big hit at the Navy base."

"Yeah, I'm sure. She's a big hit anywhere there's a group of guys."

"Don't tell him I said this," I whispered, "but I think Hunter was a little jealous when she was flirting with the sailors."

"Oh, Chase, you have to head that off. You can't let him—"

"He's a big boy. I've warned him, but he's hardheaded. Tell Clark I'm thinking about him, and keep me posted if anything changes. I'll call you from Paris."

"I will," she said. "I love you, and I can't wait to see you tomorrow."

* * *

The first leg of our flight home was uneventful except for two Belarusian flight attendants who enjoyed having someone else on the flight who spoke their language. Hunter appeared to be as smitten with the flight attendants as he was with Anya, so that helped ease my mind about her burying her claws in him.

My call to Penny, however, did nothing to comfort me.

Her tone sent chills down my spine. "It's worse than we thought, Chase."

Chapter 5
Agony

The eleven-hour flight from Charles de Gaulle to Hartsfield made me feel like a grain of sand at the top of the hourglass waiting my turn to fall through the neck. My anxiety over Clark's condition left me incapable of thinking of anything else until the captain pulled the 747 to the gate.

"Welcome to Atlanta, ladies and gentlemen. It's ninety-one degrees under partly cloudy skies. If you will, kindly keep your seats until we take care of a little business. There will be two people coming aboard to escort one of our passengers off the plane. I know you're anxious to get off, but I assure you it will only take a few more moments."

Hunter leaned toward me. "Do you think they're taking you off first to get you over to Emory?"

Anya spoke for the first time in hours. "No, is CIA coming for me. This is what I have expected. Thank you to both of you for everything. I am American in America now because of you. You will find me in some days, yes? And tell me of Clark?"

"Yes, of course I will, but it won't be the CIA. It's going to be a couple of guys from the State Department or maybe the FBI. They're not going to mistreat you," I assured her. "Be honest with them, about everything, and I'll see that you have a good place to live and maybe even some tickets to a baseball game or two."

She smiled, obviously pretending not to be nervous, and kissed me on the cheek. "Thank you, Chasechka. I promise will be last time I call you that name."

She turned to Hunter and kissed him a little less innocently, just in front of his left ear. "And to you, also thanks, *okhotnik*."

A man in a ninety-nine-dollar suit stood over Anya's right shoulder. "Please come with us, Ms. Fulton."

She stood and offered her wrists to be cuffed, but the man's expression said he had no idea why she'd be doing such a thing. "No, ma'am. You don't understand. We're here to welcome you to the States, not apprehend you."

Her smile overtook the expression of worry she'd worn for hours. "I am not to be arrested?"

"No, ma'am."

Every passenger watched Anya walk off the plane between the two men, then immediately sprang for the overhead bins and the gangway.

* * *

Penny's face lit up as if she hadn't seen me in months. Perhaps it had been that long. I didn't know what time it was, or even what month it happened to be.

Her arms flew around me in an enthusiastic embrace. "It's so good to have you home. I saw them take Anya away. Where are they taking her? What will they do with her? Do you know how to find her?"

I brushed her hair from her face. I loved the way her hair seemed to have a mind of its own and never cared what the rest of her body was doing.

"Slow down," I said. "She'll be fine. It's a little weird for you to be so worried about her."

"Oh, I'm not catty like that. After I really got to meet her in Alaska, I know I've got nothing to worry about. Sure, she's pretty and all, but she can't shoot fish and run a boat like me. And there is that one special thing I do for you that I bet she can't—or won't—do."

I grinned. "Well, there is that."

Penny flung her arms around Hunter only slightly less enthusiastically. "Welcome home, Hunter. How was the flight?"

"Long," he said. "How's Clark?"

Penny grabbed my hand. "You probably don't have any bags, do you?"

"No, we're empty-handed," I said.

"Good, 'cause we need to go. He's not doing very well."

Imagine watching a hundred thousand baby sea turtles hatch simultaneously and start their mad dash for the sea. That's what the Atlanta airport parking lots look like. Penny wisely found a way around that issue. I chose not to ask how she pulled it off, but waiting curbside as we left the terminal was a white SUV with "Emory Hospital Security" emblazoned down each side, and a set of flashing lights affixed to the roof.

The driver pulled away from the curb as if his life depended on escaping the airport, and soon, we were northbound into the city of six million souls. In a hospital bed somewhere downtown was the man from whom I'd learned more about staying alive than anyone else on Earth.

* * *

A lab-coat-clad man in his mid-fifties stuck out his hand. "I'm Dr. Pembroke."

"Chase Fulton. I'm Clark's partner."

The doctor looked back and forth between Penny and me as I impatiently waited for him to continue.

Finally, Penny cackled. "No, they're *business* partners. He's my husband."

Dr. Pembroke blushed. "I'm sorry. I wasn't putting the picture together. Forgive me."

"It's fine," I said, trying to hurry him along. "What can you tell us?"

"Oh, yes, of course. Mr. Johnson is suffering from vertebral osteomyelitis and discitis with epidural abscess. Essentially, that means he has a serious infection in his spine."

The lump in my throat grew as everything else I'd been thinking dissolved from my head. "So, what are you going to do about all of that?"

Dr. Pembroke cleared his throat. "Well, first, we've started him on aggressive IV antibiotics, but ultimately, a neurosurgeon will have to debride the affected tissue."

"I don't know what that means."

"In short, it means we'll clean and remove affected tissue from the spine to allow improved circulation, which will, in turn, promote healing."

"So, this is easily remedied?" I asked.

"No, it's not that simple. This is a very serious case, but we have some of the best neurosurgeons in the world right here in Atlanta. Your . . . partner . . . is in very good hands, and we'll do everything in our power to make sure he enjoys the best possible recovery."

"But he will recover, right?"

The doctor looked at the floor between my feet. "Time will tell, but this condition has gone untreated for several days, and it's impossible to know how much actual nerve damage has occurred."

"What do you mean several days?"

Penny put her hand on my arm. "Chase, you know how he is. He's been in a lot of pain, but he wouldn't tell anyone. We couldn't have known."

I pushed past the doctor and through the door into Clark's room. What I saw left me terrified.

In the time I'd been gone, Clark had lost so much weight, the flesh of his face stretched across his bones like a drum. He slowly opened his eyes as if it required all of his strength. "I guess embracing the suck didn't work this time," he said, barely above a whisper.

"Why the hell did you let it get this far? Why didn't you say something?"

He tried to shrug. "I didn't want to sound like I was complaining."

"Complaining? My god, Clark. You're going to die if they can't fix this."

"I don't really need you yelling at me right now, College Boy."

The realization of my behavior sickened me. "I'm sorry, man. I didn't mean to . . ."

"It's okay," he groaned. "Just sit awhile, will you?"

I pulled a mechanical reclining chair beside his bed and pretended to make myself comfortable.

"I heard you were bringing Anya home with you."

His voice was raspy and painful to hear, but he and I had been apart far too long. We had a lot of catching up to do, and I knew it was killing him not chasing bad guys on the far side of the world with me."

"Yeah, we brought her back. The State Department has her now. Who knows what they'll do with her. But she made quite a find aboard a sub in the Black Sea."

"You put her on a sub in the Black Sea?"

"Yeah."

"Why?"

I had to laugh. "That was the only ride out of there we could find after we sank the boat."

He tried to smile. "I can't wait to hear this story."

"I'll tell you all about it, I promise, but for now, I think you need to get some rest."

"I've had nothing but rest for two months. I'm sick of rest. I need to be back on my feet."

"Yeah, I know, and you will be soon enough, but this thing's pretty serious," I said. "Are you still hurting?"

He shook his head in abbreviated motions. "No, I'm on so many pain-killers, you could cut my feet off and I wouldn't know it."

"I'm sure nobody else is telling you the truth, but you look like hell."

"I'm still prettier than you."

Even at death's door—for the second time in as many months —Clark Johnson still threw his jabs at me.

I told him the story of the operation to convince the Russian Foreign Intelligence Service that I was turning into fish food on the bottom of the Black Sea, and he kept his eyes open throughout most of it.

I expected two dozen questions when I finished, but instead, Clark whispered, "I'd like to see my brother."

I held up one finger. "Wait here. I'll be right back."

He coughed. "Where would I go?"

I waved him off and found Penny just outside the door. "Get Dominic and Tony up here. Clark wants to see his brother, and I think Dominic needs to know how bad his son's condition really is."

Dominic Fontana was far more than my handler. He was also Clark's father and a former operator like me. He'd spent most of Clark's childhood saving the world, so theirs had been a rocky relationship for the first twenty-five years of Clark's life. Only after

Clark became an American covert operative, had he and his father reconnected, sharing the common bond of doing whatever freedom required to keep America afloat. Clark's brother, Tony, was a Coast Guard rescue swimmer and former boyfriend of my analyst, Skipper.

Penny shoved her phone into her pocket. "Tony's in Savannah, and Dominic's on his way from Miami. They'll both be here later tonight."

"Where's Skipper?" I asked.

Penny glanced at her watch. "She's at the hotel across the street getting some rest. We've got a suite of three rooms, but if necessary, we can get more when Dominic and Tony get here."

I squeezed her shoulders. "You're really good at this sort of thing."

She shrugged. "It's what I do."

I returned to Clark's room and found him either asleep or unconscious from the pain meds. He needed the solitude and rest, but I couldn't leave him. We'd been through too much together for me to leave him fighting for his life in a hospital bed while I slept across the street in luxury. He'd lain in a cave at the top of the Khyber Pass, knocking on death's door until I'd brought him home, and I wasn't going to let him go through anything like that again without me by his side.

The jet lag and physical and mental exhaustion of the mission I'd just completed beckoned to my body and mind to sleep, but the responsibility I felt for my partner kept me camped in that chair all night long, never taking my eyes from the man who'd been my brother, teacher, tormentor, and friend for five years. I owed him my life and everything else I could muster. I'd been shot, stabbed, blown up, and beaten until I couldn't see, but nothing I'd ever endured ten thousand miles from home, or in my own backyard, hurt as badly as seeing Clark Johnson helpless, broken, and confined to a hospital bed less than six feet away.

Chapter 6
You're the Reason

At just before 7 a.m., a phlebotomist arrived with a cartful of empty, vacuum-sealed test tubes. "I'm sorry to wake you, Mr. Johnson, but I need to draw some blood."

Clark forced his eyes open and offered the young woman his left arm. She soon had five tubes of blood and vanished as quickly as she'd appeared.

Seconds after her departure, an institutional plastic plate landed on the wheeled table next to Clark. Nothing on the plate except for the single slice of an orange was identifiable as actual food.

"Thank you," came my partner's raspy reaction to the delivery.

The realization that I was powerless to help him felt like a mule kick to my gut. I couldn't rescue him from the microscopic enemy eating his spine. Outnumbered, outgunned, and unsupported, Clark Johnson and I could stand shoulder to shoulder and fight our way out of almost any scenario anywhere in the world, but fighting an enemy crawling inside his body that couldn't be killed with bullets or blades was too much for either of us to swallow.

Clark dragged a spoon through a glob of porridge mostly confined to one partitioned section of the plate, but he couldn't seem to gather the wherewithal to lift the goop to his mouth. That's when Maebelle made her first appearance of the day.

"I'm sorry I'm late, but that two-burner, piece-of-crap stove in the hotel isn't exactly the same as cooking at home. How are you feeling this morning?"

He smiled and reached up for the young woman who treated him like a god and looked at him like a smitten schoolgirl. She set her oversized bag on the rolling table and nestled close by his side. She took both of his hands in hers. Surprise overtook her expression when she spotted me splayed across the least comfortable chair on the planet. "Oh! Hey, Chase. I didn't know you were here."

"Hey, Maebelle. I've been here all night."

"Yeah, Penny said you were staying with Clark, but it slipped my mind. I was too focused on making sure he has something good for breakfast."

She stood, lifted the plastic plate, and headed for the bathroom. The sound of the flushing toilet echoed through the small room, and she began unpacking her bag.

Scrambled eggs, bacon, a pair of biscuits big enough to scotch a truck tire, and a bowl of gravy took their rightful places where the hospital plate had been.

Clark's crooked smile, even buried in a weathered, weakened shell, made its appearance. "Now that's what breakfast is supposed to look like."

He situated himself upright in the mechanical bed, and Maebelle rolled the table until it was parked perfectly in front of his chest. Although the bites were small, he ate some of everything. Maebelle blew across the mug of coffee she poured from her thermos and then tasted it before offering it to Clark. I'd never seen anyone care for another living soul with such sincerity. Although he was a decade and a half her senior, she loved him as if she'd been put on Earth for no other purpose. Women had fawned over Clark for the five years I'd known him, but none were like Maebelle, and I'd never seen him return the loving stares with anyone else the way he did with her. If he survived the battle he was waging, I believed he'd follow Maebelle Huntsinger to the ends of the Earth and beyond, just as I'd do for Penny.

* * *

"Good morning. I'm Dr. Collins, one of the neurosurgeons here at Emory. How are you feeling this morning, Mr. Johnson?"

As the doctor and a throng of medical students filled the space, Maebelle wiped the corner of Clark's mouth with a napkin and rolled the table to my corner of the room.

Clark extended his hand. "Forgive me for not standing to shake, but I've had better days, doc."

"No worries. We'll have you back on your feet before you know it. I hear you have a pesky little infection gnawing at your back."

"That's what they tell me," Clark moaned, "but I'm afraid it's moved from gnawing to chomping."

"That's why I'm here. The pill-pushers believe they've got you on enough antibiotics to keep the infection under control, but until we get in there and clean up the area, you're not going to see much improvement."

"He sounds more like a mechanic than a surgeon," Maebelle whispered to me.

One of the med students overheard her and leaned toward us. "Dr. Collins is the best spinal surgeon on Earth. His techniques are taught all over the world. He's a genius."

Maebelle squeezed my arm. "Did you hear that, Chase? He's the best in the world."

"That's why they sent him here," I said. "Between Dr. Collins's scalpel and your biscuits and gravy, I think Clark will be back in the game in no time."

"How would you feel about me opening you up and having a look inside this afternoon?"

Maebelle was right, I thought. Collins did sound like a mechanic.

"I'll have to check my calendar, but I think I'm free this afternoon," Clark said.

Dr. Collins glanced at the remaining feast on the rolling table. "I'm afraid you're not going to be able to finish your breakfast. I'd like for your stomach to be relatively empty when we start the procedure, so we'll keep some fluids running, but nothing else to eat today, okay?"

Clark nodded, and I pulled the table toward me. "This looks too good to have it go to waste."

Maebelle giggled. "I've got some honey in my bag for that second biscuit if you want it."

I did want it.

When I'd polished off the breakfast, Maebelle said, "Why don't you go get cleaned up and get some rest? I'll stay with him, and I'll call you if anything changes."

* * *

By the time I made it back to the hospital, our caravan had grown. Clark's brother, Tony, and his father, Dominic, had arrived, and each had spent some time with Clark before they rolled him into the operating room.

Skipper and Tony sat at opposite ends of the bank of chairs in the surgical waiting room. Their romance had ended after Tony hadn't been as monogamous as she'd expected. Young men make stupid decisions, but young women sometimes cause those stupid decisions to worsen exponentially.

Lift with your knees to save your back, and think with your big head to save your ass. That's how Dr. Richter, my favorite psychology professor, mentor, and friend had put it. Tony probably hurt more than his back.

Six hours later, Dr. Collins stood in front of us in the waiting room, looking battle-weary. "It was worse than I expected. I don't know which of you talked Mr. Johnson into getting his butt up here to Atlanta, but whoever it was, you saved his life. The infection was bad. It's still bad, but it's better than it was."

We were all anxious, but Maebelle couldn't contain her anxiety. "Is he awake? Can we see him? Did the surgery go well?"

Dr. Collins wiped his brow with the surgical cap he'd pulled from his head, then wadded the cap into a ball. "We're not finished. I'm going back in. I just came out to let you know what's going on. You can expect at least another four hours. He's doing fine under anesthesia. He's young, incredibly strong, and in far better shape than most twenty-year-olds. Barring some unforeseen complication—and those do come up from time to time—we'll wake him up, and you can see him in a few hours. I won't be back out again until we're finished, so just sit tight."

A pair of pneumatic doors opened, and Dr. Collins was absorbed back into his realm—a world none of us could understand, but one where we all hoped the doctor was king.

Maebelle wrung her hands. "Well, I guess that means I should go cook some dinner for everyone since it's going to be at least four more hours."

I took her by the arm. "Stop worrying about us, and focus your energy on Clark. We're all grown-ups and perfectly capable of feeding ourselves."

"Yeah, I know, but I just feel better when I cook."

"I understand, but I don't think any of us has much of an appetite today."

She looked up at me with sad eyes. "What's going to happen to him, Chase?"

I led her away from the others, across the vast waiting room, and sat beside her on a surprisingly comfortable sofa. "He's going to be fine," I began. "You heard Dr. Collins. Clark is strong and in great shape. He's in very good hands."

She shook her head. "That's not what I mean. I have faith the surgery is going to go well, and that he'll beat the infection, but what happens after that?"

"I don't know what you mean."

"I mean, I don't know what you guys do . . . not really. I know a little, but even if they get all the infection and Clark heals up, will he be able to go back to work with you?"

"I'm ashamed to admit it, but I don't know. I don't know how much damage the infection has done to his already injured spine. I just don't know."

"He loves working with you, Chase. He tells me that all the time."

I slowly nodded. "And I love working with him. Just like that doctor, Clark's the best there is. He's one of the elite."

She lowered her head. "*Was*."

"What?"

"He *was* one of the elite. It's not the infection that's going to kill him. It's the fact that he can't go back to work with you. That's what'll kill him. Doing his job is what he lives for. He believes that's the reason he's alive. You know that better than anyone."

She was likely correct. Clark had been a soldier for over half his life. It's all he knew. Polite society doesn't have soft spots for old warriors to land. Men like Clark don't put on a suit and tie and start working nine to five when their days as an operator come to an end. Most of us never retire; instead, we die in frozen, forgotten corners of the globe, doing things no one will ever know, and we wouldn't have it any other way. As much as I wanted to believe I'd wade into the hell of battle with Clark Johnson by my side again, I knew Maebelle was wise beyond her years, and those days were behind Clark Johnson—the man both Maebelle and I would love until we drew our final breath.

* * *

Five hours later, Dr. Collins dragged himself through the pneumatic doors again. He stood before us, covered in sweat, exhaustion pulling at every inch of him. "We got it all. They're closing now, and we'll be waking him up in a few minutes. What does Mr. Johnson do for a living?"

Every eye in the group turned immediately to me. "He's a . . . um, well, he's . . ."

Maebelle saved me. "Clark is an overseas security consultant."

"I see," Dr. Collins said. "A consultant. Well, that must be a more dangerous profession than I realized. It would appear that someone's been shooting at our *consultant*. I removed half-a-dozen bullet fragments from his spine while I was in the neighborhood. I'm sure there's a good explanation for that, but I'd rather hear it from him when he's back on his feet. You'll be able to see him in less than an hour."

Maebelle embraced the doctor, and he didn't resist. "Thank you, doctor. I mean it. Really. Thank you."

Through a weary smile, he said, "No, ma'am, thank you. I suspect you're the one who talked him into coming to Emory. You're the reason he's alive."

Chapter 7
Who's That Lady?

The body's reaction to emotional stress is remarkable, and even though some scientists would disagree, impossible to accurately measure. It is, however, not only possible, but also quite easy to feel in the shoulders, neck, arms, and facial muscles. The suddenly relaxed postures of everyone in our group spoke volumes about how we'd spent the past several hours of our lives. Clark was going to wake up, and he was going to smile at all of us again with his crooked smile that made women melt and men wonder what he knew that they did not.

Dominic suddenly reassumed his tense posture, and I followed his gaze toward the double doors of the waiting room. Gliding through the doors as if she'd just walked off a Hollywood set, was an elegant woman who appeared to be in her mid-forties, carrying herself with the confidence of a runway model. Whoever she was, the woman had Dominic's undivided attention. I was intrigued and quickly formed a plan to sit as patiently as possible while the coming scenario played out.

To my surprise, it wasn't Dominic who rose first. It was Tony. "Mom. I can't believe you got here so fast."

Mom? Clark and Tony's mother?

I didn't need a mirror to know my face shone with shock and disbelief. I immediately knew exactly where Clark's bone structure that women adored came from. If Ms. Johnson and Anya were in the same room, not a man in sight would notice the Russian.

Tony and his mother embraced, and she leaned back, taking in the sight of her younger son. "I just cannot believe you are your father's child. Look at you. You are a specimen of a man. How are you not clawed half to death from these women pawing at you?"

I shot a glance at Skipper just as she rolled her eyes, and I motioned toward the woman and mouthed, "That's his mom?"

Skipper shrugged and mimed "I don't know" in exaggerated motions.

When she finished admiring her son, she turned her attention to Dominic. "Look at you, you old scoundrel. Perish the thought, but you still make an old gal's heart flutter. How've you been, Dom?"

He reached for her hands. "Wanda, you are as stunning as the first time I saw you. It's delightful to see you again, but I wish it could be under better circumstances."

The two shared a brief hug before she asked, "Where is my little Mud Pie?"

Mud Pie? That's too good to be true. He can't die now. I'll never call him anything other than Mud Pie.

"He's still in surgery, but Bobby just came out and said he got it all and that Clark should be awake soon."

Relief poured over Wanda's face. "Oh, that's wonderful. So, you got Bobby Collins on this?"

"Of course I did. I've got it all covered. I spoke with the CEO of the hospital and made sure she knew we'll spare no expense. Clark is to receive only the finest care from the finest physicians, and Bobby Collins is the best."

Wanda hugged Dominic again, this time with a great deal more affection. "Oh, Dom. I knew you'd take care of everything."

The two shared a moment, and I wondered how long it had been since they'd seen each other. I'd never heard Clark talk about his mother. In fact, he rarely spoke about his childhood at all. I had a lot of questions, but that wasn't the time nor the place for any of those.

Wanda playfully slapped Dominic on the shoulder. "Stop being rude, and introduce me to these people."

Dominic glanced down the row of chairs. "This is Maebelle Huntsinger. Maebelle, meet Clark's mother, Wanda Johnson."

Maebelle leapt to her feet and threw her arms around Wanda as if she were a long-lost friend. "Hey, Ms. Johnson. It's so nice to meet you. I'm in love with . . ." A look of horror overtook her face as she realized what she'd almost said, but Wanda saved her the embarrassment.

"Maebelle, it's so nice to meet you, and I understand exactly what you mean. Everybody's in love with my little Mud Pie. You can't help it. How do you know my son?"

"I'm his chef," she blurted out.

"His chef? Well, Clark is moving up in the world to have a beautiful young lady like you as his personal chef."

"No, ma'am. I'm not his personal chef. I'm just a chef, and I'm worried about him, so I've sort of appointed myself as his caretaker."

"Thank you for caring so much for my son. He's lucky to have you."

I stood and offered my hand. "Ms. Johnson, I'm Chase Fulton."

She slapped my hand away and pulled me in for a long, intense hug. "Oh, I knew you the minute I walked in, Chase Fulton. I love you already because Clark loves you. He just gushes on and on about you. Chase this, Chase that. You should hear him. You'd just die. I swear you would."

To say the least, I was surprised. Clark had told his mother about me, but never vice versa.

"Your son has made a habit of saving my life. He's the dearest friend I'll ever have."

"And this absolutely has to be the lovely and incomparable Penny."

My wife rose from her chair, and Wanda had her in a full-on bear hug before she'd gathered her balance. "It's nice to meet you, Ms. Johnson."

"Girl, what's with this Ms. Johnson bologna? You call me Wanda." She motioned toward me with her head. "Clark says you're too good for this one, but I'll sure bet you keep him in line, now, don't you?"

"I do my best, but it's not always easy. These boys get themselves wrapped up in some messes."

Wanda reached for Maebelle's hand and pulled her into a triangle with Penny. "We'll talk later, and I'll tell you some stories you won't believe, but first, is that Elizabeth down there?"

Penny and Maebelle glanced toward Skipper. "Yes, ma'am. That's Elizabeth, but we all call her Skipper."

Wanda covered her mouth. "Oh, my. Skipper, indeed. You'll forgive me, but I have to talk with her. My boys are a lot of things, but cheaters ain't on that list."

Penny and Maebelle shared a look but didn't say a word.

"Elizabeth Woodley, I'm Wanda Johnson. I've heard so much about you from Tony."

Skipper shot a look at her ex-boyfriend and back at Wanda. "Is that so?"

Wanda sat beside her, and I listened closely, unable to pretend I wasn't interested. "It most certainly is so, and I want you to know my Tony was—and still is—head-over-heels goo-goo-eyed for you."

Skipper huffed. "Well, he sure has a funny way of showing it."

Wanda cleared her throat. "I'm not sure you know exactly what you're talking about, young lady."

I didn't want to see the claws come out, but I couldn't look away.

Skipper lowered her chin, and I could see the courteous demeanor leave her eyes. "Is that so? Well, I'll have you know that I read the emails, and there was one from somebody named Tiffany that said, 'We're waiting for you, party boy. Get your ass over here. The girls can't wait to climb in your lap.' Just what would you think if you read that?"

Wanda tilted her head and reached into her purse. "Well, Little-Miss-Jump-To-Conclusions, let me show you a picture of Tiffany and the girls from that email."

Skipper's face was growing redder by the second as Wanda unsnapped her wallet and unfolded several photographs from a plastic sleeve. "This is Tiffany, my brother's daughter. As you can see, she's about a thousand months pregnant with her fourth child, and these are the *girls* who just can't wait to climb onto their cousin Tony's lap."

Skipper's face immediately flushed pale. "But I didn't . . . but . . ."

Wanda patted her on the wrist. "No, sweetheart, you didn't. You never stopped to think that my Tony was supposed to visit his cousins and their little girls while he was in Puerto Rico, where they're stationed with the Navy. You just assumed that gorgeous man down there was cheating on you, and you didn't even give him a chance to explain."

For the first time in my life, I saw Skipper speechless. I was both amused and relieved.

The infamous pneumatic doors opened, and a nurse stepped through. "Okay, he's awake, and the first words out of his mouth were, 'Go tell Chase I'm alive,' so I don't know which one of you is Chase, but he's alive." We shared a chuckle, and the nurse said, "I can only let two of you come back at a time, and only for a few minutes. So, who's first?"

Wanda grabbed Maebelle's hand. "We'll go first. I'm his mother, and she's his fiancée."

Maebelle grinned, and the two followed the nurse through the double doors.

When Wanda and Maebelle returned to the waiting area, Dominic and I followed the nurse down the corridor to Clark's room. Clark's narcotic-induced smile greeted us.

Dominic laid his hand on Clark's shoulder. "How're you feeling, son?"

"I'm going to be okay. At least that's what they tell me."

I looked down at my mentor, teacher, and dearest friend. "You had us worried, old man."

He let out a breathy chuckle. "No need to worry, College Boy. Just rub some dirt on it. Everything stops bleeding eventually."

I laughed. "Yeah, well, I didn't bring any dirt, so I'm glad to see you're doing well."

The three of us talked until the narcotics lulled Clark back into the spirit world. When we returned to the waiting room, Tony and Skipper were talking quietly in a secluded corner. They rose in unison to take their turn. I didn't have the heart to tell them they weren't going to get much conversation out of Clark.

Penny poked my side. "Do you think that story Wanda told Skipper was the truth?"

I laughed. "For all I know, those pictures may've come with that wallet. But I'm happy to see her and Tony talking again."

After everyone spent a few minutes with Clark, Maebelle and

Wanda decided they would stay overnight while the rest of us went back to the hotel to get some much-needed rest. The road ahead would be bumpy, but Mud Pie was going to make it, and maybe Skipper and Tony would, too.

Chapter 8
Maybe We Can Help

Although time at Emory Hospital crept along at a snail's pace, Clark showed marked improvement with every passing day. Two days post-surgery, he was on his feet and walking the hallways, but never without Maebelle close by his side.

In a rare moment alone with Clark, it was time for a confession. "I was worried about you, my friend."

As had become his routine, Clark waved a dismissive hand. "It's going to take more than a little infection to put me in the ground, College Boy."

"I was still worried," I said. "You had us all concerned, and I've got a few things I want to tell you."

He shook his head. "You're not about to profess your undying love or something like that, are you? Because Penny wouldn't understand."

"I'm serious, Clark. I've never thanked you for . . . well, for everything. I've learned more from you than I ever learned at The Ranch. I don't know if you set out to become my sensei, or if it was part of some grand plan from your dad, but I mean it. I really appreciate what you've done for me."

He rolled his eyes. "Cut it out. There was no plan. You were just a green rookie who'd never been shot at when I showed up.

Somebody had to teach you how to stay alive, and I was the only one around. You never have to thank me. Besides, I didn't do it for you. I needed to make sure my partner knew how to keep me alive when the shit hit the fan, and God knows we've seen our share of fan blades covered in crap."

I couldn't suppress my smile. "I knew you'd say something like that, but I want you to know I appreciate what you do for me, and you're right—I'd have been dead two dozen times if it weren't for you. Now, I have to ask you a serious question."

My tone apparently got his attention because he sat up and focused intently on my face. "What is it?"

I swallowed hard. "I have to know why your mother calls you Mud Pie."

He snatched a pillow from behind his head and hurled it toward me, but I deflected the missile in classic wax-on-wax-off Daniel-san style. "Come on, Green Beret. Spill it."

Clark had never been a pointer, but he aimed his index finger between my eyes. "If you ever call me that name, I won't kill you in your sleep. I'll wake you up and cut your throat."

"Oh, come on," I jabbed. "If you don't tell me, I'm just going to ask your mom. In fact, I think that's a better idea anyway. Her story's going to be far more amusing than yours."

"Okay, okay," he said. "I'll tell you, but I mean it. You're not getting away with calling me that name."

"No promises," I said. "But let's hear it."

He cleared his throat. "It's not as good as you think. Honestly, it was the last fight I ever lost. I was seven years old and got into a tussle on the playground with a bully. The kid shoved me down into a puddle. I was covered in mud, so the teacher had to call my mom to bring me some clean clothes. When she showed up at school, she said, 'Aww, look how cute you look. Like a little mud pie.' That's all there is to the story."

"Well, that's disappointing. I really wanted it to be better than that."

"Yeah, well, that's all there is to it. But you've never heard Tony call me that name, have you?"

I considered his question. "No, I guess I haven't."

Clark gave a single, brisk nod. "That's because I beat his ass the first time he did, and he's never done it again."

I gave him a long, appraising look. "I don't know for sure, but I don't think you can kick my ass today, sensei."

He didn't hesitate. "Maybe not today, but if you know what's good for you, you won't risk it."

"Okay, I'll let it go this time, but—"

"You'll let it go *every* time, and you're welcome."

I shot a curious glance. "What?"

"You're welcome," he said. "You're one of the best students I've ever had, but don't get too cocky. I've still got a lot to teach you."

* * *

Dr. Collins made an appearance at just past three that afternoon. "Well, soldier, it looks like you're shipping out."

Clark had long abandoned the hospital bed and taken up residence in the chair by the window with Maebelle encamped nearby. "It's about time, doc. What took you so long?"

"The bloodwork shows no signs of infection, and we've done all we can do for you here. It's up to you and the physical therapists now. Normally, I'd recommend a home healthcare service, but. . . ." The doctor cast his eyes toward Maebelle.

She grinned. "Trust me, Dr. Collins. He's not going to get any better home healthcare than he'll get from me."

The doctor smiled. "Yeah, we've all figured that out. He's lucky to have you."

"So, are you kicking me out today?" Clark asked.

"No, we have to milk one more night out of the insurance company, but we'll send you home tomorrow morning. We can arrange for an ambulance for the ride home if you need it."

I said, "No, that won't be necessary. There's no reason he can't fly, is there?"

Dr. Collins shook his head. "No, flying is fine as long as he's comfortable."

"Penny and I'll drive back to Saint Marys this afternoon and get the Caravan. That'll be a much better ride than an ambulance. It's just over an hour-long flight back home."

The doctor shrugged. "That sounds perfect. Have you got room for a couple more? We've got a place in Fernandina Beach, just across the water from Saint Marys."

"No kidding?" I said. "We've just inherited the Bonaventure Plantation. Of course we've got room. Our Caravan is on floats, so we can drop you at your dock."

Dr. Collins threw up his hands. "Oh, if only I had the time. Perhaps our paths will cross on the coast sometime."

"I hope so." I reached for his hand. "And thank you for what you've done for Clark."

"I've known Clark's father for years," he said, "and I'd met his mother a few times, but this is the first time I've actually met him and Tony. Fine young men they are."

"As fine as they come," I said.

He looked around and motioned for me to follow him to the corner of the room. After casting a questioning look toward Clark, I followed him and leaned in as he whispered, "I'm not trying to pry, but is everything okay with Wanda?"

"What do you mean?" I asked. "I just met her for the first time, so I don't know her well enough to say."

He shot a glance back toward Clark. "Something's going on. It's my job to notice things others don't."

"That's my job, too, doctor, but like I said, I don't know her well enough."

He grimaced. "It may be nothing, but I overheard her and Dominic talking about a kidnapping. It caught my ear. That's all."

"A kidnapping?"

"Yes, but I didn't get any details. I just heard the word *kidnapping*."

"I'll talk with Dominic and find out what's going on. Thanks for the heads-up, doctor."

He shrugged again. "It may be nothing, but I don't know."

I returned to Clark's side of the room. "How do you feel about an airplane ride tomorrow, old man?"

"If it means getting out of this hospital, I'd be happy to walk home."

"I think the Caravan is a much better idea. We'll be back to get you in the morning."

I found Dominic in the hallway on his cell phone, and I held up one finger, letting him know we needed to talk. He nodded and looked at his watch. Raising three fingers into the air, he either told me to wait three minutes or thirty minutes. It didn't matter. The conversation we were about to have was important enough to wait three days if necessary.

It turned out to be three minutes.

"Chase, I'm glad you're still here. I need to talk with you about a situation that's come up."

I narrowed my eyes. "Does it have anything to do with a kidnapping?"

Dominic shot a look across his shoulder. "You don't miss much, do you?"

"What's going on, Dominic? And how can I help?"

"This one's off the books, Chase. It's a friend of Wanda's. His granddaughter's been taken, and they're asking for money."

"Money? Am I supposed to finance a ransom for some kid I don't know?"

"That's not exactly what I have in mind," he mumbled.

"Exactly what *do* you have in mind?"

"They have the money," he said, "but paying kidnappers is like feeding stray cats. They keep coming back for more."

"Hostage rescue isn't my forte, Dominic."

"I know, but Hunter, Singer, and Mongo have been through the schools."

I let his suggestion bounce around inside my skull for a few seconds. "I'll talk with them and see what they have to say, but I'm going to need a lot more details."

He placed his hand on my shoulder. "I've known Wanda Johnson for forty years, Chase, and she's never once asked me for a favor . . . until now."

I licked my lips and took a long, full breath. "I'll talk to her."

Back in the waiting room, Wanda was checking her makeup in a compact mirror.

"Let's go for a walk," I said, reaching for her arm.

As if she'd been expecting me, she stowed the compact, stood, and threaded her hand inside my elbow.

"They're letting Clark go home tomorrow morning. I'm going to St. Marys to get my airplane tonight, and I'll fly back up and take him to Bonaventure tomorrow morning."

"That's wonderful," she said. "I'm sure he's ready to be home."

"He's ready to be back in the field with me, but for now, home is a pretty good step in that direction."

She squeezed my arm. "That's not what this walk is about, though, is it?"

"No," I said. "Tell me about the kidnapping. Maybe we can help."

She took a look over her shoulder and poured out her soul. "Chase, it's just terrible. My dear friend—I just love him to death

—his name is Graham Lightner, and he's a talent agent in Nashville who represents songwriters. It's his granddaughter. Graham has made a lot of money, and he's more than capable of paying the ransom, but Dom says there are other options. Are you one of those other options?"

I took her hand. "I don't know, Wanda, but for now, try to calm down and tell me what you know. If we can help, we will, but until I've heard the whole story, I can't do anything."

"Okay, so Graham's daughter married this scumbag, and they had a daughter. She's just precious—the sweetest thing you've ever seen. The scumbag thought he was marrying into money, but my friend Graham believes people should work for what they have; otherwise, it has no value to them. That's why he doesn't throw money at his kids like some rich fathers. He pays for them to go to school, and he helps them get a nice place to live, but after that, they're on their own financially until he dies someday. It's not likely that'll happen anytime soon. He's in great shape."

I jumped in. "Listen, Wanda. We have to focus on the kidnapping. Tell me the mother's name."

"It's Patricia."

"What's her last name?"

"Lightner. She changed her name back to Lightner after the divorce because she was—"

"Focus, Wanda. What's the little girl's name?"

"Melanie, but her last name is Gibson. That was the scumbag's name, Donny Gibson. He's a—"

"We'll get to scumbag in a minute," I said. "But first, let's talk about the timeline. When was Melanie taken?"

"Today's Wednesday, right?"

I nodded.

"That would've made it Monday afternoon."

I suddenly wished I had a pad and pen, but my mental notes would have to suffice. "Give me the details of what you know. I need to know when, where, and especially how she was taken. We'll get to the aftermath in a moment."

She swallowed hard. "Melanie was supposed to be at her friend Katherine's house. Katherine's mom is a floating dumpster fire. She can't get anything right . . ."

Keeping Wanda Johnson focused on a linear conversation was like trying to pet a porcupine. "Okay, Wanda. I'll ask direct questions, and you give me simple, direct answers. Okay?"

"I'm sorry. I'm not good at this sort of thing."

"Nobody's good at this sort of thing, but to know if I can help, I need the bare facts without getting sidetracked. Let's start with the *where*. Do you know where Melanie was when she was abducted?"

"It was definitely from the community pool. They've got this summer program for kids. It's a great program. They have swimming lessons, archery, summer reading—all sorts of things."

I lost all ability to avoid laughing, and Wanda palmed her forehead. "I guess I'm a bit of a dumpster fire, too, huh? First it's Clark, and now this. I'm so relieved Clark is going to be okay, but I'm just worried sick over little Melanie."

"Okay, let's try again," I said. "Melanie was taken from the community pool on Monday afternoon. When was the first contact from the kidnappers?"

"Monday night."

"How was the contact made? Was it a phone call? An email?"

"That's one of the scariest parts. He knocked on Patricia's door at about nine o'clock and handed her a lock of Melanie's hair. He said he was going to keep delivering body parts until he got five million dollars. When he got his money, he said he'd deliver what was left of Melanie, but if she called the police, he'd shove Melanie's severed head in her mailbox."

A shiver ran down my spine, but I maintained my composure. "Has there been any further contact?"

"I don't know," she breathed. "But will you get her back?"

I closed my eyes and let a thousand scenarios play out in my mind. My involvement made every scenario worse. When the time I'd spent thinking grew uncomfortably long, I asked, "Does Graham have the money?"

"No, not all of it. That's a lot of money."

"Yes, it is. If he had the money, would he pay the ransom?"

"Probably."

I squeezed her hand. "This isn't the kind of thing I do, but I have a team made up of people like Clark. I'll discuss it with them, and if they believe they can help, I'll have them on a plane to Nashville before the end of the day. Does Graham know you've come to us for help?"

"He knows Clark's a Green Beret, and I told him I'd ask his advice, but that's all he knows."

"Okay, that's good. Let's keep it that way for now. I'll have an answer for you in less than an hour."

She wrapped her arms around me as if I'd told her she'd won the lottery. "I can't tell you how much this means, Chase. Thank you."

I returned the hug. "I've not done anything yet, but we'll see what we can do. Oh, I almost forgot. Clark told me the story about the bully shoving him down on the playground and how he's been Mud Pie to you ever since."

She grinned and placed her lips close to my ear. "Did he tell you that *bully* was Suzie Burkhardt?"

Chapter 9
Landlord

Penny did the driving while I worked the phones on the ride back to Saint Marys. It took less than three minutes to brief Singer, Mongo, and Hunter on the information Wanda had taken half an hour to deliver.

"So, what do you think, guys? Is this something you're interested in taking on?"

Singer was the first to speak. "It sounds like you're leaving this one to us. Why aren't you in, Chase?"

"If the three of you are willing to take it on, I'll provide the financing, equipment, and logistics, but I'm not trained for anything like this. I would only be in the way."

"How about Skipper?" Hunter asked. "We'll need an analyst. But yeah, count me in, especially since it's for Clark's mother. He's one of us, so *his* family is *our* family as far as I'm concerned."

Singer said, "I'm in, too. I'll get the doc to cut this cast off today, and if he won't do it, I'll have Mongo rip it off."

"No problem," Mongo said. "I'll get that thing off your leg in no time. And I'm with these guys. We'll get that little girl back if we have to tear some heads off to do it. You can't be messing with little kids."

I breathed a sigh of relief. "Skipper's all in, and she's all yours. She'll write the checks, and I'll pay double your daily rate and cover all expenses. There's a ten-grand bonus in it if Melanie's back in her bed by the weekend. Pick a team lead, and go to work, guys. Here's Wanda's number."

Singer asked, "Who's paying you, Chase?"

"I'll deal with that later. Just get that little girl back safe and sound."

* * *

Back at Bonaventure Plantation, I was happy to see the Judge in residence again. "Welcome home, Judge. We've missed you."

"Thank you, son. It's good to be home. I hear tell Clark had a bit of a close call."

"He certainly did, but he's coming home tomorrow morning. We just came back to get the airplane."

The Judge frowned. "You're not seriously going to carry that boy home in that One-Eighty-Two of yours, are you?"

"No, sir. We did a little horse-trading since you've been gone. I swapped a boat in which I had an interest to an old friend for a Two-Oh-Eight Caravan on amphib floats."

"Ah," he said. "That's better. I look forward to seeing it."

"You're welcome to ride with us to Atlanta tomorrow morning to pick up Clark," Penny offered.

The Judge shook his head. "No, I'll see it some other time. I need to check on things around here—you know, the horses and fence. And I'm sure nobody's checked the trotlines. They've probably washed away."

"I'm sure you're right," I said. "I'm glad you're feeling better, and again, it's good to have you home."

Penny hugged the old man, who looked as if he'd lost twenty pounds since we last saw him. "Maebelle will be home tomorrow," she said, "and she'll have you fattened back up before you know it."

He rubbed his beltline. "I could use a good home-cooked meal. Evelyn doesn't cook. She always wants to go out, and as you know, I like eating at my own table."

Penny and I descended the back steps and walked down the sloping yard to *Aegis*, my fifty-foot custom sailing catamaran. Sooner or later, likely after the Judge had drawn his last breath on Earth, we'd move into the plantation house, but the privacy and comfort of the boat was where we felt most at home.

Penny poured two glasses and settled into a settee. "The Judge looks bad. I'm worried about him."

I took a long sip of lemonade. "Yeah, he does. I suspect he went to Atlanta to tell Ms. Evelyn goodbye."

Penny pressed her lips into a thin smile. "You're probably right. Do you know how old he is?"

"I think he's ninety-four, but I'm not sure."

We sat in silence, and I imagined Penny's mind was doing exactly what mine was doing: pondering how life ashore will feel and how different our lives will become in the years ahead.

There was one thing ticking inside my head that I'm certain wasn't happening in Penny's. "After we get Clark home and this kidnapping case settled, I want to go to Athens."

Penny furrowed her brow. "Greece?"

"No, goofy. Georgia. I want to clean out Dr. Richter's house and bring the Mustang back here."

When my favorite psychology professor, Dr. Robert "Rocket" Richter, passed away, he left me, among other things, his modest house near the University of Georgia, as well as a North American P-51D Mustang that had been beautifully restored.

Dr. Richter was far more than merely a professor to me. He'd been a father figure and the most influential force recruiting me into the service of my country. He knew my parents before they were killed in the jungles of Panama, where they'd been opera-tives of the same organization I now served. They, however, oper-ated under the guise of missionaries providing humanitarian relief in the area. They, along with my younger sister, fell victim to assassins while I was still a boy. At that age, I couldn't have known that my life had been predestined for the path I was now solidly upon, following in the enormous footsteps of my mother and father, and defending freedom beneath a veil of secrecy with some of the finest men and women who'd ever live.

Dr. Richter had another secret that most of the world would never know: he was Anya Burinkova's father.

Penny's shoulders rose and slowly fell with a long, considered breath. "You're giving Anya the house, aren't you?"

I shrugged. "It's rightfully hers."

"No, it isn't," she said. "It's yours, and you can do anything you want with it. Dr. Richter gave it to you. You were just as much his son—and maybe more so—than she is his daughter. He loved you, and that's why he gave you everything he owned. To him, you were his own flesh and blood."

I sighed. "I don't know. It just feels. . . ."

She nestled in beside me and took my arm in her hands. "And that's one of the reasons I love you so much. You do what feels right when most people would be selfish and greedy. You're the best man I know, Chase Fulton, but that house is yours. I'm not suggesting you don't let Anya live there, but someday, that house is going to mean more to you than you could know right now."

Penny's ability to see into my future left me believing she might be part witch, but she was rarely wrong when she made such predictions.

"Maybe you're right," I admitted. "But I still need to get the house cleaned out and move the airplane."

"Okay, so we'll do that, and I'll be Anya's landlord," she said.

"I think the term is *landlady*."

"I think I prefer *lord*," she said in a manner that left little doubt the discussion was over.

* * *

With the wind out of the northeast at eight knots, Atlanta Approach Control cleared me for the visual approach to runway 03 Left at Dekalb-Peachtree just after nine a.m. the next morning. Thirty-seven hundred feet of asphalt was more than twice what the Caravan needed, and I continued to marvel at the capability of my new airplane.

"I think we should name her," Penny said as I shut down on the parking ramp.

"Name who?"

"The airplane," she said. "Travis McGee named his old purple Rolls-Royce pickup truck *Miss Agnes*. Why can't we name an airplane?"

"She's already got a name. The FAA gave it to her."

Penny huffed. "That's not a name. That's a registration number. She needs a real name like Miss Penny, or something equally fetching."

"Nothing is equally as fetching as Miss Penny, especially now that she's Mrs. Penny."

She kissed me on the cheek before we climbed down from the cockpit. "Nice redirect, but we're not finished discussing this."

Although I still didn't know how they kept dragging the Emory Hospital security team into our situation, I saw Skipper perched in the front passenger seat of the van with the roof lights flashing as they pulled onto the ramp.

Maebelle helped Clark from the van, and he moved gingerly across the tarmac toward the—as yet unnamed—Caravan.

"Look at you, back in the middle-aged-mutant-ninja-turtle shell," I said as he approached.

"I'll make you think middle-aged, College Boy."

I took up the fighter's stance he'd taught me. "Come on, Green Beret. Let's go a couple of rounds."

"Go ahead and have your fun now. We both know I'll kick your ass when I get out of this thing."

"Yeah, yeah, always with the idle threats. How are we going to get your crippled butt up in that airplane?"

He shot a glance up the boarding ladder to the cabin eight feet above the ground. "I can climb."

"Oh no, you can't!" ordered Maebelle. "You'll do no such thing. You wait right here. In fact, go sit back down in the van, and I'll be back."

To my surprise, Clark obediently returned to the van as Maebelle headed for the terminal.

Skipper waved silently as she strode from the van and climbed the ladder to the Caravan with her phone pressed tightly to her face and her computer slung beneath one arm. She was setting up an operations center in the back of my airplane in support of the kidnapping recovery mission in Nashville.

Moments later, Maebelle returned. She was sitting beside the driver of a mechanized lift. Shortly after that, Clark was sent aloft on the rising platform and deposited at the rear door of the airplane. By the time I'd paid for the fuel and climbed back aboard, Maebelle and Penny had lost their fight with Clark about where he would sit.

"I'll ride your lift, but I'm not sitting in the back," I heard him say as he settled into the left seat.

We pulled on our headsets, and that old familiar feeling of flying with Clark came rushing back. I'd missed it, and I liked having him beside me again, even if he was high on narcotic painkillers and encased in a plastic shell.

"I've got the radios," he said into the mic.

"Oh, I think I can manage the radios and the flying on this trip. You've had a few too many feel-good pills to be talking with ATC."

He let me win, and we landed in the North River and taxied to the Bonaventure dock eighty minutes later. "We don't have one of those fancy lifts around here, but you should be able to step from the pontoon onto the dock without too much trouble."

"Good thinking," he said, still groggy from the meds.

Soon, Maebelle had Clark ensconced in his bed, and I had the Caravan secured near *Aegis* at the dock.

Skipper moved the ops center into the house and finally hung up the phone.

"How's that going, Skipper?"

She held up one finger, the universal sign for wait your turn, and I did just that as she pounded at the keyboard. She finally looked up. "We've got it narrowed down to a half-mile radius, and we'll tighten the noose within an hour. If she's where we think, it's going to be a tricky exfil without getting the local police involved. Hunter's in charge, and he thinks once they get a positive ID, calling in the FBI is the best choice. Their hostage rescue team can snatch the girl and nab the kidnappers. If we hit them, there's likely to be some flying lead, and it's possible one or more of them will get away."

"It's Hunter's op," I said. "I trust him, so I'm not about to second-guess him. Just don't get the girl hurt, and don't get arrested."

"I'll pass the word," Skipper said as she turned back to her computer.

Penny twisted her unruly hair into a loose bun on top of her head and stabbed a pencil through it. "Is what they're doing legal?"

"I don't know," I admitted. "But even if it's not, a little girl's life is at stake, and I think it's worth the risk of cleaning up some legal drama to get her home safe and sound."

Chapter 10
A Real Spy

Penny and I landed at the Ben Epps Regional Airport in Athens, Georgia, at ten thirty the following morning and taxied the Caravan to the parking apron. A lineman emerged from the FBO and directed us to a tie-down.

"Welcome to Athens. How long will you be staying, and do you need any fuel?" the man said after I shut down the engine and stepped from the cockpit.

"Good morning. Top off the tanks with Jet-A, if you don't mind. No hurry. We'll be here a couple of nights."

Penny and I strolled into the FBO and greeted the man at the counter.

"Good morning." I slid my credit card across the countertop. "Your lineman is topping off our Caravan, and we'll need a night's tie-down, maybe two."

He glanced down at my card. "I thought I recognized you, Chase. You inherited Robert Richter's hangar and Mustang, right?"

"That's me. He left us his house, too. That's why we're here. I need to do an inventory. Have you checked on the Mustang lately?"

He typed my information into the computer. "I look in on her a couple times a month. She really needs to be flown. It's a shame for her to sit in the hangar all the time."

"I agree, but I still need to get schooled up on her. I'm not ready to fly her by myself yet."

He pulled a well-worn black book from beneath the counter and thumbed through the tattered pages. "Here's Dave Floyd's number. He's got a few thousand hours in Mustangs and has even flown yours quite a bit. I'm sure he'd be happy to get you up to speed."

I wrote down Dave's name and number. "Thanks, I appreciate that. I'll give him a call. We're going to head down to the hangar and check on things."

"Make yourselves at home. There's a golf cart out front if you need it."

I retrieved my credit card. "Thanks. We'll just walk, though. We could use the exercise."

On the way to the hangar, Penny asked, "I thought you could fly anything. Why do you need someone to teach you to fly the Mustang?"

I pushed through the hangar door, flipped on the overhead lights, and engaged the electric motor to raise the enormous folding door. As light from the morning sun and the mercury vapor bulbs flooded the hangar, the flawless P-51D Mustang glistened in the center of the massive space.

Penny gasped. "Oh, my God! I've never seen anything like that."

"Now do you understand why I'm not ready to fly her?"

Penny stood in awe-struck wonder, staring up at the old warbird. "I'd be afraid to scratch it, so, yeah, I understand."

"Climb in and have a look while I move the van outside," I said, motioning toward the wing.

Dr. Richter's brown VW Microbus sat in the corner of the hangar near the small John Deere tractor designed to tow the Mustang. It took longer than I expected to start the van, but when it finally buzzed to life, I pulled it into the sun and left it running.

Climbing into the back seat of the Mustang, I said, "What do you think?"

"It's impressive," Penny said, "but I don't know what most of this stuff is."

"Neither do I, but that'll soon change."

We climbed down from the cockpit, and Penny stared up at the seductive, dark-haired woman painted on the nose of the Mustang beneath the script "Katerina's Heart."

"Who's Katerina?"

"Katerina Burinkova was a KGB officer during the Cold War, but more than that, she was the only woman Dr. Richter ever loved. She was also Anya's mother."

"Hmm," she said. "I don't know how I feel about a picture of Anya's mother painted on your airplane."

I let my eyes roam across Katerina's face and saw Anya's unmistakable jawline and cheekbones. "Well, maybe we can do something about that when we get her home."

The VW Microbus stopped sputtering after awakening from its hibernation. Driving the old bus felt awkward from my perch above the front tire, but Penny seemed to be having the time of her life.

She spun in her seat to look into the back. "This is just like the Scooby-Doo van."

I laughed. "Yeah, I guess it is, but we won't be pulling masks off any villains on this trip."

"Okay, Shaggy, whatever you say. But I've been around you long enough to know you're not afraid to expose a bad guy or two."

"Does that make you Velma?"

"Uh, not hardly! I'm obviously Daphne."

"I was thinking more like Jessica Rabbit, but I guess you're a pretty good Daphne, too."

We pulled into the driveway of the ranch-style brick house that had been Dr. Richter's home for decades while he was filling young minds full of psychological wisdom at UGA. Like the professor himself, the house was unassuming, with far more beneath the surface than met the eye.

It had been months since anyone had been inside, so the old home smelled stale and unused. Opening every window we could pry from their sills quickly solved that issue. The hall closet held a collection of long overcoats, Christmas decorations, and photo albums, just like most hall closets, but it soon revealed secrets no one could have known existed. Sliding the coats aside, I slid a panel away, revealing a deadbolt, and my key fit perfectly.

"Follow me." I motioned for Penny, and we began our descent into the basement.

"Okay, this is some serious spy stuff," she said.

"I guess it's safe to say Dr. Richter was a spy, but he was a lot more than that."

The lights flickered to life, illuminating a space of perhaps three hundred square feet. A desk occupied one corner of the room, with a row of six file cabinets behind it. Bookshelves lined one wall and held row after row of reference material, from atlases to histories of Ancient Rome.

Penny pointed toward a bank-vault-type door consuming the wall opposite the desk. "What's in there?"

"I don't know. I haven't been inside . . . yet."

I rolled the dial, aligning the tumblers from memory, and spun the handle. The bolts withdrew, and the heavy steel door swung easily into the room. A light came on inside the vault, illuminating the confined space.

It felt as if I were entering some ancient shrine as I forced myself to step through the opening. A small section of a metal bookcase contained leather-bound volumes of some sort, and I pulled the first from its place. When the supple binding fell open in my palm, I almost couldn't believe what I was holding. It was volume one of Robert Richter's personal journals from long before he became *Doctor* Richter.

As I read the cursive script, I could almost feel the youth and exuberance in his writing: flight school, his time in the war, test pilot school, astronaut training.

I turned abruptly. "You'll never believe this. Dr. Richter went to astronaut training!"

She leaned in beside me and peered around my shoulder. "Oh, that's too cool."

"Yeah, it is. I never heard him talk about it. If I was an astronaut, I'd tell everybody."

"Maybe he didn't make it through the training," she said.

"I've got a lot of reading to do. The more I learn about that man, the more fascinating he becomes."

Penny slowly spun around, taking in the mystery that was Dr. Richter. "What are we going to do with all of this stuff?"

"We'll move it all back to Bonaventure, I guess. I don't know what else to do with it." I returned the volume onto the shelf and slid back a metal panel that revealed a collection of Cold-War-era weapons any collector would drool over. "We're going to need more help."

"Obviously," she said, "but everyone else is on the kidnapping job."

I glanced at my watch. If they haven't resolved that by now, we've got a lot more to worry about than some old guns in a basement."

* * *

Skipper answered on the third ring.

"How's it going in Nashville?"

"It's either going up in smoke or down in flames depending on your perspective," she said.

"That doesn't sound good."

"Oh, no. It's very good. I'm telling you how it's going from the kidnappers' perspective. From our perspective, it couldn't be better."

"Let's hear it."

"We isolated the house and set up a perimeter. Hunter made the decision not to move until we had definite eyes on the girl."

"And . . . has that happened yet?"

"It has, but only minutes ago. They moved her from an interior room to the kitchen near the garage. Singer spotted her, and I confirmed the ID. It's definitely her, but there's action in the house. A new face has shown up, and I'm working on identifying him now."

"Is there anything I can do to help?"

"No, not really, but if you want to listen in, we're going to hit the house any minute."

"Definitely." I pressed the speaker button on my phone so Penny could hear the action as well.

"Okay," Skipper said, "I'm going to go live with everyone's comms. Just listen and try to stay quiet."

"You got it," I said.

"What's happening?" Penny whispered.

I covered the mic of the phone and whispered, "They're hitting the house, and we're going to listen in."

Her eyes widened in fascination.

Hunter's voice came to life. "Stand by to blow the door, Singer."

"Roger."

For the first time, I could hear Singer's prayer before the action. "God, please give these idiots the sense to surrender without a fight."

It wasn't what I expected, but I wasn't disappointed. Penny almost let out a chuckle.

Mongo said, "I'm on the garage door. I'll make entry as soon as I hear the breach."

Hunter gave the order. "Hit it, Singer."

The crisp report of Singer's rifle rang through the speaker of the phone, and what followed sounded like chaos of the highest order. I let the scene play out in my head as the sounds poured through the phone.

Hunter charged through the door Singer had blown from its hinges at the same instant Mongo forced his way into the back. In my mind, Mongo did far more damage to his door than Singer did.

"Get down!" Hunter bellowed. "Get on the ground, now!"

Muffled tones came from the kidnappers as they reacted to the intrusion, but I couldn't understand what they were saying.

No gunfire so far, I thought. *That's a good sign.*

Heavy breathing filled the speaker, and Penny buried her fingernails into my forearm.

"He's running with the girl!" Mongo yelled.

Hunter calmly said, "Singer, hit the runner at the front door. He's got the girl."

"Roger."

Seconds later, the second report of Singer's rifle echoed through the phone.

"Nice shot, Singer," Mongo said. "I've got it from here."

The sounds that followed could've been thunder or boulders falling from the roof and thudding into the yard.

"It's okay, Melanie. I've got you now. We're the good guys, and we're here to take you back to your mommy."

"Was that Mongo?" Penny mouthed, and I nodded.

"The girl's secure," Mongo said, "and you missed just right, Singer."

Hunter said, "I have the two inside flex-cuffed and eating some carpet. Is the runner alive?"

"Yeah, he's still with us," Mongo huffed, still breathing hard, "but he's going to be in a lot of pain when he wakes up."

"Get him back in here with his buddies."

"You got it, boss."

Wordless shuffling and whimpering cries from Melanie filled the next two minutes. Finally, Hunter said, "Secure. Call the mother, the grandfather, then the cops, in that order. Mongo and I'll sit on the scene. Singer, I want you to hobble your crippled butt back to the truck. We don't need to try explaining to the cops why we've got a sniper in the trees."

"Thank you, God, for not making me shoot these idiots," Singer said.

Skipper made the calls just as Hunter ordered, and although I could only hear her side of the conversation, it was clear the family was thrilled with the outcome.

The conversation with the cops was a little more complex, but it didn't take long for Skipper to take control. "Look, there was a kidnapping. The victim is Melanie Gibson. My team has the kidnappers in custody, and the girl is safe. You'll find two unarmed men. One is Stone Hunter, and the other is Marvin Malloy. They're holding three kidnappers." She gave the address and hung up.

Before I knew it, the open comms went dead, and Singer was on the phone. "You there, Chase?"

"Yeah, I'm here. That sounded interesting."

"It wasn't bad. They weren't expecting to be hit, so we caught them with their pants down."

"How did you stop the guy with Melanie without shooting him?"

I blew the concrete stairs from beneath his feet. He's probably got a broken ankle, but no bullet holes."

"Nice work, Singer. Is everybody okay?"

"I think the girl is a little shaken up, but we're all okay. I'm glad you could listen in."

"Me, too. Pass my congratulations along to the rest of the guys, okay? And let me talk to Skipper."

Skipper came on. "Okay, it's over, and Davidson County and the FBI out of the Nashville field office are on their way."

"That's impressive work, Skipper. I'm proud of you."

"Hey, it's what we do. Save the world, save little girls . . . whatever."

"When the smoke clears, take everyone to Stockyard for dinner. It has the best steak in Nashville. And then get the whole team to Athens. We've got a little moving to do."

Chapter 11
Let 'er Do It

Over the next few days, we sanitized the house, removing every piece of evidence that said the place had ever been the lair of an American spy. The microbus made an excellent moving van, and once loaded to its limit, became a Cold-War-era time machine.

Thousands of pages detailed a five-decade history the world would never know. Throughout the packing, I found myself, time after time, engrossed in the handwritten script that read more like a spy thriller than a memoir. I couldn't wait to pore over every line when we got the collection back to Saint Marys, but I had another history lesson to experience before heading for the coast.

My new flight instructor answered on the second ring.

"Mr. Floyd, I'm Chase Fulton, and I understand you can teach me to fly my Mustang."

"Hello, Chase. Call me Dave. Bobby from the airport told me you'd be looking for a few hours in your new toy. I've been expecting your call."

"When are you available?"

"I'm retired, so I'm always available. Let's go this morning."

"I'll meet you at the hangar in an hour."

With the team headed southeast with my new treasure trove of Cold War history, Penny and I drove to the airport. My head was pounding with anticipation for my first lesson in the Mustang.

Dave pulled up in a Mustang of his own, but his was a 1965 convertible built by Ford, while mine was twenty years older and put together at North American Aviation.

"You must be Chase Fulton. I'm Dave Floyd."

I shook the man's rugged, grease-stained hand. "I am, and this is my wife, Penny."

"It's nice to meet you both. So, you're Bob Richter's protégé. I've heard a lot about you, and I've gotta tell you, I'm a little envious of your new ride."

I kicked at a pebble on the concrete. "I certainly didn't expect to inherit the Mustang. In fact, there are a lot of things about Dr. Richter I never expected."

"Yep, I hear you. He was quite a fellow." Dave stared up at the Mustang in a moment of reflection. "Well, let's drag the old girl out and see if she'll start. You'll never learn to fly in the hangar."

We towed the Mustang from the hangar and conducted a thorough preflight inspection. Once inside the cockpit, the interview began.

"Before we light the fire, tell me about the flying you've done. That Caravan on the ramp tells me you can fly something with a few extra knobs and levers, but I doubt you've ever flown anything like the Mustang."

"You're right," I admitted. "I've got a multi-engine commercial ticket with fifteen hundred hours or so, but zero Mustang time."

"It's good to know I'm not starting from scratch, but you'll have to forget what you *thought* you knew about how airplanes feel. Flown correctly, this one feels like a sports car, but if you try to wrestle with her, you'll lose every time."

"I'll keep that in mind." I scanned the panel that still held a few original-looking instruments but had mostly been upgraded with modern displays and an excellent stack of radios.

"You're sitting on a parachute," Dave said. "That's what the seat cushion is made of, but there's only three acceptable reasons to ever use it. Number one is a fire . . . a big fire. Two is if one of the wings comes off. These old beauties don't catch on fire, and the wings never come off."

"What's number three?"

"Two dozen Messerschmitts. You can shoot down twenty-three, but two dozen is too much to ask of anybody."

"So, you're saying I'll never use the parachute."

"Exactly. Now, let's go through the before-start checklist. That red T-handle is the hydraulic pressure release. Move it up and in. Fuel selector to the left. Always start and climb on the left tank. The carburetor overflow returns to the left tank, so if it's full and you're burning from the right, sooner or later, you'll be pissing fuel overboard out of that left tank."

We made our way through the checklist with Dave explaining everything in detail. When we finally reached the line that read "Start," the anticipation of the enormous twelve-cylinder engine roaring to life nearly stilled my heart. However, instead of engaging the starter, Dave said, "Okay, put everything back where it was, and let's do it again."

My reward would have to wait. I ran through the checklist twice more before he finally let me spin the prop. When it finally came, it was well worth the wait.

I silently ran through the sequence as my hands did the work. *Hold the brakes . . . starter . . . watch four blades go by . . . magnetos . . . mixture.*

The Rolls-Royce Merlin engine in front of my feet inhaled a mighty breath and announced its presence with a thundering voice. There's no other sound like that one. It's humbling, exciting, and intimidating all at once.

Dave yanked me from my trance. "Oil pressure!"

I shot my eyes to the gauge as the needle moved into the green arc. "Check."

"Never forget to immediately look for oil pressure as soon as she starts. That's over a quarter of a million dollars hanging out there on the nose, and the absence of fifty dollars worth of oil can send her to hell in a matter of seconds."

We taxied from the ramp to the run-up area and progressed through the pre-takeoff checklist.

"Okay, Chase, it's time to go flying. I'll get a clearance from the tower. Put us on the centerline, and lock the tailwheel."

"Yes, sir."

Less than a minute later, I eased the throttle forward and watched the world accelerate as the tailwheel came off the ground and airspeed built.

"Easy back pressure, and she'll fly right off."

He was right. *Katerina's Heart* took to the sky as if she loathed the ground.

Dave continued his confident tone. "Okay, positive rate of climb and no useable runway remaining. Tap the brakes and get the gear up. Set forty-six inches of manifold pressure and twenty-seven hundred RPMs for the climb."

I followed his instructions, and the warbird felt like an old friend I didn't know I had. The scene out the window reminded me of the innocence and ignorance that had defined me six years earlier, the first time I sat in the airplane with Dr. Richter. Back then, I had no way of knowing I would one day become not only the keeper of *Katerina's Heart*, but also the guardian of so many things my mentor held dear. Back then, I thought he was asking more of me than I could ever give, but in the years since my recruitment, I came to believe he wasn't asking anything of me. Instead, he was giving me a world I never knew existed and en-trusting me with the weighty responsibility of preserving it to be handed down to someone else when the day came for me to walk away—if I lived long enough to see the sun rise on that day.

"Okay, kid. Let's check a few boxes and then have some fun. What do you say?"

Checking boxes meant slow flight, stalls, emergency proce-dures, and normal operations. Having some fun meant letting the Mustang show off.

"Well done, Chase. It's obvious you can fly. Now it's time to learn to fly the Mustang. This airplane is a lot like a good bird dog. She wants to please you, but what she really wants to do is impress you. Well, that and shoot down a dozen Germans if she gets a chance."

For the next hour, we pushed the Mustang almost to her lim-its, and I did things I never imagined possible in an airplane.

"As much as the Mustangs loved a dogfight, strafing runs on ground targets were one of their favorite games. They can haul ass into a target, put six hundred rounds of fifty-caliber lead per minute on it, and disappear into the clouds."

Lake Hartwell, on the South Carolina-Georgia border, is formed by the dam on the Savannah River. There are dozens of islands scattered about the picturesque lake, but I doubted any had ever been assaulted by a P-51D.

"Divide your scan between the gunsight and your airspeed. You don't want to overspeed the airplane. Remember, the wing can stall at any airspeed. If you push her too hard toward the ground, the Earth is going to get mighty big right before you prang into it, no matter how hard you pull on that stick. We want to make a gun run and escape. We're not kamikazes. Any-thing above three hundred seventy-five miles per hour is going to be a lot of work to climb out of, so here's the procedure."

He took the controls. "We'll keep it below two-fifty today so the FAA doesn't write us a nasty letter, but in the war, these were done well above three hundred. Reduce the power as the nose comes down. Keep your eyes moving. Target . . . gunsight . . . airspeed . . . airspeed . . . gunsight . . . target . . . mirror."

"Mirror?" I asked.

"Yes, mirror. Those Germans were sneaky. Getting fixated on a target got a lot of American flyboys killed. That mirror gives you a chance to get a look at the guy who's about to dump a few hundred pounds of lead into your ass."

"Oh."

"Oh, indeed. Now, back to the target. Just like Lewis Grizzard said, 'Aim low, boys. They're ridin' Shetland ponies.' Your speed is going to make every shot long, so aim short and walk it in."

He demonstrated the gun run, and I could almost imagine a German airfield with Messerschmitts lined up like Rockettes just waiting to be chewed up by the six fifty-caliber machine guns in the wings.

"When it's time to run, check that airspeed again, and then gently pull the stick. It doesn't take much. She wants to climb and turn left, so let 'er do it. Don't add power until the airspeed starts to bleed off. You've got more than enough horses out there to pull you out of any mudhole, but don't be overanxious to spur them."

The strafing training was the most fun I'd ever had in an airplane, even without real guns in the wings, but I couldn't imagine I'd ever have a reason to put my newfound skill to use.

The remainder of the day was spent landing the Mustang.

"Always make a three-point landing, with one exception. If you ever get an unsafe gear indication, gently feel for the ground with a wheel landing. If the gear collapses or isn't there at all, that'll give you the ability to fly away and come up with another plan. This airplane's worth a fortune. It'd be a shame to slide it in on its belly."

Four days and eighteen flight hours later, Dave Floyd took Penny by the hand. "It's time for you to go for a ride with your husband."

And for the first time in my life, I held *Katerina's Heart* in my hands alone.

Chapter 12
It's What We Do

When I made the decision to fly the Caravan to Athens, I didn't consider I'd be returning to Saint Marys with two airplanes, neither of which Penny could legally nor safely fly. That made the return trip a three-legged affair involving three different airplanes. Penny could fly the One-Eighty-Two, but she wanted to ride back in the Mustang with me, so we flew *Katerina's Heart* home together and returned in the One-Eighty-Two to pick up the Caravan. It made for a long day of flying, and other than burning a lot of airplane gas, accomplished little.

* * *

Singer's leg was mostly back in one piece, even though its diameter was significantly smaller than its counterpart. That would resolve itself after a few dozen hours in the gym. A sniper's legs are almost as important as his eyes. Without the ability to get to —and more importantly—get away from a firing position, all the long-distance shooting skill in the world is worthless. Singer wouldn't allow the thousands of hours he'd spent perfecting his craft to ever become worthless. Second only to his faith, his mastery of the art of death-from-a-distance defined the man.

Mongo became the stable boy. Almost as big as most of the horses in the barn, he seemed to develop a natural connection with the animals that I never would have. Nothing about the horses interested or intrigued me. I disliked and distrusted them and made no effort to remedy either. Between Mongo's affection and Penny's fascination, the vile animals didn't need anything from me.

Clark continued healing, but that didn't stop Maebelle from doting over him. Her world revolved around caring for Clark first, the Judge second, and feeding the whole clan third. In time, Clark came out of the clamshell and slowly progressed toward the warrior I'd known him to be prior to his pair of near-death experiences. His drive and determination were greater than any I'd ever seen. His mind pushed his body to strengthen itself and claw at every barrier between him and his goal of returning to the field with me. I watched the sweat meld with his tears as pain, determination, and resistance became one. The strength his body had once known beckoned to him but proved unattainable. The speed and quickness that once defined his movements were gone. No matter how hard he pushed himself to reclaim the physical prowess he'd known, it simply wouldn't come. Seeing what he considered failure broke my heart and led to another of our rocking-chair prayer meetings on the back gallery of Bonaventure.

"I knew the day would come when I couldn't do it anymore," he began, "but I never thought I'd live through it."

"What do you mean?"

He dug the toe of his boot into the oak planking of the porch. "I figured I'd take a bullet I couldn't shake off, and I'd lay down and die in the dirt in some place nobody's ever heard of. In some ways, that's how I wanted it to end. This is a lot worse."

For most people, Clark's confession would've been labeled a pity party, but that's not what my partner was doing. Just as he'd become my teacher in all things tactical, I'd become his confessor, and that was a title I was proud to hold. He didn't need or want me to explain to him how it was far better to be alive than dead at the hands of bandits on the far side of the world. He didn't need reassurance that people loved and needed him regardless of his ability to operate. He needed someone to shut up and listen. As difficult as it was, I gave my partner exactly what he needed. We sat in the ancient chairs, watching the North River flow slowly to the sea, and each of us mourned silently as the reality of never digging another foxhole together poured over us on that muggy, marshland afternoon.

We all have roles to play in the lives of people we care about. Mine was well-defined with Clark. Our relationship had been forged in the fire of battle and beneath the blows of enemy hammers pounding us into the men we were—the warriors our country required us to be. I knew exactly what to expect of him every time he moved, flinched, or spoke. I knew every time Clark Johnson pulled a trigger, a bad guy would fall to the earth, and I knew every time someone struck out at my partner, exactly how the fight would end. I knew more about him than I knew about myself. Or so I thought.

"I don't care if she was born when I was fifteen. She loves me, and I love her, and I'm going with her."

I turned to face him. "I've watched women throw themselves at you from Bangladesh to Baghdad. I never thought it'd be a chef from South Georgia who'd hang her hooks in you, but I've got to say, I wouldn't have it any other way."

"I talked to the Judge about it, you know."

I smiled. "Really? And what did he have to say?"

"He told me a story about how people make relationships more complicated than they need to be. Then he told me to love her the way biscuits love gravy."

I shook my head. "What does that mean?"

He laughed. "I've been giving that a lot of thought, and all I can come up with is that biscuits by themselves are fine, and gravy is, too, but when you put the two together, there's not a whole lot of things on Earth that are better. So, I guess that's what he meant."

"The old man does have a way with words," I said. "Does she know you're going with her?"

He picked a fleck of something from his jeans and flipped it across the porch rail. "Not yet, but I'd like to take her sailing on your boat and ask her if she'd be okay with me tagging along wherever she decides to hang her shingle."

I looked at *Aegis* tied to the dock. "Everything I own is as much yours as it is mine. Take the boat anytime you want for as long as you want."

"Thanks, College Boy. I appreciate that. I may take her up to Hilton Head for a few days if you wouldn't mind."

* * *

While Clark, Maebelle, and Charlie the black lab were gone aboard *Aegis*, meals at Bonaventure weren't nearly as elegant. Penny was an excellent cook aboard the boat, but feeding Mongo, Singer, the Judge, and me, wasn't the same as grilling a snapper.

"I guess we're going to have to get used to dinner without Maebelle's magic touch," I said as I forked the last bite of store-bought apple pie into my mouth.

"Yep, I reckon so," said the Judge. "It's time for her to spread her wings and cook for folks who'll pay a hundred dollars a plate, unlike us freeloaders."

"Where do you think she'll go?" Penny asked.

The Judge wiped his mouth. "I've got it on good authority that there's a place in Miami just beggin' to be turned into the best restaurant that place has ever seen."

I turned to the Judge. "Good authority, you say? And just who would this good authority be?"

The old man winked. "Oh, I think you know who it might be. In fact, I think you probably work for the fellow."

Knowing Maebelle would be opening a gourmet restaurant in a city of six million hungry mouths that just happened to be the same city where Dominic Fontana ran his branch of the agency I worked for, suddenly made Clark's future look far brighter than I'd feared.

Rather than responding, I offered the Judge an abbreviated nod, and he returned the gesture.

* * *

I fell asleep with Penny's head on my shoulder in the upstairs bedroom. Sleeping in a bed that wasn't rocking gently with the waves felt bizarre, but knowing I'd soon be answering to Clark when Dominic passed the torch gave me the comfort to sleep on a barbed-wire fence if necessary.

The ringing of my phone yanked me from my sleep long before dawn. "Yeah, hello."

"Chase, it's Clark. I need you to gather your wits and let me know when you're awake."

I rubbed my knuckles into my eyes and yawned. "Okay, okay. I'm awake. What is it?"

"Have you ever heard of a Russian ship called the *Viktor Leonov*?"

"What? Why are you waking me up in the middle of the night to ask me if I've ever heard of a Russian ship that nobody's ever heard of?"

"Because we would've hit it if the radar alarm didn't go off."

Suddenly, I was wide awake. "Where are you?"

"We're twenty miles off Tybee Island," Clark said.

"Wait a minute. You're twenty miles off Savannah, and you almost hit a Russian ship. Is that what you're telling me?"

"Exactly, College Boy. And she's running dark."

"Is it a cargo ship?"

Clark scoffed. "I wouldn't be calling you about a cargo ship. She's a surveillance boat if I've ever seen one."

"What is a blacked-out Russian surveillance ship doing twenty miles off the East Coast?"

"Now we're asking the same questions," he said. "Radar puts her at thirty-two degrees, two point zero four minutes north, and eighty degrees, forty-eight point nine three degrees west. She's making eight knots, course one-nine-five degrees."

My heart sank. "Clark, please tell me you didn't have the AIS turned on."

Aegis is equipped with the Automatic Identification System that tells other ships her identity, speed, and direction. On my latest mission in the Black Sea, I sunk an *Aegis* look-alike in an effort to convince a Russian SVR colonel I was on my way to the bottom of the sea. If the *Viktor Leonov* was a spy ship and she had just identified *Aegis*, it wouldn't take long for Colonel Nicholai Sokolov to get the news.

"I'm not sure," Clark admitted. "As soon as I identified the *Leonov*, I shut everything down except the radar, but I don't know for sure if I had the AIS on before I went dark."

"Okay," I sighed. "There's nothing we can do about it now. Just make sure you don't bring the AIS online when you fire back up. I'll pass the word to Dominic and Skipper, and we'll go from there."

"Keep me posted. You know our destination. I'll keep the satphone handy, and of course, I'm scrambling."

"I'll be in touch. Is Maebelle okay?"

"She's sleeping like a baby," he said. "And I intend for her to stay that way."

Skipper was back in Silver Spring, Maryland, and would answer before the second ring. My gut wanted her on the job and feeding me all the intel she could find on the *Viktor Leonov*, but protocol required that I notify Dominic first. He wasn't so prompt to answer.

In a groggy, sleep-filled voice, he mumbled, "Yeah."

"Dominic, it's Chase. There's a Russian spy ship off the coast of Savannah."

Suddenly, the tiredness was gone from his voice. "How far?"

"Twenty miles."

He belted, "How do you know, and what's her name?"

"Clark almost hit her with *Aegis*. She was running dark, and she's the *Viktor Leonov*."

I could almost hear the wheels turning in his head. "If you're right about her being the *Leonov*, that's a *Vishnya*-class boat. She's a SIGINT platform, and she has no business being anywhere near Savannah. Is Skipper on it yet?"

"Signals intelligence is exactly what I was afraid of," I said. "Clark isn't sure if he had the AIS turned on when he encountered her. And no, Skipper isn't on it yet. I called you first."

"Oh, shit . . . the AIS," Dominic whispered. "That's not good. But there's nothing we can do about it now."

"My thoughts exactly."

"Okay, you've done what you were obligated to do. I'm authorizing limited action. Get Skipper on it, and I'll send it up the chain. We'll brief at zero eight hundred."

"Done." I immediately pressed speed dial for Skipper, just as Penny rolled over and opened one eye.

"Is everything all right?" she asked.

"Probably not, but I'll tell you about it when I get off the phone."

Skipper answered as if she'd never been asleep. "Chase, what's wrong?"

"We have a mission," I began. "Write this down. A *Vishnya*-class Russian SIGINT boat called the *Viktor Leonov* is twenty miles east of Savannah. Clark spotted her. Dominic authorized action, and we'll brief at zero eight."

"Do you have a lat/long?"

I gave her the coordinates Clark had reported.

"I'm on it," she said. "Do you want to hold, or should I call you back?"

"Call me back," I said as I hung up.

Penny was wide-eyed and sitting up in bed. "What's a SIGINT boat?"

"It's a spy ship," I said. "And it's running dark twenty miles off the coast of Savannah. Clark spotted it on the way to Hilton Head."

She smiled and slowly shook her head. "I knew it. You boys will never be happy unless you're right in the middle of an international incident."

I shrugged. "Hey, it's what we do."

Chapter 13
Who Says?

After the zero-dark-thirty phone call from Clark, there was no chance of going back to sleep, so I descended the stairs and started a pot of coffee. I took my first cup on the back porch, watching the sun peek over Cumberland Island.

"Mind if I join you?"

Hunter's voice startled me from my sunrise trance. "Oh, hey. What are you doing up so early?"

He glanced at his watch. "I've been up for over an hour. I was running down by the river and saw the light up here."

"Come on up. There's coffee in the kitchen, and I've got something to tell you."

He ascended the steps two at a time and returned with a steaming mug. "Okay, let's hear it."

I pointed toward the empty rocking chair. "Have a seat. This isn't the kind of thing you hear standing up."

He raised an eyebrow and took the seat.

"I got a call from Clark about an hour ago. He and Maebelle are about twenty miles off Tybee Island on their way to Hilton Head."

Hunter blew across his coffee. "So, he just called to report his position at five in the morning?"

"Not hardly," I said. "He came across a ship running dark and got a radar collision alarm. The ship is a Russian SIGINT platform called the *Viktor Leonov.*"

He rested the mug on the arm of the rocker. "A Russian spy ship twenty miles off Tybee Island. Are you sure?"

"Yep. I don't think Clark is the type to make up something like that."

"Have you sent it up the chain?"

"Of course. I called Dominic as soon as I hung up with Clark. He authorized Skipper to go to work, so she's on the job now, and he's sending it up the flagpole to see who shoots at it."

Hunter nodded. "When's the briefing?"

"Eight."

He took a tentative sip of his coffee. "Do you think they're looking for you?"

"Me?" I asked incredulously. "No. Why would they send a ship all the way over here to look for me?"

"They sent a yacht to the Bahamas to try and sink you. What makes you think the *Leonid*, or whatever you called it, wasn't part of that operation?"

"*Viktor Leonov,*" I said. "And I can't imagine the Russians thinking I'm important enough to send a spy ship after me. There has to be more to it."

He shrugged. "Okay, believe what you want, but you pissed in a lot of Russian Cheerios, and they're not known for under-reacting."

I sighed, hoping he was wrong, but like Clark, Hunter wasn't wrong very often. "We'll know more at eight. Until then, all we can do is drink coffee and be thankful the *Leonov* isn't an aircraft carrier."

Hunter slurped another sip. "Whatever you say. You're the boss."

The passage of time is far from perceptually fixed. For a child, it takes eons for the night before Christmas to pass. For Hunter and me, it felt like eight o'clock would never come. By the time the phone rang, we'd polished off two pots of coffee and devoured the sausage biscuits Penny retrieved from Hardees.

"Hey, Dominic. You're on speaker, and Hunter is here."

"Hello again, Chase, and good morning to Hunter. Hang on a second while I patch Skipper in with us."

A few clicks later, Skipper said, "Okay, I'm here."

Dominic called the meeting to order. "Here's what we know. The ship is definitely the *Viktor Leonov*. The Coast Guard picked it up two days ago, and they've been tracking it. DOD and State are both on board and watching and waiting. There's not much we can do militarily. She's technically in international waters and not behaving aggressively."

I interrupted. "She's running dark, though. Isn't that reason enough to suspect she's up to something sinister?"

Dominic said, "What do you want them to do? Board her and write the skipper a ticket for not turning the lights on?"

"Okay, I'm sorry. I'll shut up."

He continued. "What we don't know is why they're out there. We don't have anything going on that should be of particular interest to them. The only active exercises we have happening right now are off the coasts of Maine and Norfolk. It would make sense for the *Leonov* to be up there, but all's quiet on the southern front. Any ideas?"

"All my sources agree with Dominic," Skipper said, "but I do have some unofficial reports that the *Leonov* was patrolling south of Cuba about six weeks ago and then vanished. I'm scanning satellite imagery, but she's a tiny ship as ships go, at just a hair over three hundred feet. If I can find her, I may be able to put together a track history, but it's going to take a while."

"What's her draft?" I asked.

She shuffled some papers. "At max displacement of just under thirty-five hundred tons, she draws four-and-a-half meters. That's just shy of fifteen feet. Why?"

I said, "Hunter's got a theory that she's here listening for me. If she was the support vessel for the attempt on my life in Honeymoon Harbour, she'd have to draft less than sixteen feet. Something with power and relatively shallow draft dragged that crippled yacht off the reef."

The phone grew silent until Dominic asked, "And this was Hunter's idea?"

I looked up at Hunter.

He said, "It was just the first thing that popped into my head when Chase told me about the ship. It's just a gut feeling, not based on anything solid."

Dominic cleared his throat. "Sometimes our guts know more than our heads."

I said, "Do you have anything else, Skipper?"

"Yeah, I've got tons of stuff, but it's mostly just data. You know . . . crew size, armament, propulsion. Stuff like that."

"Armament?" I said.

She shuffled more paper. "Yeah, it's nothing major—just enough to defend herself a little. She's got a pair of AK-Six-Thirty Gatling guns. Those are thirty-millimeter, six-barrel guns. And the only other kicker is a pair of SA-N-Eight surface-to-air missiles."

Hunter asked, "Aren't those shoulder-fired MANPADS?"

Skipper said, "Yeah, they're man-portable air-defense systems. I've got the data on them if you want it."

"No, that's not necessary. I know the specs. They're bad-ass, supersonic missiles that run about nine hundred knots and can track an F-16 nose-on. They're serious weapons, but what makes you think they only have two of them on board?"

She shuffled some more. "That's what the Defense Intelligence Agency reports. I'm just quoting DIA data."

"Hmm," Hunter moaned. "They could have a thousand of those things on board."

Skipper said, "Yeah, I guess they could. It's not like it's a ship-mounted rail system."

"We're getting off track," Dominic said. "Until they start shooting them, we don't care how many missiles they have on board. Right now, we need to know what they're doing and why they're doing it. The Pentagon isn't going to want us out there messing with them, but since one of our guys—that's you, Chase—might be the reason they're here, we've got a vested interest in working the problem."

"Agreed," Hunter said.

I shook my head. "The keyword here is *may*. I *may* be the reason they're here, but I think that's highly unlikely."

It was Skipper's turn to sound off. "That's how we work these things, Chase. We start with what we know, then move to what's probable, and then what's plausible. Finally, we move all the way down to possible but unlikely. Right now, the only reasonable theory is that the *Leonov* is the boat that ran the op on you in Honeymoon Harbour."

"I don't think that's likely."

Dominic said, "It doesn't matter what's *likely* at this point. For now, that's the best theory we have. Skipper, I want you to work from that angle until you find a better one."

"Yes, sir."

As if he were thinking out loud, Dominic muttered, "We're going to need a fast little boat. Hey, Skipper, what's the *Leonov*'s top speed?"

This time, there was no paper shuffling. "The official top speed is sixteen knots, but the hull design and engine configuration *should* make closer to eighteen if my computer hasn't forgotten how to do math."

"Okay, so we need something that'll do at least twice that speed."

"My RHIB from *Aegis* will do that," I said, "but twenty miles offshore is a terrible plan in a RHIB."

Dominic said, "No, we need something heavy and fast, but still small enough to make a poor target if we get under their skin too deep and they spin up that Gatling gun."

I grinned. "What about something that can go twenty times the speed of the *Leonov*?"

"There's never been a boat that can do three hundred sixty knots," Dominic argued.

"Who said it has to be a boat? I've got a Mustang."

Sometimes, when people say *no*, they mean *maybe*. Dominic Fontana is not one of those people. Dominic's *no* is non-negotiable.

"You think flying a World War Two fighter across the deck of a Russian spy ship is a good plan?" he roared.

"I didn't say the Mustang was a *good* plan. I just said I have one."

"And if you want to keep that gorgeous piece of history, and your life, you'll keep it as far away from that ship as possible."

"So, does that mean you'll think about it?" I asked, just to see if I could make him explode.

He didn't take the bait. Instead, he sat in silence, presumably waiting for me to say something less crazy.

I finally gave in. "Okay, I get it. I don't get to strafe any Russian decks with my fifty-cals. How about a boat like the SEALs use—the Mark V fast patrol boat? They're good offshore and definitely capable of thirty-six knots."

"How many Mark V fast patrol boats do you have lying around, Chase?"

It was my turn to go on the offensive. "I'm not the boat guy. That's your area, but what if I knew a guy who knew a guy who just happened to have a few Mark V's at his disposal?"

Dominic cleared his throat. "Then I'd say you should get your *guy* on the phone."

"In that case, I'll give the president a call."

Chapter 14
Ask Daddy for the Keys

I'd never come to grips with the fact that I had the direct telephone number to the president of the United States. So far, I'd never dialed the number except to ask for a favor. Sooner or later, that well would dry up, so it was time to come up with a new strategy.

"Please hold for the president," came the pleasant but professional voice of the staff duty officer who answered exactly four seconds after I pressed send.

I heard the president's muffled voice. "Hold on a minute, senator, I have to take this. Well, hello, Chase. How are things down south?"

"Hello, Mr. President. Thank you for taking my call. I hope I'm not interrupting anything too important."

"No, no, not at all. I was just having an argument with the senator from Ohio. Well, actually, I wasn't arguing. I was simply explaining to him why he is wrong. Would you care to weigh in on the topic?"

"No, Mr. President, I'd rather not, but it's safe to say I'd agree with you if I did."

"As you should, my boy. What can I do for you?"

I swallowed hard. "Actually, sir, I'm calling to ask what I can do for you. I've stumbled into some information about a certain, shall we say, foreign boat drifting around off the coast of Georgia with a few too many antennae sticking up off her decks."

"And just how did you stumble onto this bit of information?"

I redirected. "Let's just say I don't miss much when it happens in my backyard. It's my guess that sending a destroyer out to run that particular boat away isn't an option. I thought I might be able to have a little fun with her and repay at least a small portion of the enormous debt I owe you."

"Are we keeping score now, Chase? Is that what we're doing?"

"No, sir, but I'm a man of my word. I told you I'd always help if I could. So, now, with this, maybe I can."

"Maybe you can, indeed. Let me confirm that the good senator from the great state of Ohio has come around to my way of thinking, as any sensible man would, and I'll call you back."

"I'll be right here waiting for your call, Mr. President."

Penny sat with her eyes closed, continually shaking her head.

"What is it? You don't approve of me calling the president?"

She sighed. "Oh, no, I approve. But I still can't believe I'm married to a man who can do that whenever he wants."

"You should answer when he calls back. You can say, 'Please hold for Mr. Fulton.'"

She giggled. "Yeah, I'll do that. But seriously, what are you doing? You want the president to lend you a fast patrol boat, so why did you offer your services instead of asking for the boat?"

I tapped my temple with my index finger. "I'm the psychologist here. I'm going to convince the president that he *wants* to give me a fast patrol boat, and I'll agree to take it because it's my duty to serve my country by doing what my president needs of me."

"You're going to play head games with the president of the United States? I think you meant *psycho* and not *psychologist*, secret agent man."

"Trust me, my dear. I know what I'm doing."

She threw a flip-flop at me. "Trustworthy people never say 'Trust me.'"

I kissed her forehead and handed her my phone. "Answer it if it rings. I have to hit the head. I'll be right back."

When I rounded the corner into the hallway, I hid behind the ornate door casing and waited for the phone to ring. I didn't have to wait long.

"Chase! It's ringing. Get in here!"

I turned my head to sound farther away. "Answer it. I'll be right out."

Timid isn't a word anyone has ever used to describe Penny Fulton. She's one of the most confident women I've ever known, but hearing the little girl who answered the phone made me bite my lip to contain my laughter.

"Uh, hello?"

"Yes, sir. Uh, just a minute. He's, um . . . well, he's in the bathroom, Mr. President."

I couldn't hold it any longer, and laughter erupted from way down in my gut. The look on Penny's face was fury laced with embarrassment of the highest order as she shoved the phone toward me and started a barrage of slaps with her remaining flip-flop.

I tried to compose myself as I pressed the phone to my ear. "I'm sorry for making you wait, Mr. President."

Penny's attack didn't stop, and the echoing report of her rubber flip-flop filled the earpiece of my phone.

"Penny's hitting you with her shoe, isn't she, Chase?"

"Yes, sir, I'm afraid she is."

"Tell her to add a couple shots for me. You deserve it. Now let's get down to business. You seem to know more about our uninvited guest than you should. We'll deal with how you found out later. For now, let's talk about what we can do about it."

"I'm all ears, sir. If what you need is within my power, I'm at your service."

"I didn't get elected to the highest office in the land by being played, young man. You wouldn't have called unless you already had a plan, so let's hear it. What do you want from me so you can go harass Comrade Commander Krusevich?"

I made a mental note of the name of the man I assumed was the captain of the *Viktor Leonov.* "Penny was right, again, but it was worth a shot."

"No, it wasn't, but you're welcome to keep trying as long as I'm living at this prestigious address. Perhaps you'll get better at it in the next six years."

"You've got my vote, sir."

"I'm going to hold you to that, son. And you better get out and round up a few thousand of your closest friends to check the same box and pull the handle in the voting booth next November. So, what do you want, Chase?"

"I want a boat. A Mark V fast patrol boat, preferably without any U.S. markings on it, sir."

"Ha! You don't ask for much, do you?"

"If you could send a platoon of SEALs out there and board that ship, you'd have already done it, Mr. President. I'm offering you a chance to let me do the dirty work for you with not only plausible deniability, but absolute deniability. Give me a boat, or tell me where I can get one, and then have the National Reconnaissance Office pipe a satellite feed into the Oval Office so you can enjoy the show."

The president let out a long, low sigh. "I like the way you think, Chase. You have yourself a great evening, and next time, listen to your beautiful wife. She's a lot smarter than you."

The line went dead before I could respond.

"What did he say?" Penny demanded.

"He said you're a lot smarter than me."

"Duh. Everybody knows that. But what did he say about the boat?"

"He didn't say anything about the boat. That's what's called plausible deniability. Oh, and he also said for you to stop hitting his right-hand man with your flip-flop."

"He did not."

I shrugged. "Well, he said something like that."

"So, are you getting the boat?"

I continued my shrug. "I don't know. We'll see."

"So, is that it? Now we just sit and wait?"

"How should I know? Just because I have his phone number doesn't mean I have any clue what he's going to do next."

"And you're supposed to be the one to save the world. Some spy you are."

"We're not spies!" came a resounding cry from all over the house.

Hunter, Singer, and Mongo appeared from their hiding places. Mongo's hiding place just happened to be a little bigger than the others.

"So, we're getting the boat?" Hunter said.

I laughed. "I don't know, but it sort of sounded like he'd be dispatching Santa Claus to drop a fast patrol boat down our chimney."

Mongo chuckled. "I've worked for a lot of people over the years, but I've got to say, this is the craziest outfit I've ever been part of, and I love it."

Singer, ever the serious member of the team, said, "What are you, or we, going to do with this boat if and when it does come down the chimney?"

I thought I'd have an immediate answer, but none came. As I stood glancing between my team members, Penny came to my rescue. "The boat wasn't Chase's idea. Dominic is the one who said we needed a fast boat. Chase wanted to pretend it was nineteen-forty-four again and go after them with the Mustang."

Hunter raised his hand. "For the record, I like the Mustang plan, but only if I get to come, too."

Mongo furrowed his brow as if he just realized the world was coming to an end.

"What's wrong?" I asked, sincerely concerned.

He let out a painful sigh. "I miss Maebelle."

I shoved the giant, but he didn't move. "You miss Maebelle's cooking."

"Maybe a little," he admitted.

I laughed. "Come on. Let's do the Riverside Café for dinner. It's on me."

The only Greek restaurant in Saint Marys sits next door to a submarine museum and is across Saint Marys Street from the Cumberland Island ferry landing. Everything on the menu is magnificent, but it's the desserts that keep customers lining up night after night. The portions are enormous—almost big enough for Mongo—and the folks behind the counter are some of the friendliest in town.

We ate for an hour, gorging ourselves on dishes we couldn't pronounce, and then passed plates of cake, pie, pastries, and of course baklava around the table until we'd stuffed ourselves to overflowing.

"Do we really have to walk all the way back to Bonaventure?" Hunter whined.

I poked at his stomach. "It's less than a mile, you wuss. After that meal, you need to walk it off. Now, let's go."

The city of Saint Marys is divided into two distinct districts: the old waterfront district and the new side of town. Bonaventure Plantation was nestled neatly between the old district and the North River—the perfect place for me. Aside from aboard my boat, I'd never felt more at home anywhere on Earth.

When we survived the arduous forced march back to Bonaventure, I felt just like a kid on Christmas morning. "Would you look at that? Santa Claus *did* come, but he didn't drop it down the chimney."

Tied to my dock, where *Aegis* would've been if she weren't in Hilton Head with Clark and Maebelle, was a nasty-looking, haze-gray Mark V fast patrol boat with absolutely no markings of any kind. All that was missing was a big red bow tied to the arch.

Hunter said, "I should've known."

"Should've known what?" I asked.

"That's the boat from Kings Bay we used when we played aggressor during training exercises. The SEALs beat it all to hell and even sank it. We yanked it off the bottom and drug it ashore. That thing's been sitting in the dry dock for at least a year."

"Santa Claus must live on Pennsylvania Avenue," I said.

"Yep, and he must have a few elves at the submarine base, too," Singer added.

Suddenly, we forgot all about our overfilled bellies and headed for the dock. The aluminum hull was battered and beaten, but the deck was dry. The weapons mounts sat empty, but that was easy enough to solve. We had no shortage of guns.

Mongo planted his huge foot on the gunwale and gave it a shove. "If we're going to play tag with the Russian Navy with this heap of junk, I think we oughta at least take her out for a sea trial."

The rest of the team and I wordlessly agreed and hopped aboard. I stepped behind the wheel and pressed the starter switches. The engines spat, coughed, and belched their way to life, but it was far from impressive.

Penny was still standing on the dock with eyebrows raised, her question obvious.

I left the pilothouse and reached for her hand. "Come aboard, my lady. You have the helm."

A perfect smile replaced her questioning expression, and she leapt over the gunwale, landing like a cat on the deck beside me. "I have the helm."

Hunter and Singer cast off the lines, and seconds later, we were backing away from the dock. One of the old engines died twice before Penny let the bow fall off downstream and opened the throttles. What was left of the engines did their best to push the heavy boat through the brackish water, but she definitely didn't perform like the craft Lieutenant Schauble, the SEAL commander, used to intercept *Aegis* in the Gulf Stream. Penny nursed the throttles, coaxing all the power she could get out of the engines, but it was clear a tune-up was in order.

She turned and met my gaze, instantly recognizing the disappointment on my face. "Don't worry, Chase. Earl can fix it."

Chapter 15
Stud Muffin

Although I loved my BMW, Dr. Richter's old VW Microbus was quickly becoming my new favorite ride. The team had driven it home from Athens and unloaded everything we'd taken from what would become Anya's house . . . if we ever saw her again.

As far as I knew, the State Department still had her tucked away in the wilds of northern Virginia, debriefing every detail of her life out of her. I didn't envy her situation, but it had to be better than living above Yuri's bar in a Siberian hotel on the edge of nowhere.

Penny and I pulled into the St. Augustine Municipal Marina, and the microbus bus buzzed to a stop. I don't know if the folks at VW meant for it to make that sound, but I loved the personality of the old bus.

I punched in my old code, and surprisingly, it still worked. The gate swung open, and we strolled down the dock, hand-in-hand. A flood of memories poured over me as the smells and sounds of the Matanzas River filled my senses.

"This is where you clocked the gangster who was pretending to be a cop. Remember that?"

Penny rolled her eyes. "How could I forget? Look, the blood-stain is still on the dock."

I dragged my toe across the dark stain. "You're pretty lethal with a boat hook."

She leapt into some sort of cartoon kung-fu stance and let out a ferocious sound that wouldn't have frightened a fly.

I laughed. "What's wrong with you?"

"Apparently, quite a bit. I married you."

I playfully gave her a little shove toward the water. "Best decision you ever made."

She ignored my jab. "Come on. Let's see if we can find your supermodel girlfriend slash boat mechanic."

Earl, the best marine mechanic I'd ever met, wasn't hard to find. Her mother named her Earline, but she'd stab a screwdriver through your hand if you called her anything other than Earl. We found her—well, the bottom half of her—sticking out of the engine compartment of a dilapidated boat that was far older than the microbus.

I yelled across the stern of the boat. "Nice butt, baby girl!"

Her echoing, disembodied reply came from the bowels of the engine compartment. "Is that you, Stud Muffin?"

She shimmied, or rather, wallowed her bulbous frame out of the compartment and wiped a blob of greasy sweat from her brow. "I knew that was you, Stud Muffin. I could feel my loins getting all warmed up."

She tumbled across the transom of the boat and landed on the dock like a walrus. The sixty-something, spikey-haired woman was taller lying down than she was standing up. When she finally made it to her feet, she threw her arms around me in a bear hug that would've made a wrestler proud.

"How've you been, old girl?"

"Me? You know how I've been. I've been greasy, overworked, and sexy. The question is, *where* have you been?" She motioned toward Penny with her chin. "I see you're still draggin' that skinny thing around with you. Oh my God. Is that a wedding ring?"

Penny stuck out her left hand. "Hey, Earl. It is. I finally made an honest man of your stud muffin."

She grabbed Penny's hand and pulled it close to her squinted eyes. "Man! That's some kind of ring. You done good, boy. But you know, she's way too good for you, so when she gets her head straight and runs off, you know momma's gonna be right here waitin' for you."

"It's always nice to have a fallback plan, Earl. It's good to see you."

She laughed that Green Giant sound she used for laughter and hugged me again. "So, I know this ain't no social call, so what'd you break, and how much you gonna pay me to fix it?"

It took significant effort to get my long arms around the woman, but I returned the hug with everything I had. "Believe it or not, this time, I didn't break it. It came to me already broken."

"Well, what is it? And where is it?" She spun around, looking for my boat.

"It's a Mark V fast patrol boat, and it's up in Saint Marys. I sort of inherited it, you might say. It runs, but just barely."

The wrinkled, weathered skin of Earl's face stretched smooth as her eyes turned to saucers. "A Mark V? How the hell did you get your hands on a Mark V? I knew there was more to you than you were lettin' on."

I looked away. "It's for an article I'm writing."

"Yeah, sure it is, and I'm on a diet gettin' ready for my cover girl photo shoot for this year's swimsuit issue."

I shot a quick glance at Penny. "Make a note to order a thousand copies when that swimsuit issue comes out."

She laughed. "No way, big boy. We can't have that much sexy lying around. I need your attention on me."

"Yeah, yeah, screw you two. So, what's wrong with them motors on your Mark V for your so-called article?"

"Like I said, they run, but most lawn mowers make more horsepower than those two engines."

"If they ain't seized up, I can fix whatever else is wrong with 'em. Let's go."

"Let's go?" I said. "You're going to need to pack a bag. This may take a few days."

"Hell, I've got a relatively clean pair of panties in the truck, and these are my travelin' shoes. I can make it a good four or five days with what I've got on."

Earl followed us back to Saint Marys in her beat-up F-350 dually that she called a classic. I don't know if I'd agree with it being a classic, but it was exactly the truck a diesel mechanic of Earl's caliber should be driving.

When we pulled into the circular drive at Bonaventure Plantation, Earl stood on the crushed shell driveway and looked up at the antebellum mansion. She let out a long low whistle. "Baby Boy, this is some kind of place. That make-believe writing job of yours must really pay good."

"It covers the rent," I said. "Come on, I'll show you what's left of the boat."

"Can I drive in the yard?" she asked. "You know, all my tools is in the truck, and I don't want to hurt my back totin' 'em down there. You know, with my photo shoot comin' up and all."

"Sure you can, Earl. Drive around this way, and you'll see the boat down at the dock."

Earl beat us to the dock and was already pacing back and forth, taking in the tattered remains of the once-remarkable Mark V.

"So, what do you think?" I asked.

She did the whistle again. "She's gorgeous, and she's a lot more boat than those old Vietnam river rats. Let's get a look at them motors."

"Make yourself at home, Earl. Whatever you or the boat needs, just let me know. We'll be up at the house while you two get to know each other."

* * *

Three hours later, Earl made her way up the steps to the back door, and in her usual, subtle style, yelled through the kitchen into the house. "Hey, Stud Muffin! You in there?"

Hunter shot a spray of ice water from his nose. "Is that what your mechanic calls you?"

I walked through the kitchen and opened the door for her. "Come on in, Earl. There's a bunch of people in here who can't wait to meet you."

"I ain't got time for socializin', but I do have some good news. Is there a good weldin' or machine shop in town?"

"I'm sure there is. What are you building?"

"It ain't your motors that's the problem. They're fine. I mean, real fine. That boat's been underwater, and somebody put a pair of brand-new motors in it when they got it up. Didn't you even look in the engine room?"

"No. Honestly, I don't know the difference between a carburetor and an ignition coil. It wouldn't have done any good for me to look in there."

She threw up her hands. "Well, lucky for you them motors ain't got carburetors nor coils. What you do have is two aluminum tanks full of rotten diesel fuel and bacteria."

"Are you telling me all that's wrong with the boat is bad gas?"

"No, it ain't gas. It's diesel . . . or it used to be diesel before it turned into goopy, rotten sludge. I'm gonna rebuild the whole fuel system from the tanks to the injectors. It ain't gonna be cheap, but . . ."—she looked around Maebelle's commercially-equipped kitchen—"from the looks of things, you ain't too worried about spendin' money."

"Let's say we've got a maintenance fund for the boat. How much?"

She wiped her nose on the sleeve of her filthy T-shirt. "It's gonna be every bit of ten grand by the time I get done, and that's just parts. It's the labor that's gonna really burn ya."

The Judge ambled into the kitchen with curiosity in his eyes. "Afternoon, Chase. Who's your friend?"

"Judge, this is Earline, the best diesel mechanic on the East Coast."

He offered an abbreviated Southern bow of his head. "It's a pleasure to meet you, Earline. I'm Bernard Huntsinger, but call me Judge. Everybody does."

"It's nice to meet you, too, Judge. And call me Earl. That and a few other names I can't really say in polite company; them's the only names I answer to."

"Well, all right. Earl, it is . . . while we're in polite company. Did I hear you say something about needing a machine shop?"

She wiped her nose again. "Well, really, alls I need is a good welding machine—some good heavy aluminum or stainless steel would be even better—a brake, and a drill press. I can do the work. I just need the tools and materials."

"Well," said the Judge, "I've not been out there in some time, but I think you'll find everything you need in the shop beside the horse barn. Fergusson Metal Works is about four miles away, and I'm sure they'll have the material you need. What are you building?"

"All right, then. This job is gettin' better by the minute. I'm fixin' the fuel system on Stud Muffin's Mark V."

"Stud Muffin," the Judge said. "Indeed. That must be the boat the men from the Navy yard dropped off yesterday."

I nodded. "Yes, sir. That's the one. We have a job offshore that requires a little more boat than your Carolina Skiff, so the Navy was kind enough to let us borrow one they had lying around."

Earl huffed. "Ha! A writer, my ass."

The Judge gave her a knowing smile and pulled on the door of the refrigerator. "When is Maebelle coming back? An old man could starve to death like this."

Penny made her appearance and took the Judge by the arm. "Come with me, Judge. I'm taking the boys down to Lang's for lunch. You can join us."

"Great idea," I said. "Bring back a plate for Earl and me, if you don't mind."

I hated missing a trip to Lang's. It was a great waterfront seafood restaurant situated diagonally across the street from Riverside Grill. Everything they serve was swimming not long before it found its way into Lang's kitchen.

I rode in the passenger side of Earl's dually as we bounced down the path to the shop.

"So, is this place yours or the old man's?"

"It's a long story," I said. "It's technically still his, but believe it or not, he's my great-great-uncle, I think, and this place has been in our family for almost two hundred years. He left it to me. And Maebelle, who I guess is my second or third cousin, is the only other living heir. She's a chef. That's why everyone's so hungry around here. She's gone off with Clark to Hilton Head aboard *Aegis*."

"Why didn't she get this place?"

"She doesn't want to stay here. Like I said, she's a chef, so she's moving to Miami to open a gourmet restaurant. She's using her portion of the inheritance to finance that venture."

Earl raised her eyebrows. "So, Pretty Boy and a chef, huh?"

I grinned. "Yep. Believe it or not, a woman finally got her hooks into Clark. He got hurt pretty badly overseas, so he's moving on to the next chapter of his life with Maebelle and his father in Miami. Clark's dad is sort of in the boatyard business down there."

"Is that so?" she said. "Well, if that man looks anything like Clark, you can tell him you know a damn fine diesel mechanic who'd love to move to South Florida."

"I'll do that, Earl. Here's the shop. Just pull in beside the small door."

Bonaventure never ceased to amaze me. The horse barn, which would fit nicely on any Kentucky thoroughbred farm, was surprising enough, but "the shop," as the Judge called it, looked like an engine plant for Ferrari. It was spotless with every imaginable machine lining the exterior walls. A large, open area with a hydraulic lift and overhead crane consumed the center of the space. Stainless-steel workbenches on locking casters were situated neatly around the space, and nine rows of overhead lights lit up the area like an operating room.

Earl's whistle returned. "Boy, this is what momma calls a shop. Skinny Penny may not be a gold digger, but she sure done good latchin' on to you, Stud Muffin."

I grinned. "To tell you the truth, this is the first time I've been inside this place. I'm just as surprised as you. So, do you think you'll have everything you need in here?"

"I've got everything I could *ever* need in here. If this place had a bathroom and a hot plate, I'd never leave."

I pointed toward a pair of heavy double doors. "Something tells me you just might find one of those back there."

I was right. Through the doors was a bathroom, two offices, and a kitchenette.

Earl examined the space. "Yep, I'm movin' in. We can swap out the rent in work and 'special favors,' if you know what I mean."

"The Judge was a lawyer in his younger days, so I'll see if he can work up a rental agreement for us, but you're going to have to be a little more specific about those special favors."

* * *

A trip to Ferguson's and a stop by the auto parts store cost me just over six thousand bucks, but Earl assured me we weren't finished spending money.

"So, come clean. What are you doing up here with all this money and fancy military boats? What's really going on, Chase?"

I sighed. "It's a long story, Earl. Let's just say I'm not really a writer, but you've probably read a book or two about people like me. Have you ever heard of an author named Cap Daniels? He writes about people who do the kinds of things I do."

"I knew it. You can't fool Earl. This old girl's been around. I don't do much readin', but I bet this Cap Daniels fellow ain't never really met nobody just like you. Maybe I'll look him up next time I'm perusing the library. Come to think of it, I don't even know where the library is."

I laughed. "Maybe we can find you a coloring book. I'm going to get out of your way so you can work. Do you need anything?"

"I could use a sandwich and a beer."

"Penny will be back with lunch soon, and I'll hook you up. In the meantime, I'll be in the house if you need me."

"Just feed me soon. You won't like me if I get hangry."

"Hangry?" I said.

"Yeah, that's hungry *and* angry. Not a good combo."

As I walked back to the house, I peered through the trees, hoping to catch a glimpse of the Mark V, but my new favorite toy was practically invisible against the backdrop of shadows and gray water. The thought of my boat being invisible sent the synapses firing, and I knew exactly how I was going to stroll right through the Russians' back door without them ever knowing I was there.

Chapter 16
A Tough Crowd

Penny returned with a stack of Styrofoam boxes from Lang's, and I promptly delivered one to Earl in the shop. I found her inside a rectangular, stainless-steel tank, her Weeble-like form backlit by a blue welding flame.

"Is that my new gas tank?"

The flame stopped, and Earl's voice echoed from behind the welding helmet. "Nope, it's a diesel tank. I'm going to teach you the difference sooner or later. Did you bring me something to eat?"

I placed the box on the table. "I did, and I even managed to find a beer, but only one as long as you're working."

She shuffled out of the tank. "Tanks a lot. You're the best."

"I see what you did there, but you'd better stick to mechanic work. I don't think a career in comedy is in the cards for you."

"Weld, it was funny to me," she jabbed.

"Stop it. You're killing me. Eat and get back to work."

She waved me off with a gloved hand and tore open the box.

Back at the house, I locked myself in the office and called my handler. "Hey, Dominic. I got us a boat."

"Do tell," he said.

"It's a Mark V fast patrol boat, but it needs a little work. I've got the mechanic here now building new gas, I mean, diesel fuel tanks, and rebuilding the fuel system."

"How on Earth did you score a Mark V?"

I smiled, proud to have surprised him. "I can't tell all my secrets, but it's good to have friends in high places."

"Regardless of where, or how, you got it, it's an excellent choice. Can I do anything to help get it ready to go? It sounds like it needs some work."

"That's why I'm calling. I need the two electronics technicians you sent to sweep *Aegis* for bugs. Can I borrow them for a few days?"

"Sure," he said. "They're finishing up a radar installation on a sportfisher now. I'll send them your way. What do they need to bring?"

I gave him my shopping list, and it was his turn to whistle. "I like your style. It'll take a few hours to get everything together, but I'll get them on the road tonight. They should be there tomorrow afternoon."

"I can run down and pick them up in the Caravan if that'd be easier."

"That's even better. Come down tomorrow morning, and I'll have everything you need plus two top-notch technicians."

"Great. I'll see you tomorrow, late morning."

"Before you go, I want to thank you for helping Wanda's friend with that thing in Nashville. That showed a lot of leadership, and it was an excellent result."

"Thanks, Dominic. I knew it was out of my league, but this team I've put together has skill sets that aren't easy to find."

"That's exactly what I'm talking about. Knowing the capabilities of your team is one of the marks of a great leader. Resource management is hard to teach, but I think you're quickly becoming a master."

"I'm not used to compliments, but thanks again. I'll see you tomorrow."

"Oh, one more thing, Chase. I have to know. Did you call the president?"

"Come on, Dominic. Don't you think I can scrounge up a special operations combat boat without calling the leader of the free world?"

"I thought so," he said, just before the line when dead.

* * *

The flight down the east coast of Florida wasn't as pleasant as some I'd flown. We had to dodge a dozen thunderstorms and towering cumulus clouds as the morning air warmed up in the subtropical sun.

Hunter splashed the Caravan into the canal beside four monstrous cruise ships at the Miami Seaplane Base as if he'd done it a thousand times.

"Well done," I said. "We need to get your seaplane ticket finished up soon so you can do that without me beside you."

Dominic met us at the ramp with half a ton of equipment and the two technicians still wearing their hard rock T-shirts, but they'd traded their AC/DC and Metallica shirts for Black Sabbath and Mötley Crüe. We refueled, loaded the plane, devoured a pair of sandwiches, and blasted off back into the world of dodging thunderstorms.

A line of severe storms forced us to land at New Smyrna Beach to wait out the weather. I didn't mind making the stop. It gave me a chance to visit with Earl's brother, Cotton Jackson, an A&P mechanic I'd met a year earlier when a mafia button man tried to send me to the Promised Land with a well-placed explosive charge on the engine of my Cessna 182.

When we taxied to the ramp, I saw Cotton standing just inside the maintenance hangar, watching the rain come down in sheets. I shut down as close to the hangar as I could and made a mad dash for the cover of the building.

Cotton's eyes lit up as he recognized me. "Chase? Is that you?"

I jogged to a stop a few feet from him, water pouring off my shoulders. "Hey, Cotton. It's good to see you again."

"I'll be darned. I thought that was you. It looks like you upgraded from the One-Eighty-Two. That's a good-looking Caravan."

"It's not an upgrade—just an addition to the fleet. I've still got the One-Eighty-Two. I couldn't bear to get rid of it with that brand-new engine you stuck in her."

"That's good to hear. What brings you down this way?"

I watched Hunter and the two techs gallop into the hangar through the rain, and introductions were made.

"I actually stopped in to get out of this weather, but while we're here, I figured you might take a look at the Caravan. It'll need an annual inspection in December, and I'd love for you to do it."

"Sure, I'd love to. It's always good to have work lined up ahead of time."

"That's not all," I said. "Do you know anything about Rolls-Royce Merlin engines?"

"Like the ones in the P-51s?" he asked.

"Exactly like that. I picked up a Mustang that I'd like to add to your maintenance schedule."

His low whistle sounded just like his sister's. "You've been spending some money. Did you hit the Powerball?"

"No, unfortunately not. I inherited the Mustang, and I did some boat trading for the Caravan."

"Lucky you," he murmured.

"Yeah, lucky me. Do you have time to come to Saint Marys for a couple of days to go over the planes?"

He stared back into the depths of the hangar. "Yeah, I guess I could get away for a couple of days. I just finished up a landing gear refurb and a prop job on that King Air. The overconfident owner ran it off the end of the runway. I've been waiting for the weather to break so I could take it up for a maintenance test flight."

"Great," I said. "When the weather breaks, do your test flight and then hop in with us. We'll have you back by the weekend. Earl's at my place doing some diesel work for me, too. It'll give you two a chance to visit."

He shot another long look into the brightening sky. "Looks like the rain's 'bout gone. You wouldn't be interested in flying the King Air with me, would you? It's either you, or I'll have to go get one of them cocky young guys up at the flight school. I hate those guys."

"Sure, if you did the work, I'll fly it with you."

The sky cleared, and we blasted off in the King Air—me in the left seat and Cotton running maintenance checks from the right. It was my first maintenance test flight, and I felt a knot in my belly every time he cycled the landing gear. They came up and down exactly as they should every time, but that didn't quash my anxiety. The props behaved well, and Cotton declared the airplane to be better than new. I greased a landing and silently celebrated the fact that the gear didn't collapse.

"All right, let me do the paperwork and grab my toolbox, and we'll get going."

Hunter, the techs, and I made use of the facilities and checked the weather. Half an hour later, we were climbing out of New Smyrna Beach into a clear blue sky. We flew to the west to avoid the line of storms moving off to the northeast and landed in Saint Marys just before three o'clock.

I called Penny and asked her to pick us up in the microbus and to bring Earl. In typical Penny style, she *almost* followed my instructions. She and Earl pulled up ten minutes later in the dually, not the bus.

When Earl saw her brother, she bounded from the truck and grabbed him with even greater energy than she'd used for my bear hug two days before.

They had a family reunion moment while the techs unloaded the equipment from the plane and into the bed of Earl's truck. We left Cotton in the hangar with *Katerina's Heart* and headed back to Bonaventure.

The techs wasted no time poring over the Mark V.

"So, can you do it?" I asked.

Black Sabbath said, "It's already done, mostly. You see this coating?" He pointed to the gray hull.

"Yeah, it could use a paint job," I said.

He shook his head violently. "No! That's not paint. That's radar-absorbing coating, the same kind Lockheed-Martin uses on the JASSM missile."

I leaned in close to the hull and scratched at the coating. "Well, how about that? How effective is it?"

"Greatly effective against civilian radar systems, but the high-tech, mil-spec systems can still get a target—just not a big one. That's nothing to worry about, though. The mods and gear we're going to install will make this beast disappear like magic. Do you mind if we play some music while we work?"

"Sure, just try not to scare the neighbors."

He joined his partner and vanished inside the boat. Seconds later, to my surprise, the sound of Bill Monroe and the Bluegrass Boys came wafting from the depths of the boat, singing "Man of Constant Sorrow."

Earl showed up just before dark with a pair of shiny new diesel tanks. "Hey, Chase, you think you could get that giant of yours to help me with these tanks?"

Mongo and I made short work of setting the tanks in place, but Earl wasn't happy. She grabbed my arm and motioned toward the techs. "Who are those guys, and what are they doing on my boat?"

"Your boat?" I asked.

"Yeah, it's mine until it's running again, and then I'll give it back, but who are they?"

I laughed. "They're electronics techs installing some gear to make us a little harder to see."

"Oh, a Romulan cloaking device," she replied.

"Well, not exactly, but close. I didn't figure you for a Trekkie."

"Are you kidding me?" she said. "If they'd've had me on the Enterprise, I could've shown Scotty a thing or two about getting another warp factor out of that hyperdrive."

"You're too much, Earl. Get back to work. I promise the techs won't get in your way."

"If they do, I'll put their scrawny asses in the water."

"I don't doubt that for a second. When you finish, come up to the house and bring those guys with you. Penny's working on supper for everyone."

Penny's supper would've made Maebelle proud. Even the Judge was impressed. It was fried chicken—Texas-style, whatever that means—green beans, mac-n-cheese, biscuits, and of course, a pecan pie.

The Judge wiped his mouth, leaned back in his chair, and declared, "Miss Penny, you have fouled up this time."

Panic overtook her face. "What did I do? Don't you like my pie?"

"Oh, no. I like it just fine. That's the problem. You've gone and shown all of us that you can do nearly as good as Maebelle."

He leaned forward conspiratorially and whispered, "But don't you tell her I said so."

That garnered a round of laughter from around the table.

The Judge said, "It does an old man's heart good to see so many young folks gathered around his table and fellowshipping over good food. I like having all of you here. There hasn't been this much life in this old house in thirty years or more. I don't know what you're working on out there, but I hope I live long enough to get a look at whatever it is—and to get a ride in that Mustang of yours."

"We'll definitely make all that happen, Judge. I promise. Earl should be finished with the boat in the next couple of days, and her brother, Cotton, is running through the Mustang. I don't see any reason we can't do a boat ride and P-51 flight this weekend if you're feeling up to it."

The old man smiled broadly. "I can't imagine a better weekend unless I got to spend it with Mildred. I don't think I'll ever stop missing her. Take it from me, don't let the ones you love go a day of their lives without tellin' them how much you care. I'd give every penny I've ever had to tell Mildred I love her just one more time."

Silence filled the dining room, none of us knowing what to say . . . except Singer.

"She knows, Judge. God knows how much you loved her, and she's with him. He'll never let her forget."

The Judge wiped a tear from his eye. "Thank you for that, Singer. You know, you're the only hope this merry band of heathens has to stay out of Hell."

"Don't I know it, Judge. I'm doing the best I can, but it's a tough crowd."

Chapter 17
Dignity

I opened my eyes the next morning to see my beautiful wife staring down at me, her hair blossoming around her head in a gravity-defying performance, and my first smile of the day won its battle with what would've otherwise been a yawn.

"Good morning," I whispered.

"Good morning. Is it creepy that I like watching you sleep?"

"A little," I admitted. "But don't stop."

She tried to smile, but the sadness in her eyes was impossible to dismiss.

I ran my fingers through her wild hair. "What's wrong, sweetheart?"

She looked away. "I'm worried about the Judge. What do you think that was all about at the table last night? I've never heard him talk like that."

"I don't know. I've been thinking about that all night, too."

"Do you think he's all right?"

I sighed. "No, I don't think so, but I'm taking him flying, and if Earl gets the boat running, I'm taking him for the ride of his life."

She closed her eyes. "You're a good man, Chase Fulton, and I love you."

"I love you, too, Penny. I'm lucky to have you."

She kissed me gently on the tip of my nose. "I didn't know we had a cat."

"A cat? What are you talking about?"

She pressed two fingers beneath my chin, pushing my mouth closed. "We must have a cat because it smells like he pooped in your mouth overnight. Go brush."

"Oh, you're funny," I breathed, deliberately exhaling in her direction.

By the time I'd showered, brushed my teeth, and made it downstairs, Earl was already working on the boat, and Hunter had arrived with a bag of biscuits.

"They're not as good as Penny's, but they'll have to do."

"Thanks," I said. "What's on the agenda for today?"

He took a look at his watch. "Earl says she'll have the boat running by the end of the day. She said something about rebuilding an injector pump, but I don't know what that means. Do you?"

"Ha! I'm the least mechanically inclined dude you know. I'm just happy to have Earl around when we need her."

He agreed. "Yeah, and Cotton seems to know his stuff, too. He was saying something about a worn lobe on the cam in the Mustang last night. You should probably talk to him about that."

"Is he up yet?" I asked, scanning the first floor of the house.

"I've not seen him, but he strikes me as an early riser."

I nodded. "Penny's worried about the Judge."

Hunter looked at his boots. "Yeah, I get that. He seemed out of sorts last night, didn't he?"

"A little bit."

Singer came into the kitchen in shorts and a shmedium T-shirt.

"Been doing your own laundry again, Singer? That shirt's a little tight, isn't it, buddy?"

He flexed both biceps. "Just showing off the guns on my run this morning."

"We were just talking about the Judge. What do you think's going on with him?"

Singer poured himself a glass of orange juice and joined us at the table. "I think he's coming to terms with what he believes is the quickly approaching end of his time among the living. And I'd say he's doing it exactly how he's lived his whole life—with admirable dignity."

"That's what we're afraid of," I said.

"Don't be afraid. The Judge is ready to go. He's a man of great faith. I've had a number of conversations with him, and it's obvious he's not afraid of what comes next for him. In fact, it's my belief that he's well prepared for it."

"It's not nice to talk about an old man when you think he's not listening."

The three of us spun in our seats to see the Judge leaning against the ornate door casing between the kitchen and dining room.

I said, "We're just worried about you, Judge."

"Don't worry about me, young man. This is your season. I've had mine, and I made the most of it. I think you fellows should do the same."

I asked, "Have you checked the weather for today, Judge?"

"Another beautiful summer day in the marshlands. It'll probably rain late this afternoon, but other than that, I plan to sit in my gazebo and talk to the river."

"How do you feel about a Mustang ride this morning?"

He grinned. "I believe I'd better have another piece of Ms. Penny's pecan pie before we go—if there's any left."

I stood and pulled what was left of the pie from the top shelf of the refrigerator while the Judge poured himself a cup of coffee.

An hour later, we gently helped the Judge into the cramped cockpit of *Katerina's Heart*.

"Do you really think there's any reason for me to wear this silly parachute?"

"It's built into the seat, Judge. Besides, I'm a terrible pilot. You may want to get out before we land."

He chuckled. "I can promise you one thing, son. Even if you get out, I'm staying with this thing 'til she's safely back on the ground."

"I believe I'll do the same, Judge. Let's see if this old girl will start."

I felt the resistance of the Judge's hands and feet on the controls as I flew the Mustang off the ground. I leveled off a thousand feet above Cumberland Island.

"Look at the horses running on the south end of the island, Judge."

"I see 'em. They sure are beautiful. I've watched those mustangs on the island for almost a hundred years, but this is the first time I've ever seen the mustangs from inside a Mustang."

I made a few gentle turns around the island and then overflew the plantation and Saint Marys waterfront.

"It's a beautiful place, Chase. Take good care of it, will you?"

"You know I will, Judge. I'm coming to love Saint Marys almost as much as you do."

"I'm not just talking about Saint Marys. I'm talking about our country, son."

I swallowed hard. "Same answer."

We flew in silence for several minutes, exploring the rivers, and eventually across Fernandina Beach and Fort Clinch. Turning south, I rolled to the right, showing the top of my beautiful airplane to the hundreds of tourists enjoying the beach. I questioned my own vanity for wanting to show off my Mustang, but a quick glance over my shoulder gave me a view of the Judge waving down at the crowds and grinning from ear to ear. I gave myself a pass on my vanity.

I gently rolled into a climbing left turn out over the Atlantic Ocean and felt the Judge, once again, on the controls.

"How's your stomach?" I asked as we climbed through three thousand feet.

"I've got an iron gut, son. Let's have a little fun."

Checking my speed to make sure I was staying below the FAA-mandated two hundred fifty knots below ten thousand feet, I rolled into a steep turn with the left wing pointed directly at the water. I felt the gentle pull of the moderate-G turn and asked, "You okay back there?"

He grunted lightly. "Oh, yeah."

I had no idea what effect a three-G turn would have on a ninety-year-old man, but by all indications, he was having one of his best days in a long time.

When I rolled the wings level, heading north, I felt his grip tighten on the stick. I smiled and loosened my grip, finally relinquishing the controls to the Judge.

"Ease the stick to the right and pull slightly," I said, and he did exactly as I instructed.

The nose came to the right and rose slightly above the horizon. I added enough right rudder to coordinate the turn and let the Judge fly us through a three-hundred-sixty-degree turn to the right.

"Now, try one to the left."

He did, and I felt the left rudder pedal depress without my input.

Who says you can't teach an old dog new tricks?

We rolled out, heading northeast and farther out to sea.

With a little hesitance in my voice, I asked, "How do you feel about a barrel roll?"

"I thought you'd never ask. Let's do it."

"Follow me through the controls."

I pulled the nose a few degrees above the horizon to begin a gentle arc. The airplane was more than capable of performing a nearly endless series of snap rolls, but I wanted this one to be as gentle as aerodynamically possible. Just before the top of the arc, I added enough left aileron to send the world in front of us slowly rotating to the right as we rolled left. I felt my weight press against the shoulder harness as the canopy pointed directly toward the blue water of the Atlantic. I was tempted to glance back at the Judge, but instead, I kept my eyes on the horizon and completed the roll, softly adding enough back pressure to stop our slow descent.

"Do it again, son. Do it again!"

Who could say no to that?

"You do it this time, Judge. I'll keep my hands on the controls and help if you get lost, but I think you can do it."

"All right," he said. "Just don't let me make these parachutes necessary."

"You've got this. Make it happen."

He started the roll without raising the nose, so I made enough control input to correct the problem. His roll was a little more aggressive than mine, but with my help, we survived it, and he rolled the wings relatively level, having lost only four hundred feet of altitude.

"Not bad, Judge. It's too bad they didn't make you a fighter pilot instead of a lawyer."

"The Army doctor said I had asthma and wouldn't live to see forty. Otherwise, I may have died in one of those wars. So far, I've outlived his death sentence by nearly fifty-six years."

"Are you really ninety-five years old?" I asked before I could stop myself.

"I'll be ninety-six if I live to see August sixth."

What must it be like to have watched nearly a hundred years pass?

I had to ask. "What's the most important thing you've learned in ninety-five years on the planet?"

He didn't flinch. "Love. There's nothing more important. Just imagine how great this old world would be if we all just went to loving one another."

Wisdom like that is priceless and ageless.

I checked our position and found us to be about twelve miles east of Saint Simon Island. "I guess we should head back before they start worrying about us."

"What kind of ship do you think that is just in front of the right wingtip?"

What I saw when I turned my head set a knot in my belly and sent a chill down my spine. I'd memorized every detail of that ship from the pictures Skipper sent. I knew every curve of the hull and every antenna that protruded above her decks.

Every fiber of my being wanted to roll in on the *Viktor Leonov* and show comrade Commander Krusevich my face, but discretion being the better part of valor—or something like that —I took a deep breath. "I don't know. It could be some kind of cargo boat, I guess."

"I don't think so," he said. "Let's get a closer look."

Discretion be damned. I rolled in and imagined the six fifty-caliber machine guns in my wings still being useable as the *Leonov* grew larger and larger in my useless gunsight.

Sanity returned, and I raised the nose, added right rudder, and broke off to the southwest. "I think you're right, Judge. It's not a cargo boat. I think it's one of those research vessels NOAA uses."

"You're probably right," he said. "I was hoping for something more exciting."

Forty miles from Saint Marys, the Judge said, "Why haven't you asked me yet?"

"Asked you what?"

He let out a long breath. "Why haven't you asked me what I did with Loui Giordano, the hit man you delivered with my cannon last year?"

There were a thousand reasons I hadn't asked. First, it was none of my business, but perhaps more importantly, I didn't really want to know. Assumption led me to believe the Judge had buried him beneath the cannon after a long, painful talk.

I finally said, "I can't dwell on things like that. In my line of work, that's the best way to drive yourself insane. I just do my job and move on." A glance into the mirror designed to give Mustang pilots a glimpse at the Germans on their tail revealed the Judge's satisfied, peaceful smile on his weathered face.

"I let him go," he said.

"You let him go? Why?"

"I looked him in the eye, pressed the barrel of my old forty-five to his cheek, and told him I forgave him. Then, I cut his handcuffs off with a pair of bolt cutters, and I spent the rest of the day talking to God and Mildred."

Singer was right. With dignity is exactly how Judge Bernard Henry Huntsinger lived every day of his life.

Chapter 18
A Flounder Promise

Squeezing the Mustang, Caravan, and Skylane into one hangar at the Saint Marys Airport was a bit like a four-million-dollar game of Tetris. It frightened me every time, but so far, we hadn't scratched any paint. Perhaps a hangar expansion or acquisition was in my future. The investment would not only ease my nerves about denting airplane skins, but would also give us more room to comfortably maintain our seemingly ever-expanding air force.

When we pulled into the drive at Bonaventure, the Judge laid his hand on my shoulder. "I don't know how to thank you for this morning, Chase. It was one of the grandest experiences of my life. I know it was just a common flight for you, but it's important to remember that the things that appear simple and even meaningless to you may be the things that others see as remarkable and unforgettable. Don't take these things for granted, son. The gifts God has given you—like that beautiful, faithful wife of yours, those friends you call a team, and this grand life you lead —are perishable if not protected, and the best way to protect them is to be thankful for them every day. I don't mean just flippantly saying thanks. I mean devoting a part of every day of your life to meditating on how much they mean to you and how empty your life would be without them. Love those people with everything you have because even if you live as long as I have, life is fleeting. So many people and things are gone in the blink of an eye."

I sat, staring back at the weathered skin of his face and the wisdom in his deep-set dark eyes. "Thank you, Judge . . . for everything. Especially for this morning with you."

He nodded, patted my shoulder, and climbed down from the microbus.

The front entrance to Bonaventure felt far too formal for me, so I rarely used those doors, preferring instead to walk around the house and enter through the kitchen door from the back gallery. As I rounded the corner of the house, I heard the beautiful rumbling of a pair of big diesel engines coming from the dock, so I wasted no time jogging for the water's edge.

"That sounds a lot better," I said across the gunwale to Earl's backside.

She peered across her shoulder with a look of satisfaction and pride. "That's how they're supposed to sound, but we're gonna need to find a diesel pump. These things are thirsty, and the tank in my truck only holds a hundred gallons."

"How big are the tanks you built?" I asked.

"The original pieces of crap I took out were thirteen hundred gallons each, but mine are upgrades. If my math is right, you'll be able to carry almost twenty-eight hundred gallons."

"Whew! That's a lot of gas."

"I done told you too many times, it ain't gas. It's diesel. Are you ever going to learn?"

"I know, old girl. I just do it to keep you on your toes. What kind of range will we get with twenty-eight hundred gallons of *diesel* fuel?"

"If you'll stay out of the throttles, I figure you'll get around a thousand miles, but if you open her up, you'll cut that in half."

"We'll definitely need to do some testing to determine burn rates. I can't afford to guess when we'll run out."

She grinned. "Those two little geeks you've got wiring this thing have already taken care of that for you. That fancy computer they put in does all of that for you."

"Thank God for the geeks."

"Yeah, that ain't all they did, neither. They had me solder up a set of copper pipes that looks like the worm on a whiskey still to wrap these motors in. We're gonna pump seawater around these big heaters so them heat seekers have a hard time finding something hot to home in on. I don't know what kind of stew you're gettin' into, Stud Muffin, but if somebody's shootin' heat seekers at you, you'd better not take Clark with you. They'll home in on his hot ass if you ain't careful."

"In that case, I guess we'd better leave you behind, too."

"You know it, Baby Boy. Now get out of here and let me finish up. We'll be ready to run this thing in a couple of hours."

I spent the next hour of my life negotiating diesel prices. Lang's, as it turned out, was not only a great seafood restaurant, they were also a commercial fishing operation with a fleet of diesel-burning behemoths, necessitating a pair of fifty-thousand-gallon tanks at their dock and a ten-thousand-gallon tanker truck. I arranged for a delivery and promised I wouldn't eat grilled flounder from anywhere except Lang's for the next month.

The techs finished their work just before three o'clock, and the fuel truck arrived as they were packing up their tools. Twenty-seven-hundred and fifty-five gallons later, I'd spent a total of slightly more than twenty-one thousand dollars rebuilding, repairing, refurbishing, and refueling my Mark V fast patrol boat. All that remained was learning how to employ it to wreak as much havoc as possible against the *Viktor Leonov* that was prowling the waters just across the horizon.

"Come on! We need a driver," I yelled through the kitchen door. Penny bounded onto the gallery with the anticipation of a child on her way to the county fair.

The Mark V was designed to carry sixteen fully equipped Navy SEALs, allowing them to sit in high-quality seats or stand on a platform supported by pneumatic and gas shocks designed to absorb the shock of rough seas, leaving the SEALs unfatigued when they reached their objective. Although considered a boat, the Mark V is no small craft at over eighty feet long and displacing over fifty tons. In the confined waters of the North River, she looked like a battleship, but on the open sea, she'd be little more than a gray dot on the endless blue.

Our crew for the sea trial hardly scratched the surface of what the boat was capable of carrying. Penny manned the helm, of course. The techs stood by, monitoring everything with electrical current flowing through it. Earl wedged herself into a corner near her beloved engines. I stood behind Penny, and the rest of the team—Hunter, Singer, and Mongo—roamed the decks, getting a feel for every inch of the space. With Mongo's help, the Judge strapped himself into the command seat, overseeing everything. Through the weariness of age and failing health, the eyes of the fascinated little boy still inside him gleamed like beacons of light.

The North River snakes its way through marshland and finally empties into Cumberland Sound and what some call Saint Marys Bay. To see the area on a map would confuse even the craftiest cartographer. There appears to be a dozen or more rivers named Saint Marys River. I'd long since given up trying to keep track of all of them, but the GPS system the techs installed made navigation in the complex and winding waterways a breeze. As much fun as the rivers were to negotiate at high speed, it was the open ocean where the Mark V would have to perform at its best.

Penny opened the throttles as Fort Clinch passed off our starboard side in a blur. The tide was running in the pass with a westerly wind blowing at our back, which made for seas of greater than five feet for most of the exit. The hull cut through the waves like butter, and the articulating seats and platform made the ride feel like a Sunday afternoon drive down a lazy country lane. To say I was impressed was a wild understatement.

Once on the open ocean, Penny cast a glance over her shoulder toward the Judge. "Are you doing okay back there?"

Rather than yelling back at her, he gave a broad grin and two crooked thumbs up.

She pressed the throttles to their stops, and the fuel flow gauges lit up like Christmas trees. At full throttle, the boat burned more fuel per minute than all three of my airplanes combined.

"I'm going to try some high-speed maneuvers," Penny yelled.

I moved into position closely beside the Judge so I could relay any discomfort he felt to the helm. "She's going to make it dance a little, Judge. Let me know if it gets to be too much for you, and we'll back off, okay?"

The grin continued, and the thumbs up returned.

Penny put the boat through its paces with several hairpin turns and speed changes. It handled every demand as if it wanted more, reacting like the precision piece of military hardware it was designed and built to be. Unlike the production models that come from VT Halter Marine in Gulfport, my Mark V had a suite of electronics those guys never dreamed of, as well as a custom-built fuel system and heat shielding system to make us a lot harder to hit in a hostile environment. I had no way of knowing if the Russians would shoot at us, but if they did, I wanted every advantage I could buy, borrow, or steal on my side. The upgrades made my boat slightly more survivable in a high-threat environment. When originally designed, the boat was intended for service under conditions of low to moderate threat levels, but I planned to push it well outside those levels.

Over the next hour, we took turns at the helm. I had no intention of Penny being aboard when we started our campaign against the *Leonov*, so it was an absolute necessity that everyone aboard be fully competent at the controls.

Finally, we headed for the pass that would take us back into one of the Saint Marys Rivers, and I turned to the Judge. "She won't do a barrel roll, I hope, but she's all yours if you'd like to drive."

His answer came in the form of a hasty attempt to unstrap himself from his seat. Penny ran him through the basic controls, and his arthritic, bent hands grasped the controls as if he were twenty-five again.

Instead of easing us into the pass, he powered the boat up to sixty percent and made a dramatic turn back out to sea. Every face on the boat lit up with excitement. After twenty minutes without the grin leaving his face, the Judge turned to me and yelled, "How fast will it go?"

The only appropriate answer was, "Let's find out."

I monitored the radar screen while every other eye on the boat scanned the horizon, and the Judge pushed the throttles to their stops. Nobody got in our way, and the huge chunk of aluminum and electronics cut across the wave at sixty-one knots before the Judge eased the throttles back to twenty percent.

"Okay, now that I've shown you how it's done, sonny, you can have your boat back."

I laughed and helped the Judge back to his captain's chair. We pulled up to Lang's dock and refilled our tanks, carefully checking fuel quantities against the calculations of the tech's computer system. Just as expected, it was spot on.

Everything was falling into place, and that meant it was time for a conference call with Dominic and Skipper. I was ready for a plan, a mission brief, and execution, but nothing could've prepared me for what awaited me on the gallery back at Bonaventure Plantation.

Chapter 19
Keeping Score

Penny nestled the boat against the Bonaventure dock with the skill of a seasoned Navy coxswain, and we tied off as if we'd done it a thousand times. We secured and locked the boat to make sure it would still be there when we awoke the next day and headed up the yard in a loose formation with the Judge leading the way, everyone satisfied with the day's accomplishment.

The Judge squinted toward the house. "Who's that on the gallery?"

Penny shot a slicing glance at me, and I sighed, unsure of what to do or say.

"Trouble," Penny said. "Trouble is who she is."

Anya Burinkova rose from a rocking chair only seconds ahead of the two men in cheap government employee suits.

"That is Mark V fast patrol boat used by American special operations. Is very nice. I did not know you had this." These were the first words out of Anya's mouth. The second were, "You do not look happy to see me."

"Well," I began, "your timing isn't the best, but I'm pleased to see you're still in the States and not behind bars."

She held up her thin wrists. "Nope. No more handcuffs or bars for me. I am now American girl for real, and I am here to help with mission."

"What mission would that be?"

Anya scanned the group. "I do not know if all of these people have clearance and need to know, but,"—she pointed toward the Mark V—"that mission."

The G-man on Anya's left asked, "Is there someplace we can talk . . . privately?"

"Sure. Come on in. We can talk in the library."

I led the two agents and Anya to the library with Hunter and Penny following closely behind.

Anya locked eyes with Penny at the door to the library as if to question her presence, but Penny didn't slow down. "Oh, I have both clearance and need to know."

We took our seats, and the first G-man started his spiel. "I'm Donald Brady with State, and this is Glenn Franks with DIA."

Hmm, State Department and Defense Intelligence. This should be interesting.

"As you know, Ms. Burinkova-Fulton has been undergoing a rather intense debriefing over the previous weeks. She's been remarkably forthcoming with information, intelligence, and operational details of her former comrades. All indications lead us to believe her former countryman bought your little charade in the Black Sea, hook, line, and *sinker*, so to speak."

"That's encouraging," I said. "Especially since they seem to have gone to a great deal of trouble and expense to send an intelligence-gathering ship all the way across the Atlantic just to make sure I don't turn up back here at home."

"That's why we brought her here," said Brady. "The White House believes she'll be of great value to your operation."

"Does that mean I get to keep the boat when this is over?" I asked.

The two G-men shared a knowing glance, and Brady said, "What boat?"

I offered an abbreviated, knowing nod. "Please continue."

"I have a set of documents for you verifying the State Department's position that Ms. Burinkova-Fulton possesses the necessary clearance to operate under your direct supervision in support of missions in defense and preservation of the United States, its allies, interests, and other duties pertaining thereto."

I held up my hand. "Wait a minute. This is all starting to sound like a truckload of responsibility I don't think I want. If the Kremlin couldn't control her, what makes you think I'll do any better?"

"Our boss," Brady said.

"*Your* boss? You mean the secretary of state?" I asked.

Brady shook his head slowly. "No, his boss. The one on Pennsylvania Avenue. He wanted you to know that if you're still keeping score, you're now winning."

I closed my eyes and swallowed hard. Dominic said this would happen. When I started trading favors with the leader of the free world, there would come a time when I couldn't say no. It looked like that time had come.

"Let me see the paperwork," I said, holding out my hand.

He placed a sealed document carrier in my hand, and I carefully read every word. The taste in my mouth soured more with each sentence. When I finished, I read it again and tossed the packet on the desk. "I don't have a choice in any of this, do I?"

"Of course you do," Brady said. "But when the Saint Marys Airport becomes the property of the U.S. Government, the nearest equivalent airfield is a long way from Bonaventure Plantation. Oh, and that boat you mentioned earlier? The government thanks you for the upgrades."

I dug my heel into the hardwood flooring and spun my chair to face the window. The pain in the pit of my stomach left me hoping Anya would "gut me like pig" and get this over with.

"How long?" I asked.

Brady spoke with the confidence of a man who had an armored tank division behind him. "That's up to you, Mr. Fulton—you and the voters next November."

I growled, "If she goes rogue, I'll shoot her in the head."

"If I feel desire to go rogue," Anya said, "I will shoot myself in head. I owe to you my life, Chase. I will not be problem for you."

"Where do I sign?" I asked impatiently.

Brady smiled. "There's nothing to sign, Mr. Fulton. When Franks and I return to D.C., we'll either have an empty back seat or the body of a dead Russian. Either way, she's not our problem anymore."

For the first time, Penny spoke. "Can you cook?"

Anya smiled. "I can make borsch, fish stew, hot tea, and sometimes lemonade, but I think my lemonade makes people fall asleep."

I slid the State Department documents back into their carrier and locked them in the safe. Turning back around to face Anya, I said, "We don't have any beets, so I guess it'll be fish stew for dinner."

* * *

I briefed Singer and Mongo, and they took the news far better than I did.

"Look at it this way—she probably knows a lot more about that spy ship than any of us," Singer said. "Maybe she'll come in handy. God sends us what we need sometimes."

"Yeah, and sometimes He sends down fire and brimstone," I said.

Just before dark, an old familiar sound came rolling from the backyard, and I walked through the kitchen where Anya seemed to be deeply devoted to an enormous pot on Maebelle's stove. Two steps onto the gallery, my suspicion was confirmed. Clark was back and tying *Aegis* on the wrong side of the dock because the upstream side was occupied by my new toy.

I jogged down the steps and across the yard to greet him and Maebelle. "It's good to have you home. How was Hilton Head?"

Clark ignored me and pointed toward the Mark V. "What's up with that thing? Are the SEALs here for dinner?"

"That one doesn't belong to the SEALs. That one is ours."

His smile replaced curiosity. "Well done, College Boy. I like where your head's at."

Maebelle leapt from the catamaran and landed silently on the dock beside Clark. "Ooh, that's sexy."

Clark shook his butt. "Thanks, but you've been looking at it for a week."

She slapped at his arm. "Stop it. That's sexy, too, but I was talking about the new boat."

"Thanks, Maebelle," I said. "It's good to see you. We've been starving to death without you."

"Don't you worry," she said. "I'm home now, and I'll take care of that."

I glanced back toward the house. "Uh, well, actually, we've sort of imported a cook for tonight."

"Imported a cook?" she said.

"Well, sort of. Anya's back, and she's making something. I think it's fish stew, but I'm not sure."

Maebelle headed for the house. "I'll take care of this."

Clark eased himself across the gunwale of the patrol boat and pulled a flashlight from his pocket. "This is nice. How'd you come by this thing?"

"It's a long story, but basically, your dad said we needed a small fast boat if we were going to mess with the Russian ship, so I made a call, and this thing showed up."

"It just showed up, huh? That must've been some call you made."

"Yeah, it was, and I may have stolen more chain than I can swim with this time."

Clark sighed. "I thought that might be the case when you said Anya was back. It sounds like you've been relegated to babysitter."

"How did everyone else see that coming and I didn't?"

"You'll see it next time," he said.

I briefed him on the new systems and upgrades the techs and Earl installed on the boat.

"So, are we planning to hit them or just pester them?"

"*We* aren't planning anything," I said. "*You* are staying here. Beyond that, we don't have a definitive plan yet. I'm going to have a conference call with Skipper and Dominic later and make some decisions. Regardless of the plan, though, we're ready to go."

He seemed to ignore my admonition. "We need to hang some guns on those mounts."

"I've been thinking about that, and I don't know if I want to show up strapped to the teeth, or nice and subtle."

"Subtle. That sounds like a tactic the Russians would never expect."

"I like the idea of them not knowing we're there at first."

He locked eyes with me. "If that ship is what I think it is, they'll see and hear you coming from twenty miles away."

"They may, but only if they've got a satellite feed Skipper can't jam. Their radar will never see a thing, and thanks to Earl and the techs, their infrared isn't going to see much of a heat signature either."

He nodded his approval. "So, when are we going?"

"Like I said, partner, the *I* of we will go when Dominic says to, but the *you* of we ain't going nowhere."

He laughed. "I guess we'd better go make that call, and you can keep pretending I'm not coming with you."

I was afraid of what I might find when I opened the door to the kitchen. Part of me expected to see Maebelle and Anya in a standoff, each wielding butcher knives, but I was pleasantly surprised. Maebelle stood over Anya's pot with a tasting spoon in her hand, giving instructions, and making a stirring motion with her hand. Anya appeared to be listening intently. We didn't interrupt whatever that was.

I gathered the team in the library and started my briefing. "The time has come to put our preparation into action. We've got the equipment, the manpower, and the objective. Is there anything you want to discuss before we call Dominic and Skipper?" I looked around, waiting for someone to speak.

Finally, Singer said, "If she's going with us, don't you think Anya should be in here?"

"That's one of the things I want to discuss. She may have something to add to the mission, or she may be in the way. I haven't decided yet. I'd like to hear your thoughts."

"When has she ever really been in the way?" Clark asked.

Penny spoke up. "Oh, I can think of a few times."

"During a tactical scenario," Clark added.

Singer, ever the voice of reason, said, "It comes down to whether or not you trust her and if you think she has anything to add to the mission. What skillset does she bring to the table that we don't already have?"

"I-O-K," said Clark. "Intimate operational knowledge. She knows more about how the Russians think, feel, and operate than all of us combined. She'll be able to predict their next moves if it turns into a scuffle."

"There's still the possibility that she's going to see that ship and start feeling homesick," Mongo said.

I considered his concern. "I don't think we have to worry too much about that. I believe that bridge has burned."

"So, you trust her?" came several voices.

"No, not entirely. But I trust that she doesn't want to run home to the Kremlin like the prodigal daughter. She had that chance in the Black Sea. What she did over there, plus her decision on the submarine to point out Gregory Sidorov, the Russian spy, makes me believe she's on our side. The thing that scares me is the fact that she's not a team player. She's almost always going to do what's in her best interest. If it benefits the team, that's great, but we're not going to be her first priority."

Penny reminded me, "She took a bullet for Skipper."

I let out a long sigh. "Of all people, why do you have to be the one to bring that up?"

Penny tried to smile. "Because I love Skipper."

Chapter 20
It's Your Turn, Son

"Let's make the call," I said. "We need Dominic and Skipper's input."

"You're the operational commander, Chase."

At first, I wasn't sure who said it, but when I looked up and saw Singer staring back at me, I knew he was right, and ultimately, the decision to take Anya or leave her behind was mine.

I repeated, "Let's make the call."

Dominic and Skipper answered simultaneously, and I started the meeting as officially as I knew how.

"Good evening. Present are Singer, Mongo, Hunter, Clark, Penny, and me. It's time to proceed with a plan of action and determination of rules of engagement. Being the operational oversight officer, Dominic, I think we should hear from you first."

Dominic spoke up. "Thank you, Chase, but I think an intel update from Skipper is in order first. Do we know where the *Leonov* is?"

I interrupted. "I know where she is."

In stereo, Dominic and Skipper said, "How?"

"The Judge and I saw her this morning."

Again, in stereo, they said, "What?"

"I took the Judge flying in the Mustang, and we flew out over the Atlantic. I swear it was completely coincidental. I wasn't hunting her. In fact, the Judge is the one who saw her first."

Dominic's tone turned firm. "Tell me you didn't dive on her!"

"As badly as I wanted to, I did not. I made a turn toward her and immediately broke to the southwest back toward Saint Marys."

"So, where exactly?"

"We were about fifteen miles east of Saint Simons Island."

"She's been loitering there for the past thirty-six hours," Skipper said.

"So, you've been monitoring her?" I asked.

"Of course I have. What did you expect?"

Dominic asked, "Did the boys get all the gear set up on the new boat?"

"They did," I said. "And Earl installed the new fuel systems and built the heat shielding system designed by the techs. We did the sea trials this afternoon. and everything works like a charm."

"That's good news. So, can I have my two best technicians back now?"

"They should be getting on a plane in Jacksonville as we speak. They were just as anxious to get home as you are to have them back."

Skipper said, "Is it my turn yet?"

"Sure, go ahead. What have you got?"

"I think I know the real reason that ship is out there."

"Let's hear it," I said.

"Well," she continued, "do you know about degaussing?"

I said, "Sure, that's when they change the magnetic and electronic signature of a ship."

"Right," she said. "It's like changing a ship's fingerprints. I think that's why they're lurking around off the coast of the only nuclear sub base south of Groton, Connecticut. They're listening for electronic signatures of subs as they go into Kings Bay and as they come back out. But there's more. I think they may actually be laying a network of hydrophones on the seafloor to keep listening even after they're gone."

"How did you come to this conclusion?" Dominic asked.

"It's a long story, but I've been putting data together from historic satellite tracks since the *Leonov* made the turn north around Cuba. The track is consistent with that of cable-laying ships, and the speeds match as well."

I scratched my chin. "So, you've come to this conclusion based solely on speed and track?"

"No! That's the best part. I've come to this conclusion based on watching how they behaved when a pair of Argentinian subs showed up for degaussing five weeks ago."

"How did they know the Argentinian subs were coming?"

Skipper said, "I'm not sure, but I think they must have a pretty good satellite link—a lot like what I set up on *Aegis* so you could see who was coming and going when you sailed back from Miami."

"I'm glad you mentioned that," I said. "Can you do anything to interrupt that signal if that's what they're using? If you could, that would give us a huge advantage. We know their radar won't see us coming, or at least we believe it won't, and our heat signature is going to be so low, we'll hardly look like anything bigger than a johnboat. But with real-time satellite imaging, they'll see us coming for miles."

"I'm working on that. The problem is there are over four thousand satellites floating around out there. Finding exactly the one, or ones, the Russians are using isn't so easy. I can't just jam them all."

"So far, that's our biggest hurdle, so stay on it."

"You know I will."

I scanned the room, asking with my expression if anyone had anything to say, but no one spoke up. "Okay, back to you, Dominic. What's the plan and ROE?"

"Is Clark still with us?" Dominic asked.

"Yes, I'm still here."

"Take us off speaker, and pick up the phone."

Clark lifted the phone from the desk and pressed the button, changing the call from speaker to earpiece. "Go ahead, Dad."

The rest of us sat in silence, trying not to stare at Clark as he listened to his father. Occasionally, Clark offered brief reactions, but nothing that would give us any idea what Dominic was saying.

"Yes, I understand . . . But . . . I don't know . . . Okay . . ." He laid the phone on the desk and pressed the speaker button. "Okay. Back on speaker."

Dominic broke the brief silence. "I apologize for that, but Clark and I needed a moment. As you already know, his injuries have changed his operational profile. What you don't know yet is that he'll be moving into an oversight role, much like mine. In fact, exactly like mine. The time has come for me to hang up my cloak and turn in my dagger. I'll stay with you long enough to get Clark settled into his new role, but it's your turn, son. This operation is yours."

Every eye turned immediately to Clark, and I stood and motioned for him to trade seats with me. The reluctance in his step was obvious even though his Green-Beret brain knew he shouldn't show any hesitation in assuming a leadership role.

"This isn't exactly how I thought this would happen, but I guess baptism by fire is the way of things," Clark said.

Dominic cleared his throat. "I have to go. You can brief me tomorrow, Clark. If you need anything else, you know where I'll be, but there's a pretty girl who doesn't speak much English waiting outside, so good night." He clicked off before any of us could put up an argument.

Clark raised his eyebrows. "So, I guess that's how we do change of command ceremonies around here."

That garnered a round of uncomfortable laughter, and he continued. "Dad, uh, Dominic has kept me up to speed on the developments over the last few days. I knew I'd be moving into a higher support role, but I didn't know it was going to happen on this mission. So, with that in mind, we're doing this one together. I'll take the heat if it goes south, but I'm not a dictator like my father. I know all of you, and I know your capabilities. I also know your weaknesses—the few there are. We'll work *with* the strengths and *around* the weaknesses until we can turn those into strengths. Deal?"

Everyone nodded.

Clark licked his lips and fidgeted with a pen on the desk. "Okay, so, Singer was right, Chase. Anya's involvement is up to you."

I didn't hesitate. "If our first run is strictly harassment or recon, I'm taking her. If it's aggression, I'm leaving her behind."

Clark tried not to smile. "Nicely done, College Boy, putting the ball back in my court. The first run is strictly look and listen and maybe a gentle pat on the ass if you can get close enough, but let's see how they react to a relatively invisible fast patrol boat nosing around."

"When?" I asked.

"We need a weather window and a precise location. I'll get Skipper on that, and we'll give her twenty-four to forty-eight hours to try to identify the satellites they're using. If she can't narrow it down, we'll be forced to find another way to approach."

"And the ROE?" I asked.

Clark bit at his bottom lip. "For the first run, the rules of engagement are simple. No offensive engagement. Take enough weaponry to slap their hands if they start firing on you, but I don't even think the Russians are dumb enough to fire on what they'll perceive as a U.S. military vessel if they see us at all."

I made a circular motion with my index finger as if lassoing everyone except Clark. "You mean if they see *us*, not *you*, right?"

He shook his head. "Yes, you win this time. I'm not going. But if you get your asses shot out of the water, you'll wish I was there."

"So, who's briefing Anya?" I asked.

"She's your responsibility, College Boy. Brief her up, and we'll reconvene tomorrow morning after breakfast. Now that Maebelle's back, I'm sure all of you are anxious for one of her banquet breakfast spreads."

We adjourned, and I couldn't wait to see what was in the pot Anya and Maebelle were nursing.

When the six of us gathered around the table, Maebelle and Anya came into the dining room with an enormous soup tureen, six loaves of French bread, and two gallons of tea on Maebelle's favorite cart.

Maebelle announced, "It's our newest American's first attempt at gumbo. You'll eat it, and you'll like it. If anybody groans or complains, you'll never get another bite of food from my kitchen. Got it?"

"Where's the Judge?" Penny asked.

Maebelle placed a pitcher of iced tea on the table. "I fed him and put him to bed already. He was exhausted. Apparently, you gave him the best day of his life today. Thank you for that, Chase."

"I just took him flying and on a little boat ride."

Maebelle smiled. "I think it meant a lot more to him than just an airplane ride and a boat trip. Now eat up, and remember, no complaints!"

Nobody complained. In fact, although it tasted nothing like gumbo, whatever it was disappeared in a flurry of spoons and broken French bread. Anya even learned what the phrase *sop it up* means.

For dessert, Anya brought in a thin-layered pastry of some kind and served each of us a piece—Penny first.

"What is it?" I asked before anyone else.

"Is *medovik*. You would say *honey cake*. Is made with sweetened cream, and I think word is *pastry* with much honey inside."

"For the record," Maebelle said, "I had nothing to do with dessert. This one is all Anya, so if you want to complain about it, take it up with her. She's on her own."

Singer and Mongo volunteered to clean up while Hunter and I briefed the newest "member" of our team.

Anya ended the briefing by asking, "I can drive boat, yes?"

"I'm afraid you'll have to take that up with Penny," I told her.

She looked at the ceiling. "Perhaps I will not drive . . . this time."

Chapter 21
I Did Not Kill Him

It wasn't uncommon for me to be the first person awake in the house. Watching the sun show its face in the eastern sky has always held some unexplainable magic for me. I understand the science, and I know it's my planet that's doing the moving, but in those early morning moments when the first light of day chases the darkness from the Earth, it's easy to believe the sun is an avenging angel dispatched to vanquish the demons of the night.

On that particular Saturday morning in July of 2002, from beneath the Judge's gazebo, my favorite coffee mug and I had front row seats for that vanquishing. A dozen wispy clouds floated in carefree indifference to the demons above Cumberland Island, and I watched in awe as our nearest star set those clouds ablaze with colors every artist dreams of capturing but never would. Something about the scene left me on the edge of my seat, anticipating the show that would follow the rising of such a magnificent curtain on the morning's stage.

"We need to talk, my Chasechka."

Not what I needed on that particular morning.

"Good morning, sweetheart. I love you" from the perfect lips of my wife would've been an excellent next scene, but "We need to talk" from the mouth of a former Russian spy who I neither wanted nor needed in my life was not how my day should have begun.

I swallowed one more mouthful of the strong coffee and turned to face Anya. "What is it?"

"Is the Judge. I did not kill him."

I shuddered. "Well, I should certainly hope not."

"I could not sleep in night, so I come to kitchen for *zakuska*, and Judge is there with milk and *medovik*."

Almost afraid to ask, I said, "What's *zakuska*?"

"If I knew English word, I would say it. Is small food in night but not part of meal."

"Snack."

"Yes, is snack. I come for snack in night and find Judge eating my *medovik*. He said to me, 'Is delicious. Did you make?' I say to him, yes, I make. And he smile."

"Anya, your English is even worse than when we were in Siberia. What's going on? Is everything okay?"

She shook her head in tiny, jerking motions—something I'd never seen her do. "Is not, Chase. Is not okay."

I slid an Adirondack chair toward her with my foot. "Sit down and tell me what's going on."

Instead of taking advantage of the design of the chair, she nestled painfully on the edge of the seat. If I believed it was possible for Anya Burinkova to show fear in her eyes, I would have sworn that's what I saw. "Tell me in Russian if you have to, but say it. Whatever it is."

She licked her thin lips, and her eyes glistened with what, from any other human with a soul, would've been the beginnings of a tear. "Chasechka, to me he says, 'I'm having milk and honey with an angel. I surely didn't know Heaven would look like my kitchen.'"

They *were* tears because they fell, and she made no effort to wipe them away. Instead, she kept talking. "I think he is having bad dream, so I take him by arm and return him to his bed. I swear it to you. I did this exactly and nothing more. Today, when sun come, I am still awake, and I look to see he is okay, but he is not breathing in morning. I did not kill him, Chasechka. I swear it. I did not."

I closed my eyes and prayed she was telling the truth about not killing him and that she was wrong about him not breathing. I stood. "Stay here. Don't leave that chair. I swear to God, if you move, I'll shoot you and bury you where you fall. Do you understand me?"

"Yes, Chase. I understand. I will stay only here."

A chill enveloped me as I stepped through the kitchen door and saw Maebelle at the stove.

She turned, and the look on her face melted from joy into deepest concern. "Is everything okay, Chase?"

"I don't think so," I said. "But please stay here. I'll be right back."

"Chase, what's going on? What's wrong?"

"Just stay here, Maebelle. I'll be right back."

"Oh, my God. It's grandfather, isn't it?"

She slapped her hands against her apron, sending a cloud of flour billowing around her, reminding me of the mist I'd watched over the island only minutes before. She ran past me and down the hall, dragging her fingertips across the two-centuries-old plastered walls and screaming for her grandfather.

I was too slow to catch her, but when I reached the Judge's bedroom, I found Maebelle holding his face in her hands, his skin smooth and pale and lifeless. Tears poured from her eyes, and she gasped in agonizing implosions, her body quivering in disbelief and shock.

Instead of interrupting, I stepped back through the doorway and pulled the heavy door to its jamb. Its iron hinges creaked their mournful cry, and I waited just outside the door for Maebelle to say goodbye to the man who'd given her everything he could since she'd been barely able to crawl, but now lay dead in her hands. Perhaps he needed the moment alone with her as badly as she did.

When the gasping subsided and turned to delicate cries, I pressed through the doorway and took her arm. "We need to call his doctor."

She pressed her quivering lips tightly together and looked up at me. Her youth and innocence were fading, and she nodded in resolute acceptance, but instead of pulling away, she stood and buried her face in my chest and let me hold her. "You and I are now the only family there is, Chase. I love you."

Those were the words that burst the dam holding back my tears. "I love you, too, Maebelle."

We stood there holding each other, clinging to a bloodline neither of us had known existed only months before.

* * *

There was no hearse. Instead, the Judge's beloved horse Pecan, pulled the casket on a polished black wagon, starting at First Baptist Church, down Wheeler, to Saint Marys, and finally up Bartlett to the Oak Grove Cemetery. On the morning of July 23rd, 2002, exactly two weeks before his ninety-sixth birthday, we laid the Judge's body to rest beneath oak trees dripping with Spanish moss and history. The old town of waterfront Saint Marys, Georgia, locked its shops, closed its restaurants, and mourned the loss of a man, the likes of whom it would never know again.

I believed then, and will until I leave this Earth, that Bernard Henry Huntsinger was the last of the best of what men were capable of becoming. He loved without fear or reservation. He respected men for how they treated each other, ignoring the color of their skin, the god they worshipped, and the misdeeds of their past, looking instead for the respect they showed themselves and those around them. He gave unselfishly of himself, his fortune, and his wisdom, knowing far better than most that he could take none of those things with him into the life that awaited him beyond the final sunset he would ever behold, and into the loving arms of the God he served and the wife to whom he dedicated his boundless loyalty. May he forever rest in the peace that he brought immeasurable love and boundless generosity to everyone who knew him.

Chapter 22
I Didn't Kill Her

I didn't shoot Anya, and the Russian spy ship never once crossed any of our minds for four somber days.

On the gallery of Bonaventure, the afternoon of the Judge's funeral, Maebelle held my hand and whispered, "You know the last thing he ever said to me?"

I let my tear-filled eyes meet hers, but I didn't speak.

"He told me you gave him the best day of his life since Grandmother was taken from him. That's what he told me, Chase. Thank you for that."

Words wouldn't come, so I simply squeezed her small hand in mine and looked out over the marsh where even the birds seemed to mourn the passing of an old friend.

"What happens now?" she asked meekly.

"Now we live our lives the way he'd want us to—being kind to each other and doing what's right, even when it's not easy."

"That's what you guys do, isn't it?"

"What do you mean?" I asked.

"All of you," she said. "You do what's right, even when it breaks your backs and nearly kills you. I've never seen anything like it, anything like you and Clark, and all of you."

She turned and wiped her eyes. "I'm going to marry him, you know. And I'm going to have his babies. And I'm going to try to make him forget what he's been through because I love him. Do you think that's possible?"

I felt my eyebrows form the shape of a gull's wings. "Do I think it's possible for you to love him or for you to make him forget what he's been through?"

"I already love him," she said. "It's the other I don't know about."

"Don't try to take those memories from him. They're part of the man he is. They are the things that make it possible for him to sleep at night, and at times, they are the things that rob him of that sleep. It won't be easy, Maebelle. Clark is a man of action. He always has been. Part of him will die in the coming weeks and months, but you'll be there to fill that enormous void and give him something new to live for—something new to devote himself to with the same intensity and passion he gave to his work."

"He's a dangerous man, isn't he?"

I smiled. "No, not to you, but for anyone who would ever try to hurt you or those beautiful babies you'll give him, there's never been anyone more dangerous. He's the best friend I'll ever have, and he's the reason I'm still alive a dozen times over."

She returned my smile. "Thank you for everything."

"We're family. Thanks is implied."

"That doesn't mean we still shouldn't say it," she whispered.

Silent conversation followed until shadows consumed the marsh, and the river, and perhaps our souls.

* * *

It wasn't the passing of another night, nor the coming of another day that returned our focus on the task that lay ahead. It was knowing that a wolf paced at our gates, and that the wolf had to be faced and slaughtered. We were the protectors of what lived within those gates, and we owed it to them to stand fearless in the face of an enemy and beat back the pacing wolf and any who dared come after him. It was, and is, what made us warriors. It was our common need to serve the country we loved and the people who'd never know our names. The wolf's day in the sun was about to become his bloodiest, and my team and I would be the sword that would spill his blood.

We established satellite comms with Clark and Skipper and UHF comms between every member of the boat crew. An M2, "Ma Deuce," fifty-caliber machine gun rested on the deck, lashed securely in place near the weapons mount on the starboard rail. A pair of M249 squad automatic weapons, or SAWs, stood at the ready and out of sight, just inside the pilothouse. It was far from the heaviest weaponry we'd ever carried into battle, but hopefully it would return at the end of the day unfired and unnecessary. Of course, hope is for children and saints, and I was neither.

The sun met the bow of the Mark V as we broke clear of the pass into the Atlantic, mist still rising from the ocean, and shrimp boats chugging to sea with their dangling nets empty and hungry.

Penny chose to stay with Maebelle, and part of me was glad she did. Standing her in the face of danger left me sickened and terrified. Knowing she was safe and comforting Maebelle granted me the freedom to focus on the mission and the *Viktor Leonov*.

I had the helm. Hunter and Singer rode the rails amidships, eyes scanning the horizon as we cut across the waves at nearly fifty knots. Mongo stood with one foot on top of the fifty-cal and one enormous arm wrapped around the mount. Anya stood over the collection of multifunction displays absorbing the barrage of radar returns, satellite images, and data from every imaginable source.

Skipper's voice echoed in our earpieces. "She's on your bow at thirty-two miles. You should see her on the satellite imagery."

"I have her," said Anya in her cold, measured tone.

The temptation to shove the throttles through the console and rocket across the waves was almost irresistible, but getting there two minutes faster wouldn't change a thing, so I kept both our speed and fuel consumption under control.

Looking away from the horizon, I double-checked the panel for indications that the radar-scrambling systems were online and doing their best to keep us invisible.

Twenty minutes later, Hunter yelled, "Tallyho!"

The superstructure of the Russian spy ship came into sight on the horizon.

Anya said, "Bear away to starboard and pass behind them at one-half mile. If they are laying hydrophone, I will see with sonar."

Skipper said, "They're making perfect speed for it, Anya. Keep your eyes open. Don't miss it."

"What speed do you want when we pass?" I yelled.

"Do not yell. I can hear you," Anya scolded.

"Sorry. What speed do you want me to make on their stern?"

"Twenty knots. No more. If faster, I will miss."

"Twenty knots, aye." I bore away, mentally plotting a course that would take me eight hundred yards off the stern of my nemesis.

"Lookouts on deck," came Singer's voice in my ear.

"Activate the cameras," I ordered, and Anya pressed a series of controls, training the arch-mounted hi-def camera systems on the hull of the ship.

"Cameras locked and recording," she reported.

My heart pounded as the ship that had appeared so small through the gunsight of my Mustang a few days before, now loomed large less than a mile off my port bow. Antennae of every shape jutted skyward, and satellite dishes too numerous to count pointed straight up, likely sending, and more menacingly, *receiving* data from their own private collection of orbiting birds even Skipper couldn't identify.

I glanced around at my team. Hunter and Singer were laser-focused on the ship. Mongo was scanning for support vessels. I expected to see the back of Anya's head as she stared down at the displays, but to my surprise and disbelief, she stood erect, mesmerized and fixated on the ship.

I imagined the thoughts running through her head: signaling her former countrymen of our intention and vulnerability. A moment of terror ran through my chest as I thought of her disabling the radar jamming and heat signature shielding and calling in a missile attack on our position.

In angered frustration, I pounded on the bank of screens in front of her and yelled, "Focus, dammit! Find that hydrophone!"

She turned to face me and slowly shook her head. "I do not have to find hydrophone. Is there. I know this ship." She pointed furiously through the windscreen. "Look at ship. Look! She is too low in water. She was not built to sit in water like that. She is laying hydrophone, but there is more."

"What are you talking about?"

She motioned with her finger as if she were stirring. "Make circle."

"Here?" I asked, still yelling.

"No, no. Big circle around ship at five hundred meters."

I pointed my finger within inches of her nose. "If you're playing me, they'll never find your body."

"I am American now . . . especially now. Make circle."

"Are you copying this, Skipper?"

Skipper said, "Isolate!"

I reached for my comms control and cycled the switch that would isolate my voice comms with only Skipper and Clark. "Isolated."

Clark spoke his first words of the operation. "What the hell is going on out there?"

"Anya says she knows what they're doing, and she wants us to circle the ship at five hundred meters."

Anya pounded on my shoulder with a relentless hammer fist. "You must give order to mount guns. They will likely fire on us if they think we cannot shoot back."

I drove my thumb into the isolation switch, reopening the channel to my team. "Mount the guns!"

I didn't have to wait for an audible response. The movement on deck told me that my orders were being executed without question.

Back on isolation, I said, "We're mounting the guns. Anya thinks—"

Skipper cut in. "I know. I can still hear her. I had her comms wired for open channel."

"What does she think they're doing?" Clark howled.

"She thinks they're laying mines." Skipper's low, husky voice was full of dread from a thousand miles away.

"You can't lay mines from an intel ship," Clark said. "They're not built for that."

"That's what she meant by the ship's sitting too low in the water. It's been modified."

"Get out of there, now!" Clark ordered.

I turned hard to starboard, following Clark's orders, but Anya drove her palm into the back of my elbow. "Make circle. You must trust me, Chase."

I stared into the eyes of the woman who had once lured me beyond my own flesh and out of my own mind, but the assassin who'd worn those eyes no longer owned them. These were the eyes of an American by choice rather than birth. These were the eyes of a warrior who'd, for the first time in her life, chosen her team instead of having it chosen for her. These were the eyes of someone with something to prove.

I thumbed the comms controls back to open channel. "I'm making the circle."

Instead of reissuing the order to abort, Clark said, "Roger. Report mission complete."

Anya abandoned the array of screens in front of her and climbed the arch. She clung to the aluminum structure with her left arm and hand while holding binoculars tightly against her eyes with the other, never taking her attention off the spy ship.

I gave my first order of the day. "Train that fifty-cal on the bridge, and if you see so much as a flash from that ship, blow every inch of glass out of it."

Mongo cycled the bolt on the M2 and growled, "Aye, sir."

We completed our circuit of the ship at five hundred meters without receiving or sending fire, but we didn't do it unseen. There was no question every man on that ship knew they were being orbited and watched and recorded. There's no way the Russians believed they could lay mines thirty miles off the coast of a U.S. nuclear submarine base and go unnoticed.

As we broke away from the *Leonov*, I reported, "Mission complete. RTB."

Clark replied, "Roger. Returning to base. Stow the weapons when able."

Every member of the boat crew heard Clark's order, but they all turned to me. Oversight and on-scene command are two very different things; no one understood that better than Clark Johnson. I nodded, confirming his order, and the weaponry was dismounted and stowed, still clean and unfired, except for a little saltwater spray that would be thoroughly scoured back at Bonaventure.

While the team was securing the weapons, Anya climbed into one of the crew seats and removed her left boot, pulling the padded insole from inside. I was intrigued, but I didn't ask. Instead, I just watched. She turned the insole upside down with the gray side facing up and the blue side pressed against her thigh. She slid a pen from her sleeve pocket and began sketching on the insole. No matter how hard I tried, I couldn't come up with any rational explanation for what she was doing, so I gave up and focused on getting us back into Saint Marys without the Coast Guard running out to intercept us.

We tied up at the Bonaventure dock with our pulses still pounding and my brain reeling over what Anya had sketched on the insole of her boot. Ultimately, it didn't matter. Our first mission had been a success in that we didn't get blown out of the water. We'd announced our presence and identified ourselves as a potential threat. Perhaps the Russian crew would turn for the Baltic and run home to momma, but more likely, they'd spend the next forty-eight hours trying to figure out who the insane bunch of American cowboys on the invisible boat were, and wondering if we had the guts to come out and play again. Little did they know, we were about to answer that question with a lot more than cameras and unfired machine guns.

Chapter 23
She Said That

As I climbed from the Mark V, Anya took my arm. "You need to listen to me, Chase."

"Not now," I said. "We have to debrief and send up what we have."

"But, Chase. You do not have—"

"Anya, listen to me. We're very good at this. Whatever you've got on your mind is going to have to wait. We don't delay the debrief for anything short of a gunfight. Is anybody shooting at us?"

She shook her head and released my arm.

The weapons were shouldered and returned to the Judge's vault built into the northern wall of the house. We'd temporarily claimed the space as our armory until we could have something more substantial built.

Clark called us into the library, where he and Skipper were already planning what to do next. As I hustled through the kitchen, Penny took me by the hand. "I know you have to go, but is everybody all right?"

I leaned down and kissed her, taking her hands in mine. "Yes, everything went great. Everybody's fine, and we have a lot of new information to work with. We'll be back out in a few minutes."

I tried to pull away, but she clung onto my wrists. "What about her?"

I shot a look toward Anya's back. "What about her?"

"Did she do anything, you know . . . wrong?"

"No, she did everything right this time."

We closed the door, and each of us gave our version of what happened. The varied experience of every operator tends to shape his perspective of events. A sniper looks at the world quite differently than a bomber pilot, even though both of their jobs involve destruction from afar. Our team's makeup was even more diverse than snipers and bombers. We had a baseball player, a combat controller, a sniper, a giant, and of course, a former Russian assassin.

Hunter went first. "She's clearly vulnerable at the stern where all ships are. There are limited fighting positions aft of amidships and no stern-mounted weaponry. There's no question that's our way in if it comes to a boarding."

Mongo said, "I didn't detect any support vessels of any kind. She appears to be completely autonomous. I can't say I'd want to be thirty miles off the Russian coast in a tub like that one without out a carrier group for backup."

Singer, our sniper, had an eye for detail the rest of the team lacked. "I only saw two men on the bridge, eight on deck, and four on high watch. Of the two on the bridge, one never took his eyes off us, and the other never looked up. The four on high watch used handheld comms and binoculars from the sixties. The crew on deck appeared to be AB sailors on typical maritime duty keeping the ship running. There was no exposed armament and no position on the ship from which a full range of defensive fire would be possible from one gun. I agree with Hunter about the soft stern."

When Clark finished his furious scribbling, he looked up at me. "What did you see?"

"I saw a relatively soft target that wasn't maneuvering well. It looked gangly, to tell you the truth. I expected her to be intimidating, but her attitude in the water was awkward at best."

Skipper chimed in. "That's because, just like Anya said, the *Leonov* has probably been modified as a minelayer. There's no other explanation. I've already written up the intel report, and I'll get it to you as soon as we're done here. I recommend we get it to the Pentagon as soon as possible. They need to know the Russians are laying mines under the submarine highway in and out of Kings Bay."

Clark said, "The intel report comes to me first."

"Of course," Skipper said. "That's the chain."

Our new boss flattened his hands on the desk. "Okay, let's talk about you ignoring the order to abort."

Until that day, I'd never worked beneath Clark, only at his side, so reporting to him felt nothing like my debriefings with Dominic. I stared at him and waited for a direct question.

After a long, uncomfortable moment of silence, he said, "So, let's hear it. Why did you reengage after I ordered you to abort?"

"Because you're not a dictator like your father, and we're doing this one together. Isn't that what you said?"

Anya squirmed in her seat. "Because of me—"

Clark either intentionally ignored her or chose to talk over her. "Yes, that's exactly what I said, and if I had been on that boat with you, I would've most likely made the same call to continue the mission, but it's different from here. We'll learn the new organizational structure, and we will always work together. Nobody got hurt, and we picked up some valuable intel, but if the Russians had started shooting—"

"But they didn't," I interrupted. "Not this time. But you're right. I should've aborted. I put my team and your command at risk. It was my call, and it was the wrong one. It won't happen again."

An almost imperceptible nod between Clark and me closed the subject and sealed our agreement.

Clark turned to the speakerphone. "Skipper, have you got anything else to add?"

"No."

"Anyone else?"

No one spoke, so Clark leaned back in his chair. "If the Russians are laying mines like Anya says, this just became somebody else's mission. We'll pass the intel we've gathered up the chain, and it'll be out of our hands by sundown. Most likely, the SEALs or Delta will take it from here. What you did out there today was remarkable. I wish I could've been with you. I never thought I'd say this, but I'm glad Anya was there with you. Without her knowledge of that ship, none of us would've known about the minelaying operation. So, thank you, Anya. I, for one, am glad to have you."

Every eye turned to the only member of the team without an American birth certificate. She wore the stern look I'd come to know so well in years past when determination superseded everything else she was feeling.

It was an odd moment for that look, so I said, "I think Clark speaks for all of us. We're all glad you were there today. You may have saved a great many American lives and prevented an international incident of monumental proportions."

If anything about her expression changed, it was that it grew colder. "I said nothing about mines." She pointed toward the speakerphone. "*She* said that."

"What?" came the response from the room.

Anya shook her head. "I did not say the *Viktor Leonov* is laying mines. I try to tell you many times, but this is assumption you make. Is possible for mines, but I do not think this is so. I think you should not send intelligence report to Pentagon until we look closely at video."

Clark squeezed his eyes closed and sighed. "This is not what I need."

I pulled the video memory cards from my pocket and slid them across the desk. Soon, the high-definition video was playing on the computer screen, and everyone leaned in.

"May I tell about ship?" Anya asked.

Clark slapped his forehead. "Yes . . . yes. For God's sake, tell us about the ship."

She lifted a pencil from the desk and pointed to the water just astern of the *Leonov*. "Look at water here. Ship is with two propellers, but I think is only using one."

I leaned forward and pointed to the screen. "She's right. The only disturbance is on the starboard side. The port screw isn't turning."

"So, maybe they're conserving fuel," Hunter said. "I can think of a thousand reasons they'd only be turning one screw."

Anya said, "No. You can think of one thousand reasons you would not be turning screw, but not Russian crew putting hydrophone on bottom of sea. Maneuvering with only one propeller is difficult enough if only moving ship, but when laying hydrophone or other things—even like mines—is not possible."

Clark waved toward the screen. "Go on. What else?"

She drew an imaginary line with the eraser end of the pencil across the bottom of the screen. "Look also how ship is not level. Is, uh, I do not know word. Maybe tilting?"

"Listing," I said.

"Thank you. Yes, listing is what ship is doing. I think maybe ship is wounded and maybe also flooding."

Skipper jumped in. "She could still be laying mines. Or if it's just a hydrophone, the cable is fouled."

"What cable?" I asked, demonstrating my ignorance.

"If they're laying hydrophones," she said, "the network is built on several heavy sections of steel cable designed to weigh down the microphones and hold them in place on the seafloor. When the NOAA research vessels lay hydrophone networks to listen to whales or whatever, they do it from a ship with these huge spools of this cable on deck, and they feed it off the back like commercial fishing boats do with their nets. That lets the cable play out behind the propellers and rudder so they can go as fast as they want . . ."

A communal "Ahh," rose from the team.

"That's right," Skipper said. "If they modified the *Leonov* to lay cable or mines, they would've had to do it from a moon pool setup in the belly of the ship—you guessed it—*ahead* of the props and rudder. That means she'd have to move so slow that the cable would be dragged behind her and into the props. If they got anxious when they saw you coming and tried to close up shop, maybe, just maybe, they fouled a prop."

Clark bit at his lip. "I don't like it. There are too many maybes. It could be mines, but Anya doesn't think so. It could be a fouled prop, but we don't know. It could be taking on water, but the listing could also be caused by poor ballast control or maybe one of these big spools of cable they've got buried in that ship rolled over to the wrong side. We need a way to see the belly of that ship without them knowing we're there."

Hunter drummed his fingers on the desk. "I can score an ROV from the Navy, but it's tethered. We'd have to be practically tied up alongside that ship to get a look underneath, and between their satellite links and lookouts on deck, there's no way we could get that close without them seeing us."

A crack of thunder rattled the windows and caused the house to shudder as another South Georgia afternoon thunderstorm rolled across the marsh.

I looked past Clark and through the library window as the rain fell in sheets and erased the landscape. "Exactly how long is the tether on the ROV?"

Hunter cast his eyes toward the ceiling. "Two thousand meters, I think."

I grabbed Hunter's collar and dragged him toward the window. "Look out there. Can you see two thousand meters in this storm?"

Hunter grinned as if he'd just won the lottery. "Are you brave enough to take the Mark V out in this weather?"

I grinned back. "Are you cowardly enough not to come with me?"

He nodded. "I'll make the call."

As Hunter dialed his contact at the Navy base, Singer said, "Are you going to let the rest of us in on the big secret?"

I pointed toward the computer monitor. "We can't get near that ship because they can see us on the satellite imagery and the lookouts on deck."

"Right," Singer said.

Then I pointed out the window. "Satellites can't see through those clouds, and lookouts can't see the tips of their noses in weather like that. It storms just like this every afternoon. All we have to do is hide in one of the big nasty squall lines and get close enough to that ship to hover the ROV underneath her for a few minutes. Then we'll know everything that ship is capable of doing from every angle. If it's a minelayer, if it's a cable layer, if it's a milk truck, we'll know."

Clark sat back, satisfaction dripping from his face. "I like it."

Anya said, "Is good plan, I think, but what is ROV?"

It was easy to forget American acronyms may not be Anya's strong suit. "It's a remotely operated vehicle—an underwater robot on a cable."

Apparently satisfied with my answer, she asked, "And this ROV has camera, yes?"

Hunter hung up the phone. "To answer Anya's question, no, it doesn't have a camera. It has nine cameras. And it's all ours whenever we're ready to pick it up."

Our Russian sat with a look of utter disbelief in her eyes. "This is how Americans plan mission always?"

I smiled and sat on the windowsill. "Oh, no. It's usually a lot more chaotic than this."

Chapter 24
Tink . . . Tink . . . Thud

Predicting summertime thunderstorms along the southeastern coast of the United States is like shooting fish in a barrel. If it's summertime, the storms will come. The problem is predicting exactly when and where they will come. In our case, perhaps the more important concern was how long they would last.

We needed a storm large enough to obscure the sky so the satellites couldn't see the surface, and intense enough to essentially blind the lookouts on deck beyond a thousand meters or so. Even though our ROV could roam twice that range, the shorter we kept the tether, the faster we could retrieve it and make our exit. I didn't know how much a U.S. Navy ROV cost, but I didn't want to write a check for one if we had to cut and run.

There was a lot to think about before the next encounter with the *Viktor Leonov*, but the look on Clark Johnson's face told me that my stress load was little more than a drop in the bucket compared to what he was dealing with. I found him in the Judge's gazebo, which, I guess, had become *my* gazebo.

"You doing okay, old man?"

He looked up, brow furrowed, and the lines of the previous day's mission already showing on his face. So quickly, the weight of the new job was robbing him of the countenance that had made him look like a college freshman for twenty years.

The smile came, but it was slow. "Yeah, I'm all right. It's just different, you know."

I slid into one of the six Adirondack chairs and handed him a cup of coffee. "Yeah, I know. I'm feeling it, too. For me, it's always just been the two of us. I looked to you when I didn't know what to do, and we could always turn to your dad if it hit the fan too hard. But now I've got Mongo, Hunter, Singer, and Penny looking at me for direction. I can't imagine what it must be like for you."

He sipped his coffee. "Don't forget Anya."

"Oh, yeah, her too. What a mess that is. What am I supposed to do with her?"

He stared out across the marsh. "Get through this mission, and we'll tuck her away in Athens just like you planned. Maybe she'll settle into life in America and forget all about Chasechka."

"Yeah, I'm not so sure that'll happen."

"How much of our lives is based on what's likely, College Boy? You're supposed to be catching for the Braves, and I'm supposed to be retired from the Army and driving a truck somewhere. We've got an exiled Russian assassin who looks like she ought to be on the cover of the Victoria's Secret catalog, a gospel sniper, a giant straight out of *Princess Bride*, and whatever the hell Hunter is. It's like we're living on the Island of Misfit Toys."

I pointed toward a quartet of squirrels chasing each other up and down a dozen pecan trees. "There we go."

We watched the animals frolic in the morning sun until a hawk screeched overhead, and each of the squirrels froze in terror. Seconds later, the four of them ran for their lives, scampering beneath the floor of the gazebo.

Clark peered through the planks and gently tapped his toe against the wood. "They don't know who we are, but they know we won't let that hawk get 'em."

I raised my coffee cup in a silent salute.

* * *

Hunter took Mongo and Singer to pick up the ROV while I checked on my airplanes and Clark had a conference call with somebody well above my pay grade.

Cotton used his two weeks' vacation from his job as an aircraft mechanic at New Smyrna Beach to complete the annual inspection on my Mustang and spend some quality time with his sister, Earl. I found both of them lying on the right wing of my Mustang in the hangar around nine o'clock.

"Are you two enjoying your nap up there?"

My voice echoed through the hangar, and Earl and Cotton looked up simultaneously.

"Oh, hey, Chase," Cotton said. "I'm glad you're here. I've got something to show you, and I'm not sure what we're gonna need to do about it."

"That sounds expensive," I said as I approached the trailing edge of the Mustang's right wing.

Cotton had the gun access port open and another large panel removed from the top of the wing. "What do you know about these?"

I leaned across the wing flap to peer into the opening. "I know that's where the original guns were, and that bay is where the ammo would've been to feed these three guns when they were real."

"That's right," he said. "And these are the solenoids that would've fired the guns when you pulled the trigger on the stick."

He tapped on three silver cylindrical objects affixed to the sides of each of the dummy fifty-caliber receivers in the wing.

"So, what's the problem?" I asked.

He handed me a screwdriver. "Tap on the top of each of them guns, and start with the outboard one first."

I took the screwdriver from his hand and did as he instructed. The tool bounced off the first two guns with a tinny, metallic ping, but the third block returned a definite thud. I bounced the tool twice more on the receiver with the same result.

I looked up into the squinted eyes of my mechanic, and he nodded.

"That ain't no dummy gun like the rest of 'em."

I shot a glance across the airplane toward the other wing and back at Cotton.

He shook his head. "Nope, that side's all dummies, but it does have a camera. Come on. I'll show you."

He and Earl slid down from the wing, and the three of us ducked beneath the belly of the Mustang. He pointed into the left main landing gear well and at a complex arrangement of gadgets he declared to be a camera. "If you could get them geeks back up here and yank all this crap out, they could put you a good camera in there that probably wouldn't weigh more than a couple of pounds. You could dump all this World War Two stuff."

"I think I'd like to keep this World War Two stuff and add a couple of pounds of upgraded camera equipment. I kind of like the nostalgia of having the original camera still in the old girl."

Cotton shrugged. "Ain't no way to know if it was original. It could just be something they threw in there when they done the restoration."

In extreme opposition to her typical style, Earl hadn't spoken a word, so I said, "Are you okay, momma?"

She looked up. "Yeah, Baby Boy. I knew you was into something, but now that you've drug me and Cotton up here, it's just got me worried. That's all."

I slid my arm across her round shoulders and pulled her against me. "Don't you worry, old girl. It's not what you think."

She huffed. "It's exactly what I think. I know what you're doing . . . all of you. I've seen it all before. Hell, I seen my husband hop in an Air America C-Forty-Six and never come back, so don't tell me it ain't what I think. I've done all this before, and it cost me more than I had to give."

"Your husband flew for the agency?"

"I hate it when you people try to be all coy about that and call it the Agency. Call it what it is. It's the damned CIA, and everybody knows it."

"I don't work for the CIA, Earl. I never have. None of us do. We're sort of like . . . contractors."

She interrupted. "Yeah, I know how it works, but it's all the same, kid." She wrapped her arms around me. "It just brings back a lot of crap I don't want to think about."

I returned the hug. "You're a special kind of . . ."

She didn't let me finish. "*Crazy* is what you were gonna say. I'm a special kind of crazy, but I love you, Baby Boy. Just don't go off and get yourself killed. I used to look like that skinny wife of yours before Boomer got killed. Now look at me. You don't want that pretty girl turnin' into this if you go and get yourself shot up, now do you?"

"Your husband's name was Boomer?"

She yanked the screwdriver from my hand. "Give me that thing. I'm gonna stab you in the liver."

I recoiled. "That's not my liver, Earl."

Cotton got a good chuckle out of the exchange, but he was still all business. "So, what do you want to do about that gun, Chase?"

I turned from Earl. "What gun?"

He shook his head. "That's what I thought you'd say."

* * *

I was surprised to see the Mark V still not in its spot at the Bonaventure dock when I returned home, so I climbed the back steps and took a seat in a rocker that, just like the gazebo, was now mine.

My plan was simple. I'd sit on the gallery and watch for the team return with the ROV and my boat, but as is true with most of my plans, it didn't quite work out that way.

Maebelle had a habit of leaving the solid oak door standing open while she cooked. That left only a wooden-framed screen door between the kitchen and back gallery, which made sense in the mild winters and beautiful fall and spring, but I never understood why she did it in late July. The downside of the open door in the summer was the electric bill, but the upside was the eavesdropping.

"Is for you uncomfortable for me to be here, no?"

There was no question Anya was directing her inquisition directly at Penny.

"I don't know if *uncomfortable* is the right word, but I'll admit it's a little weird."

The guilt that should've been associated with listening in on their conversation didn't come. Perhaps that speaks volumes about my morality, or lack thereof, but there was no chance of me walking away. I wasn't going to miss a word.

Maebelle's footsteps crossed the floor. "Ooh, sorry. Am I interrupting?"

"No, of course not. It's your kitchen. We were just talking about whether it was uncomfortable for me to have Anya here."

Maebelle said, "You're not staying, are you?"

I had to suppress a laugh. I loved how Maebelle said whatever came to her mind.

Penny saved the moment. "She'll stay until they get this whole thing with the ship worked out, but we've got a surprise for her after that."

"I hope is good surprise. In my life, most of surprises are bad."

Penny laughed. "I think you'll like this one, but I don't know if Chase wants me to tell you about it yet."

"I am happy for you, Penny, to have Chase and for you also to have Clark, Maebelle. These are good men for you."

I heard something land firmly on the table.

"Oh, my gosh. We've got to find you a boyfriend," Maebelle said, trying to keep her giggling under control.

"I do not think I am to find boyfriend."

Penny said, "I'll tell you one thing. You can't have mine, but the way men look at you, America is ripe for the picking for you, girl."

"Ripe for picking?" Anya asked. "Is funny sounding phrase, like men are fruit."

"They are!" Maebelle insisted. "They're juicy and firm, and some of them are even sweet."

Penny said, "Oh, yeah. And when they get old, they turn soft and attract flies."

The girls had a good laugh until Anya said, "I can tell to you secret wish I have, yes, and you will tell no one?"

"Sure, we won't tell."

In her hesitance, I could almost hear Anya trying to decide if she could trust Penny and Maebelle to keep her secret.

"I wish for blind man who cannot see me—only know me."

"What?" came two confused replies.

"Is hard for me to say in English. I think men like only the way woman looks sometimes and not how she is under this looks. I wish sometimes to look like Earl, woman who works on boat engine."

The kitchen again erupted with laughter. "Oh, you poor, gorgeous goddess," Maebelle jabbed. "Life must be so tough for you."

"Life is mine," Anya said, "and only life I know until now. I do not have friends in Russia when I am little girl. When my mother was murdered, I became property of State and was trained to fight, and kill, and even to seduce men . . . and sometimes women. I do not have boyfriend or husband. I am only weapon for my country . . . nothing more. This does not make life tough or not tough. It is just life for me."

"Anya, I'm sorry," Maebelle said, "I didn't mean to—"

"No. Do not be sorry. Is fine. Is very different for me and for you. Now, for first time, I have friends, and is difficult for everyone."

Penny said, "I don't know if we'll ever be what you'd call friends. It is weird. All of this is weird, but I do want you to be happy and have a normal life. You know, those guys out there— Chase and the rest of them—they went to a lot of trouble for you."

"And I would give for them my life."

"That's not what they want, Anya. They don't want your life. They want you to pick a side, the right side, and have their backs when they need you."

After a long moment of silence, Anya said, "I think this is what you have found with Chase and Clark—men who know you are on their side and always have support and love from you, yes?"

Chapter 25
Home to Mommy

I heard them coming long before I saw Hunter, Mongo, and Singer pulling up in the Mark V, so I jogged down to the dock.

The ROV unit was significantly larger than I expected. It even came with a self-contained crane for launch and recovery. The rover itself was about the size of an ironing board, but the spool of cable took up at least ten feet of deck space.

"What took so long?" I asked.

Hunter looked up. "What do you mean? It only took about half an hour to pick it up. When we came back, you were still at the airport, so we've been out learning how this thing works."

"Oh, good. And how did that go?"

"Great," Hunter said. "It's easy and fast in weather like this, but we'll see what happens when we get a little thunder and lightning."

I turned to study the southwestern sky. "Speaking of which, have you checked the weather for the afternoon?"

Hunter smiled. "Oh yeah, and it's on. There's a line of thunderstorms running from Tallahassee to Orlando, and it's a beast."

I hopped aboard the boat and fired up the satellite imagery. The storm was, indeed, a beast, and the National Weather Service was already broadcasting severe thunderstorm and tornado watches and warnings.

I pointed to the screen. "That's the kind of weather only Russians and fools would go out in."

"In that case," Hunter said, "let's go join the Russians."

We found Clark studying the same line of storms on his computer in the library, and after a briefing on the successful ROV trials, he was ready to brief the operations order.

"Are you taking Anya?" he asked.

"Not this time," I said. "She's already given us what we need to know, and it's going to be a rough ride. In fact, I think we should keep the crew to the bare minimum. How many people does it take to launch and recover the rover?"

Hunter turned to Mongo. "That creature can do it without the crane if he has to, but it took two of us today."

I pictured Mongo wrestling with the ROV . . . and winning. "It's going to be rough out there. How's your leg, Singer?"

"I'm back to full strength," he said in his calm, assured tone. "I don't know if you remember the Bible story about the storm on the Sea of Galilee, but I think it's a good idea if you take me with you."

"I remember the story quite well, and I agree. It'll be the four of us unless you can round up Saint Peter. He might come in handy."

"Who's going to break the news to Anya?" Clark asked.

I looked back toward the kitchen. "She's making some new friends. I think she'll be okay with staying behind this time."

His look said he wanted to know more, but he let it go. "Here's what I have in mind."

He spun the computer monitor around for us to see and brought up a nautical chart with a satellite overlay from Skipper. "Here's the *Leonov*, eighteen miles off the pass, so our little visit with them didn't scare her away. I want you out of the pass and in open water before the storm hits. I'm not worried about the Mark V making it, but there's going to be a thousand idiots trying to get back in before the storm hits. We don't want to get tangled up with any of them."

"I agree," I said. "The last thing we need is to try to explain what we're doing to the Coast Guard."

Clark continued the briefing. "When the storm hits, I want you ten minutes inside the leading edge. It's going to suck, and you're going to get beat up and wet, but we need that cover. If I put you on the leading edge and the storm starts falling apart, you'll be wide open and vulnerable. Take the beating instead of the bullets."

"What if the *Leonov* turns to run from the storm?" Mongo asked.

"They won't," I said. "They'll turn bow-on and ride it out. They don't have the speed to outrun it, especially if they're down to one engine."

"I agree with Chase," Clark said. "They'll stay where they are for the most part through the storm, and that'll play to our advantage. If you can get downwind of them and stay between five hundred and a thousand meters away, that'll give you room to work without worrying about them blowing into you, and it'll give you cover to run if things start falling apart."

Everyone nodded.

"When you get into position, splash the rover, and don't waste any time. Get the best video you can, but don't get comfortable."

I laughed. "I don't think there's any chance of that. We're going to be getting our teeth kicked in by that storm."

"Just don't overstay your welcome," Clark said. "Get enough footage to figure out what the belly of that thing looks like, and get out of there. Got it?"

"Yeah, we got it," I said.

He motioned toward the screen. "Unfortunately, there is no cover for you when you head home. You'll have to embrace the suck and keep moving. It'll be up to you whether you try to get back into the river while the storm is blowing, or wait for it to pass."

"How wide is the storm?"

He made some measurements. It looks like it's about sixty miles wide, but it's moving to the east, so it'll be more like seventy-five or eighty miles cutting diagonally through it."

I ran my hand through my hair. "How about contingency plans?"

"There are none," Clark said. "Skipper will have the satellite uplink—if it'll work in this weather—for the feed from the rover, so I should be able to see that from here. Again, all of that depends on being able to keep that satellite link. If you get spotted, run. If the boat sinks, I recommend sinking with it. You don't want those Russians picking you up."

"Okay, let's gear up," I said. "Does anybody have any questions, concerns, doubts, fears, or want to go crying home to their mommy?"

Everyone raised their hands.

* * *

An hour later, the Mark V was refueled, and the weapons were loaded. This time, though, we mounted them at the dock and covered them with rain hoods. There would be no way to mount a heavy weapon in twenty-foot seas and forty-knot winds. Firing them accurately would be equally impossible in those conditions, but the weapons were spray-and-pray guns and not sniper rifles, so if the encounter turned into a gunfight, accuracy wouldn't be our top priority. Escape was our best hope.

Anya took the news well. "I understand. Is boys trip, yes?"

"Yes, that's it. A boys trip. No girls allowed."

She grinned. "The weak little women will stay behind and feed babies and milk cows while big strong men are going to play in storm."

Penny said, "More likely, we'll be laughing about how we could be doing it so much better, but we'll be nice and dry."

I kissed her and wrapped her in, what had become, our pre-mission traditional hug, each one getting longer and tighter than the one before.

She leaned back and took my face in her hands. "Be careful. It's going to be a bad day to be on the water."

I kissed her forehead. "Don't worry. We've got Singer, and he's got God on speed dial. We'll be fine."

* * *

The storm blackened the southwestern sky as we motored past Fort Clinch. Of the fifty other vessels we encountered on the way, we were the only one heading out to sea. Everyone else was running home to mommy.

The calm before the storm is a phrase we all use, but few truly understand. The ocean felt dead beneath the hull of the Mark V. Less than a foot of swell rolled across the surface as we motored south along Fernandina Beach and watched families pack up their umbrellas and beach chairs ahead of the coming wall of darkness.

The calm dissolved, and with it, the light. Rain came down in sheets so sharp they cut into our skin. The exposure suits we wore kept us relatively dry, but the sea looked and felt like the inside of a blender. Darkness enveloped us, and the sky belched angry claps of bone-jarring thunder and lightning that looked like angry tentacles of the clouds grasping for the ocean. I'd never been in a worse storm at sea, and I hoped I never would again.

The torrent overtook us at three forty-five, and exactly ten minutes later, I turned the bow toward the sea and left Fernandina Beach astern. During the eighteen-mile trip to intercept the *Leonov*, it felt like we'd traveled across the Atlantic and climbed and descended a thousand mountains. The twenty-foot seas I'd anticipated came, but instead of the long periods between crests I'd hoped for, the relentless waves pounded us in short periods of sometimes less than five seconds between wave tops. It was impossible to hold a course. I could make the boat move in the general direction I wanted, but little else. The radar returned solid walls of rain, and at times pointed straight down into the water instead of across the sea as it was designed. Even if we could find the Russian boat in the storm, holding the Mark V still enough to launch, operate, and recover the rover would be next to impossible.

The roar of the wind and waves made attempts at communication with Clark and Skipper futile. I could occasionally hear one or both of them yelling something in my earpiece, but it was impossible to make it out. Every three minutes, at the top of my lungs, I reported into my mic, "Continuing mission," hoping they'd hear and understand me.

Staring through the windscreen was like looking into a washing machine. Walls of white foam pounded the glass as the wipers flailed in vain against the torrent. Our GPS continued to work, but reading the digital display in those conditions was like reading Hemingway on a roller coaster. Skipper refreshed the *Leonov's* position on our display every few seconds, but it was turning into chaos of the highest order.

Mongo yelled, "Not bad, huh?"

I yelled back. "No. It's a lot better than I expected. Can I get you anything to eat or drink?"

"Sure! I'll have a martini, but stirred, not shaken."

I shot a look around the pilothouse, surveying my team. Hunter was wedged against the console, a toothpick clenched between his teeth. Mongo was holding on to the overhead rail, with his knees flexed to absorb the pounding of the waves. And Singer sat calmly in one of the articulating chairs, with his eyes closed and his lips whispering prayers.

Hunter lunged toward me. "Need a break?"

"I could use one. This is kicking my ass."

He reached around me and clipped into the helm station. "I have the helm!"

"Thanks. You have the helm."

Being wedged against the console was much more restful than wrestling with the controls. When I caught my breath, I pulled myself close to the display and tried to measure our distance to the target. "I think they're three miles on the bow."

"That's good to know," Hunter barked. "Which way is the bow?"

The time to make a decision had come, and it was up to me. My team would follow me into Hell. In fact, that's exactly where we were: in a hell where flames were made of salt water. Each of them had to be thinking the same as me: there was no safe way to launch and recover the ROV in these conditions.

We likely wouldn't be able to find the spy ship, and if we did, we'd never be able to hold a consistent position relative to her. I stared with diminishing hope at the multifunction display where Skipper was constantly feeding data. The weather radar image was bright red in all directions except for a yellow area about the size of my fingernail.

I drew a line through the yellow, our position, and another where I knew the *Leonov* was, and drove my finger into the screen. "There's our shot!"

The team leaned in, and I tried to explain what I was hoping for. "If that return is correct, it may be just enough relief to make this happen."

"Damn the torpedoes!" Hunter yelled. "We're doing this thing."

After a few seconds of telling God I wanted the same thing Singer was asking for, I nudged Hunter. "I have the helm. Thanks for the break."

"You have the helm," he yelled as we exchanged positions.

"See if you can filter out the rain and get a radar range to the ship. We have to be inside a mile by now."

Hunter went to work on the display. After being bounced between the windscreen and the deck a dozen times, he said, "There she is."

Somehow, he'd managed to find the Russian ship through the onslaught of water from the sea and sky. From my perspective, the two were indistinguishable.

If I was reading the display correctly, the *Leonov* was a thousand meters off our bow. I yelled, "Can you keep the target while I maneuver downwind?"

"I can try."

I couldn't take the risk of colliding with the ship from her windward side. In her lee, I could escape downwind in the event of a collision, but getting pinned against her hull with the wind and waves pounding at my back would be a death sentence at best.

I made the maneuver, keeping the boat as much under control as possible. Essentially, I was adding bursts of power when I thought the bow was pointed roughly in the direction I wanted to go, and just holding on when Poseidon whipped us about.

Between frantic control inputs, I shot split-second glances toward the weather radar. The yellow was still coming, and I was still praying. If the less intense rain also meant even slightly calmer seas, I wanted that rover in the water with cameras rolling.

Hunter looked up from the display. "All right! I think we're about eight hundred meters downwind from her."

I adjusted the throttles, doing everything I knew to hold our position until the storm took a breath. I can't put a number on the men I've fought, but I'd never faced one who fought like that storm. I felt as if I'd wrestled a thousand bears, and the real fight hadn't yet begun.

Every eye on the boat watched the weather radar as the yellow grew nearer, but I kept my eyes laser-focused on the surface radar. The oblong magenta return of the *Viktor Leonov* consumed my attention.

The air suddenly shuddered and filled with the tangible sound of thunder. It was like standing in front of a wall of speakers at a rock concert. The energy pulsed through our chests and left our ears ringing only seconds before the rain stopped driving into the top of the pilothouse like icepicks. The bow settled from its vertical cycles of twenty-five feet to half that intensity. Twelve-foot seas, for the first time in my life, felt like dead calm.

I focused on the magenta return and eased the throttles forward. "Splash the rover!"

Inching ever closer to our foe, for the first time in an hour, I thought we might actually pull it off, but a glance over my shoulder shattered that belief. The cable connecting the crane to the rover had snapped in the torrent of the past hour, and the heavy shackle had swung like an endless whip, tearing the steel of the mechanism.

Hunter stood on top of the rover with Mongo holding his waist. He lashed the remains of the cable to what was left of the steel structure of the crane. The aft deck rose and fell, seemingly disconnected from the bow as the sea around us continued to roil.

My hatred of failure left me cursing the wind and rain and dreading what would be the next words out of my mouth. I turned to give the order to abort and call my men back inside the relative protection of the pilothouse, but what I saw was not a team of men at the point of mission failure.

Chapter 26
Nantucket Sleighride

The scene through the pilothouse door would've made Atlas proud. Hunter was wrapped around Mongo's left leg like a kid riding on his father's foot, and Singer clung to the other. In Mongo's tree-trunk arms was the three-hundred-pound rover, propellers spinning and lights cutting through the rain.

The three men moved as one toward the rail, the giant hugging the ROV, and Hunter and Singer keeping him from following it overboard. I would've given a king's ransom for a camera at that moment because no one would ever believe the story.

With a mighty shove, the rover left Mongo's arms and plunged into the foamy, black abyss. It took my team ten minutes to rig a fairlead for the control tether, but they soon had it rigged and lashed to the rail. The fairlead would keep the tether and control cables from whipping across the deck, slicing everything in their path, and potentially severing themselves.

Back in the pilothouse, Hunter went to work piloting the rover toward the Russian ship. Mongo and Singer stayed on deck with the tether reel and called out distances as the cable played out.

To call it calm would be a slap in the face of Mother Nature, but Hunter yelled out, "How much longer 'til the hard stuff comes back?"

I studied the radar and watched in horror as the yellow melted into red. Once again, the sky turned into solid sheets of water followed by pounding waves and foam.

"Get inside!" I yelled through the door, praying they could hear me.

Singer came first as if he'd been launched from a cannon. "You didn't have to throw me, you big ape!"

Mongo's form filled the opening, and he looked down at Singer. "I couldn't have you getting blown overboard. Then we'd have to listen to Chase sing instead of you, and his singing sucks."

I wanted to laugh, but the situation outside was quickly turning from terrible back to hellish. With Hunter on the controls of the rover, I needed help. "One of you two get on the radar and keep me from plowing into that ship."

Singer scrambled to his feet and wedged himself between Hunter and me. "It's a mess, Chase. It's going to take a minute to filter it out."

"We don't have a minute," I yelled. "Find that ship before I find it with our bow."

It was like playing Operation while riding a rodeo bull, except the game's buzzer signaling a bad move would be replaced by the sound of a collision with a thirty-five-hundred-ton Russian ship. The zero visibility outside the windscreen only added to the confusion. I thought I knew which direction the ship was before we splashed the rover, but what I thought I knew was meaningless in the barbaric torrent of the storm.

The compass bounced in its binnacle, proving itself worthless. I was losing my patience and temper simultaneously. "Find that ship, Singer!"

"I'm working on it, but it's a solid return. There's just too much—"

Instantly, as if God himself reached down and cradled my boat in His mighty hand, the bow leveled, the waves pouring over the rails subsided, and we were left, inexplicably, in dead-calm water. Everyone froze, eyes darting in near panic in every direction. Rain continued to pour, but we weren't rolling or pitching.

Words fell from my mouth without intent. "Does anybody know what's happening?"

Singer raised his head. "I do."

"Now would be a very good time to let me in on the secret."

"There's nothing wrong with the radar. The reason it's a solid wall is because she's right on top of us. We're in her lee. She's blocking the wind and waves."

I pulled the throttles into reverse, hoping to avoid a collision, but I didn't know if the ship was in front of us or behind us.

"Hunter, any luck?"

"Hold us, Chase."

I swallowed hard. "I'm trying, but I've got no reference."

"Just hold us," he repeated with the intensity of a surgeon.

I turned to Mongo, and he nodded his boulder-sized head in reassurance. I continued my blind manipulation of the controls as everyone else focused intently on Hunter as he flew the rover beneath the punishing sea. Seconds turned to hours in the silence of the pilothouse, each of us completely oblivious to the roar of the cascading rain.

After an eternity of impatience, Hunter said, "How much money have you got, Chase?"

"On me?"

"No. The Navy will wait until we get back ashore."

"What are you talking about?" I demanded.

"You're gonna have to write a check. It's time to cut the rover free and let her sink. I've got what we need."

A cheer went up from the pilothouse as Hunter straightened and let out a breath he'd been holding for a lifetime. Singer and

Mongo headed for the deck to cut the tether, and I knocked fists with Stone W. Hunter, ROV operator extraordinaire.

Our celebration was short-lived. Mongo tumbled back through the door. "The snipper was destroyed with the crane. We've got no way to cut the cable."

Hunter spun to the controls. "I'll fly it back to us. Maybe we can pull it on board." He went back to work on our only remaining shot.

Before I could get to the pilothouse door, our one remaining hope turned into a hangman's noose.

Hunter said, "Uh, Chase, I think I just fu—"

The wind and waves made their thundering return. The bow of the Mark V plummeted like an anchor, and our stern was ripped to starboard in a violence so brutal it sent everyone on the boat crashing to the deck. It wasn't just the wind and waves. Hunter had fouled the ROV tether on the rudder of the *Viktor Leonov*, and we'd instantly become a fifty-ton skier behind a Russian spy ship, in the ride of our lives, in the worst storm any of us had ever seen.

In Herman Melville's time, teams of whalers would spear giant sperm whales from tiny whaleboats and let the whales drag them all over the Pacific until the enormous creature was too exhausted to continue. That became known as a Nantucket sleighride. The difference in Captain Ahab's white whale and mine was about thirty-five hundred tons, and I had no chance of harpooning this one.

A wall of water rose over our stern like a tsunami threatening to swamp us as we were dragged relentlessly backward through the unimaginable storm. Adding power was useless. Even crippled, the *Leonov* could pull us to China and never know we were back there. Our dire situation had just become un-survivable.

We were about to be four men without a boat or paddle, and up one well-known creek. We were going into the water, and there was nothing we could do to stop it. The Mark V couldn't endure the torture much longer. It was never built for that amount of stress or that much water inside the hull. I took inventory, locating every member of the team so we could abandon ship together. The chances of finding each other once overboard were less than zero. Chances of survival in the water, even together, were barely better than that.

Hunter was two feet to my left. Mongo was six feet away near the pilothouse door. Singer was . . .

"Where's Singer?" I yelled.

Mongo turned and vanished into the wall of black water pouring over the transom and into the boat. Hunter dived for his feet but couldn't get to him in time. Terrified I'd seen my team for the last time, I looked up, like Jesus in the Garden of Gethsemane, begging for relief from the fate in front of me.

To my disbelief, the sky outside the starboard window turned to orange belching flames, and thundering reports rattled every inch of the flooding patrol boat. The staccato bursts of the Ma Duece, fifty-caliber machine gun cut through howling wind and driving water as its supersonic, full-metal-jacketed projectiles painted invisible laces across the black water between us and the *Leonov*. Three seconds into Singer's barrage of machine-gun fire, he hit his mark by some miracle combination of sheer determination and God's grace. One of the massive fifty-cal rounds sliced its way through the tether, severing our noose and leaving us bobbing like cork twenty miles east of Saint Marys, Georgia, having survived to fight our great white whale another day.

The storm wasn't over, but plowing into the waves as we made our way homeward was far better than what we'd endured in the previous hours. No one spoke. Instead, we stood, each of us reliving the battle and wondering if we'd ever face anything like that again.

The Nantucket sleighride had nearly demolished the Mark V. The satellite comms were down, the radar was down, and the primary GPS was black. I navigated westward with a handheld compass, hoping the storm would subside and I'd sight a piece of land I recognized.

We battled our way onward for an hour until finally the wind and waves lessened, and the rain subsided to a drizzle. Outside the windscreen, the looming tower of a lighthouse stood above the backdrop of green island treetops and the clearing western sky.

"Isn't that the St. Simons light?" Hunter asked.

I threaded my arm around Hunter's left shoulder, Singer draped his hand across the right shoulder, and Mongo laid his meat-hook paws on top of all of us and said, "Not bad, huh?"

I looked up. "Nope. Not bad at all. It was a lot better than I expected. Can I get you anything? Perhaps a martini shaken, not stirred?"

There's nothing like laughter to bleed off stress, and we did a lot of bleeding in the thirty minutes it took us to motor down the coast into Saint Marys Entrance and up the North River.

Penny, Clark, and Maebelle sprinted down the steps and across the yard as I shut down the engines of the battered Mark V, and we tied the lines.

Penny leapt into my arms. "Chase! We thought you were dead."

I hugged my wife, thankful to be back in her arms. "Nope. You're not getting rid of me that easily. We just ran into a little traffic and had a slight weather delay. Everybody's fine."

Through his crooked half-smile, Clark said, "Let's debrief. I'm getting hungry."

We followed our new leader up the steps and through the screen door of Maebelle's kitchen. Of course the real door was standing wide open.

Anya stood at the top of the steps. I could see she wanted to smile, but she simply said, "Welcome home, big strong men."

Mongo stopped two steps below her and looked into her eyes. "You wanted to go, didn't you?"

"Always," she said, staring back at him.

He backpedaled to the bottom of the steps, picked a tiny purple flower, and climbed back to the gallery. He gently brushed Anya's hair aside and slid the stem of the flower behind her left ear. "I think there's a lot more to you than just a pretty face, Ms. Anya."

The smile she'd been suppressing came. "And maybe to you, there is more than just giant man, Mr. Malloy."

Chapter 27
Spy Dust

The scene on the steps that played out between Mongo and Anya was only slightly less interesting than the footage that the rover captured, sent miles into space, bounced off a few satellites, and finally landed on Skipper's laptop in Silver Spring, Maryland.

The hydrophone-laying apparatus we'd expected to see beneath the *Leonov* was there. The Russians were, undoubtedly, laying a network of devices on the ocean floor that would make it possible for them to eventually hear and record the sound of every nuclear submarine in the Atlantic fleet.

After watching the video twice, I leaned back in my chair, oddly relieved. "I guess that answers the question about them being here looking for me, huh?"

"Not so fast," came Skipper's voice through the speakerphone. "Just because they're laying hydrophones doesn't mean that's all they're doing."

"They're certainly not laying mines," I said.

"How do you know?" she asked.

I motioned toward the closed door of the library. "Go get your girlfriend, Mongo. Maybe she can shed a little light on this for us."

"She ain't my girlfriend. She's just a long way from home and probably feels like she doesn't fit in. I know a little about that feeling."

"Yeah, okay, Mr. Junior Psychologist. Just go get her."

He returned with Anya in tow and an idea. "I know you're the chief headknocker, Clark, but maybe we should let your dad take a look."

"I'm way ahead of you, Mongo. Skipper's already sent it to him and the intel guys at the Navy yard."

Mongo grunted. "I guess that's why you're the new boss."

Anya watched the video and asked to see it again. Clark replayed it, and we all watched in silent anticipation of what the only pair of Russian eyes in the room would see.

Anya spoke without looking away from the screen. "Is not microphones, I think. I mean, not only microphones, but is more complicated. How deep is ocean here?"

Clark looked at the speakerphone. "Skipper? How deep is it out there?"

"Give me a minute," she said. "I won't be able to pinpoint where you guys were when you launched the rover, but I can get close."

Clark eyed Anya. "What are you thinking, comrade?"

"I think your Navy does not care what *Leonov* is doing because it has nothing to do with submarine."

Skipper said, "It's shallower than a hundred feet until you break forty miles offshore, and then it gradually deepens to the shelf about eighty miles off, where it falls to well over a thousand feet."

Anya walked to the southern wall of the library, where a nautical chart of the waters off Saint Marys hung in a glass-covered frame. We watched her in wide-eyed wonder, anxiously awaiting something brilliant from her mouth, but she only stood, staring at the chart and measuring with her index and pinky finger against the scale.

Skipper's voice cut through the silence. "Uh, hello? What's going on?"

Clark held up a finger. "Hang on, Skipper."

Anya turned back to face the phone. "You have satellite track of *Leonov* for several weeks, no?"

"Yeah," Skipper said. "I've got a pretty good track on them since they came north of Cuba. Why?"

"Is very important. Plot track of ship against shelf where ocean becomes deep. How long this will take for you?"

The sound of Skipper's fingers dancing across the keyboard through the speakerphone would've made it easy to believe she was sitting at the desk in front of us.

She stopped typing. "It's done. I have good tracks from the time the *Leonov* moved north of Cuba. She ran along the shelf for two weeks at six to eight knots, the same speed she was making when we believed she was laying hydrophones closer in. What does that mean, Anya?"

The speakerphone clicked, and Clark pressed a button, adding a new caller to the conference. "Hey, Dad. We were just watching the video feed, and Anya thinks she's found a pattern."

"Oh, I'll bet she has," Dominic said. "The Russians are dusting."

Clark frowned. "What's that mean?"

Dominic chuckled. "I think I'll just sit back and listen to your resident KGB agent tell you all about it."

Anya didn't hesitate. "I was never KGB. Only SVR."

"Same horse, different saddle," Dominic said.

Anya stepped aside, giving us a clear view of the framed chart. "During Cold War, Second Chief Directorate, counterintelligence, and Seventh Directorate Surveillance used powder called NPPD, or METKA. It was visible only under cer-tain spectrum of light. With powder or dust, like Dominic says, KGB could track workers from U.S. Embassy and know who touched dusted documents."

Clark looked at the phone. "Is that what you're talking about, Dad?"

"It sounds to me like your new comrade knows her Cold War history."

I furrowed my brow. "I'm not following. What does any of this have to do with the Russian ship laying hydrophones?"

Dominic said, "Let's hear it from the Eastern European contingent."

Anya chewed at her bottom lip for a moment. "I do not understand science of this, but I think Dominic is right about principle. When you change electronic signature of ship . . . Uh, I do not know word for this."

"Degaussing," I said.

She continued. "When you do this, ship has new electronic signature, like fingerprint for every ship, yes?"

"Yes, that's how I understand it," I said, "but we're still a long way from spy dust."

Anya continued. "Is same. When embassy worker touches package or document with NPPD, he will leave small amount on everything he touches for many hours after. With network of transmitters on floor of ocean in shallow water, every ship or boat or submarine is put with electronic dust, and then is again done before ocean is deep. In this way, FSB . . . this is Russian Foreign Intelligence Service . . ."

"Yes, we know," came the group response.

"In this way, FSB can know which ships stay in shallow and which ones go in deep and watch for dust where ships go."

"I don't know," I said. "It seems like a lot of work just to track a ship that satellites can track with the stroke of a few keys on a computer somewhere."

Anya stared directly at me. "Where is ship exactly during storm, and what about submarine satellite cannot see?"

"Point taken," I said. "But why here?"

"I have also thought of this. Answer is because is convenient."

"Convenient?"

"Yes, is good place to test idea because of ability to degaussing at submarine base and also lucky if they catch you, Chase."

"So, you're saying they're using my backyard as a testbed for this new electronic spy-dusting gizmo and coincidentally hoping to catch me in their trap?"

"Yes, this is how Russian thinking works. Something big with other small things inside. Like Russian nesting dolls."

Clark scanned the room. "Any other ideas?"

No one spoke, so Dominic said, "Finish your debrief, and call me back. We have to send this one up the chain. The Navy needs to know, and it'll be a great opportunity for you to learn how poorly this kind of BS flows upstream."

"Do you have anything else, Skipper?"

"Yeah, I do. I'm glad you guys are safe. I was worried about you out there, and if you ever pull that crap on me again without letting me know you're okay, I'll kill you slowly . . . with a spoon. I love you guys. Bye."

Clark ignored Skipper's rant. "How badly is the Mark V damaged?"

"It's bad," I said. "Everything's gone from the arch, and she took on a lot of water. Not much is working except the engines."

"What kind of deal did you cut to get it?"

"I'm not sure," I admitted. "But I think it's ours now."

"Okay," he said. "If it's becoming an asset, I'll see if I can find the money to repair it, but no promises. Is anybody hurt?"

The four of us who were on the mission shook our heads.

"Have you got anything else for me?" Clark asked.

I spoke up. "Yeah. What if the Navy blows it off? What do we do then?"

"That's a good question, College Boy. We'll burn that bridge when we come to it, but I can't imagine the Navy looking the other way over something this big."

"Thousand-dollar toilet seats and two-hundred-dollar hammers," I reminded him.

He held up his hands. "We'll see. Anything else?"

No one spoke, so Clark spun in his chair to face Anya. "Thank you for the insight. I'm sure you know that no one fully trusts you yet, but I, for one, got a step closer today. Are you holding anything back?"

She put on her new stern American look. "I have picked side, and this is team I choose. I have many things in my mind, but it would take rest of life to tell you everything I know. When I think of other things about *Leonov*, I will come first to you."

"No," he said, "that's not how the chain of command works. You take it to Chase. He's your team leader. If he thinks I should know, he'll bring it to me."

"Is same in SVR," she said.

Clark smiled. "No, not exactly. The difference is this. If you think I need to know, and you don't think Chase is going to tell me, it's your responsibility to walk around, under, or over him to make sure I get the information. If you try that in the Motherland, you'll get shot in the face . . . won't you?"

"Is possible," she admitted.

"Okay, if there's nothing else, get out of here. I've got some calls to make. I'll brief you afterwards."

We left the library and discovered Penny and Maebelle had set the gallery for dinner. We ate cheeseburgers from paper plates and drank lemonade from Solo cups.

Maebelle passed out tiny American flags on wooden sticks. "We missed the Fourth of July, so we're making up for it tonight.

Apparently, I'm not allowed to know exactly what you guys did today, but from what I've overheard, it sounds like you did some real Boston Tea Party stuff out there. I'm really glad you're safe, and I'm so proud of all of you."

She wiped a tear from her eye as Clark scooped her up into his arms. "Now that's a Yankee Doodle Dandy girl if I've ever seen one."

We raised our cups and enjoyed being alive and together.

As the festivities drew to a close, I caught Anya sitting alone on the railing at the corner of the gallery, twirling the tiny American flag between her fingers. I wanted to walk over and thank her for coming to work with the good guys, for real this time, but my loyalties lay elsewhere, so I went to Penny's side and stuck my hands in the sink, helping her wash the American dishes.

Through the window, I was pleased to see Mongo's gargantuan form cast a long, broad shadow across the tall, blonde, former Russian with the tiny plastic flag clenched to her chest.

Just when I thought the night was going to end on a good note, Clark laid his hand on my shoulder. "We need to talk. The Navy ain't buyin' it."

Chapter 28
Blackbeard's Booty

Clark closed and locked the library door. "I've got a lot to learn."

"We all do," I said. "What's going on?"

He settled into the chair behind the desk, and I took a wing-back by the oversized globe near the window. The imperfection of the two-hundred-year-old glass in the massive window made the lights dance and swerve like a funhouse mirror. The scene made me think of how most people probably perceive reality. They sit in their comfortable, warm wingbacks, and view the world from behind a glass that distorts the reality outside, making it appear foreign and distant; a place where problems belong to others, and evil lives only in Stephen King novels and on Hollywood movie screens. Reality beyond the waves of the distorting glass demands sacrifices of men and women who know evil, those who've stood in its face and driven spikes into its bulging chest. The look on Clark's face said we were on the verge of penetrating that glass one more time.

He turned the computer screen to face me, and I read the intel brief he and Dominic had sent up the chain. Unlike what Hollywood wants us to believe, intelligence operatives do little more than watch, record, and report. Spies aren't tuxedo-wearing, tango-dancing superheroes. They are quiet, demure professionals who live their lives almost entirely invisible. Shadows are their domains—dark places where light, both actual and moral, rarely penetrate. They go about their work in silence, recording, photographing, and listening, only to pass what they learn to others who bear the responsibility of compiling, interpreting, and either passing the information further up the chain or branding it as unimportant and relegating it to a file, never to be seen again.

We were not spies. We were operators. Gathering information was only part of what we did. The leap across the great chasm between gathering information and acting on the information is what separated us from our brothers in the shadows with notepads and long camera lenses.

Clark's intel brief was concise and demonstrated a clear and present danger in my eyes, but mine weren't the eyes of political decision making. Mine were the eyes that had seen what the Russian operatives were capable of doing, and more importantly, what they were willing to do.

"That's a great brief," I said. "What are they going to do to stop them?"

He slowly shook his head. "They don't believe it's a credible threat to either military or shipping interests. There's nothing illegal about studying sound underwater. There's no authorized military action to prevent an intelligence-gathering ship to operate in international waters."

I raised my eyebrows. "So, they're not going to do anything?"

He continued shaking his head. "We asked that the intel be included in the PDB, but based on the reaction, I don't think that's going to happen."

"Is there any way for us to know if it gets into the Presidential Daily Briefing?"

"Short of calling him up and asking him, no."

Suddenly, the phone in my pocket weighed more than my boots and burned into my flesh through the material of my cargo pants. "Are you saying I should call him?"

Clark leaned forward. "Definitely not. In spite of what I told Anya, if we start going around the chain, we lose credibility and anonymity. I've got another idea."

I crossed my legs and tried to swallow the anger I was suddenly feeling over being dismissed by the chain. "Let's hear it."

He mirrored my posture—a trick I'd taught him. People tend to subconsciously trust and agree with people like themselves. By mirroring the posture of another, the psyche of the subject tends to instantly accept the other as being on the same team and of like mind and constitution. Just for fun, I adjusted my position in the chair, replacing both feet on the floor. Clark didn't follow.

He said, "If we can't take Muhammad to the mountain, maybe we can force Muhammad onto another mountain that can't be ignored."

"What?"

Clark chuckled. "Okay, that didn't work at all. I'm not very good at those, but try to stay with me, okay?"

"Okay," I said. "But no more Muhammad."

"You got it. But there is a mountain, sort of. Look." He stood and pointed toward the chart Anya had used earlier. "Have you ever heard of Blackwater Shoals?"

"Sure. That's where Blackbeard ran the *Marguerite de las Estrellas* aground in seventeen sixteen and scored the biggest booty of his life."

Clark blinked. "I don't know anything about that, but it *is* a mountain, and it is in U.S. waters. The shoals are forty miles long and four or five feet deep in places. If we can put the *Leonov* on that shoal, the Navy will have no choice other than investigating. When a crippled Russian warship piles up nine miles off the coast, it's going to make the six o'clock news."

"How do you plan to convince Comrade Commander Krusevich to put his ship aground on Blackwater Shoals?"

"I don't," Clark said. "I plan to do it for him."

"This I've got to hear."

Clark turned back to his computer and brought up the National Oceanic and Atmospheric Administration as well as the National Weather Service current and wind prediction models for the East Coast. "I'm not as good at this as Skipper is, but I think Blackwater Shoals is right here somewhere." He made circling motions on the screen with his fingertip.

I glanced back and forth between the chart on the wall and the screen. "Okay, I'll buy that."

"Good. Now look at the wind and current predictions for the next several days." He clicked through several screens showing a low-pressure system building over the Gulf of Mexico and turning the wind from the southeast over the Atlantic coasts of Florida and Georgia.

"If that low-pressure system keeps building, the wind and Gulf Stream would push a drifting ship north-northwest at maybe three knots. If that disabled, drifting ship became disabled"—he motioned toward the map—"right here, at exactly the right time, she'd end up here less than twenty-four hours later, right slapdab in the middle of Muhammad's mountain, aka Blackwater Shoals."

"I love your enthusiasm," I said. "And it would be a great plan if the ship was disabled, but it's not."

The crooked grin arrived—the one that always signaled a fair maiden was about to surrender to Clark's charms, or a bad guy was about to screw up. "That's where you come in, College Boy."

"You want me to disable a Russian spy ship in international waters so she can drift aground off the East Coast?"

"Exactly!"

"Attacking a ship on the high seas is called piracy," I said. "I think they still hang people for that."

"They didn't hang Blackbeard, did they?"

I threw up my hands. "No, they didn't hang Blackbeard. They shot him five times with muskets, slashed him at least two dozen times with swords, and then cut off his head."

"There you have it," Clark said. "They didn't hang him."

"You're insane. This new promotion has drained you of any sense you may have ever had."

"Maybe, but it does sound like fun, doesn't it?"

"Yeah, okay, it does, but you're still insane, and how would we pull it off?"

"We get them to attack *us*," he said as calmly as if he were ordering coffee.

I laughed. "That shouldn't be much of a challenge. I'm good at that."

"I'm serious. If we can get them to attack us, we can defend ourselves. Then it's not piracy. It's tit for tat."

"This is getting weirder by the minute. Is there a plan in there somewhere?"

Clark leaned forward, propped his elbows on his knees, and planted his chin on top of his fists. "I can't believe I'm about to say this, but we need a SEAL."

"A SEAL?"

"Yeah. We're all really good at what we do, but nobody in the world is better at assaulting a ship than the SEALs, and we don't have one."

I leaned back in my chair, trying to imagine the scenario playing out in Clark's mind. "How would the SEALs do it?"

He squinted. "They'd disable the rudder. With one screw already down, that ship couldn't maneuver with only the remaining screw and no rudder. She'd be a drifting rubber duck in a big saltwater bathtub."

I leapt to my feet. "We may not have a SEAL, but I know where we can get a sea lion."

I shouted down the hall. "Is Hunter still here?"

"Yeah, I'm in the kitchen."

"Get in here. We need you."

Twenty minutes later, Hunter was caught up.

"What we need from you," I said to him, "is that sea lion they use at the base to clamp buoys on divers."

When I first met Stone Hunter, he'd introduced me to a pair of astonishing and practically unbelievable animals: a dolphin named Chief Petty Officer Prowler, and a sea lion named Petty Officer Second Class Stinky. Prowler's job was to identify potential underwater threats to the submarine base, such as divers in the water. He'd then come get Stinky, who would carry a device in his flippers to clamp on the legs of the divers and float a buoy. That would allow the Navy Security Forces to haul the divers to the surface and interrogate them.

Hunter listened intently as Clark and I laid out the plan.

When we finished, Hunter reacted much as I had. "So, you want me to steal a sea lion from the Navy so we can take him off-shore into international waters and assault a warship of a foreign government with the intention of putting that ship aground in U.S. waters? Is that what you're telling me?"

"Borrow and defend," I said.

Hunter lowered his chin and glared at me.

"We want you to *borrow* the sea lion, and we're going to *defend* ourselves. But yes, you got the rest correct."

I didn't need another reason to reinforce my faith in Stone W. Hunter, but he gave me one anyway when he shrugged and said, "Okay, I'm in."

* * *

Sleep didn't come for me that night, and I assume Clark and Hunter spent most of the night kicking our crazy idea around until the sun pulled them out of bed.

We briefed the rest of the team on the outrageous plan after breakfast. Skipper was designated as the official monitor of weather, wind, and ocean currents while the rest of us set about repairing the Mark V.

Earl's metalworking skills made short work of the structural damage, and Dominic dispatched the techs to reinstall everything electronic. Remarkably, Clark found the money for the repairs without me having to foot the bill . . . again. The loss of the ROV was another story. I still had to write that check.

Cotton completed the required annual inspection of my Mustang, and as part of his compensation, I sat in the back seat while he flew the warbird all over coastal Georgia. I couldn't resist encouraging him to take us offshore, but I never caught a glimpse of my nemesis on the vast Atlantic Ocean.

Back on the ground, Cotton stood in the shadow of *Katerina's Heart*, looking up at the relic of a bygone era of both aviation and aerial warfare. "I've flown a bunch of airplanes in my life, Chase, but I ain't never flown nothin' like that. I can't tell you how much it means to me that you'd let me fly her. There ain't a man nowhere on this Earth, on land nor sea, who could look at nothin' else when that girl comes flyin' by."

Chapter 29
Failure Is Not an Option

I called Clark the second I climbed into the microbus at the hangar. "Get the team together. I'll be home in five minutes, and I know how to pull it off."

There was nothing he could say that would change anything over the next four minutes, so I hung up without waiting for him to respond. In defiance of my typical behavior, I ran up the front steps instead of entering the house across the back gallery. I noticed a package leaning against the threshold and dismissively scooped it up on my way through the door. The team was filing into the library when I came bounding in.

"I've got it," I declared as I tossed the package onto the desk.

Clark picked it up. "What is it?"

I waved my hand at the package. "Not that. I know how we"—I motioned toward the team—"or rather, *you* can approach the Russian ship without anyone on board giving you a second look."

The package landed on the desk with a light woosh as Clark released it from his grip. "Let's hear what your highly educated brain has come up with."

"It wasn't my brain," I said. "It was Cotton's. He finished up the annual inspection on the Mustang today, so I took him flying as a way to say thanks. He did most of the flying. I just kept her in one piece during landing and takeoff, but when we got back, he made an offhand statement that couldn't be truer."

Everyone was leaning in and hanging on my every word.

"He said nobody on land or sea can look away when the Mustang flies by. Of course, he didn't put it exactly like that, but he's right. All we've got to do is get them looking the other way long enough for you to get that sea lion close enough to the boat to plant the charge."

Clark slapped the desk with enough energy to send the team leaping out of their seats. "Man, I love my job! We're about to distract the crew of a Russian spy ship with a World War Two fighter plane, long enough to plant an explosive charge on their rudder with a U.S. Navy-trained sea lion, so we can send them aground where an eighteenth-century pirate got some booty."

I laughed. "I'm starting to think you may not fully understand the term, 'got some booty,' but other than that, you nailed it."

"There's just one decision remaining," Clark said. "We need to determine the approach angle. All of you have seen the ship from every angle. Where's her blind spot?"

Everyone, except Anya, began talking at once. She silently removed her boot, slipped the insole from inside, and tossed it onto the desk.

Clark leaned back, raising his hands in surrender. "Okay, that's nasty."

Anya pointed toward the sketch on the bottom of the insole. "Is diagram of *Viktor Leonov* sight and angle-of-fire limits."

Clark marched with drill-team precision to a position just in front of Anya and stood as erect as a statue. The former Russian spy looked up at him with utter confusion consuming her face. He reached down, took her face in his hands, and with animated flourish, kissed her squarely on the forehead.

Back in his seat, he studied Anya's boot-sole sketch and passed it around the team. Most were slightly hesitant to touch it, but not Mongo. I got the feeling he didn't want to give it back.

After a little discussion and a few crude foot-odor cracks, Clark said, "So, do we all agree the approach angle is ten to fifteen degrees to starboard of the stern?"

Everyone nodded.

I said, "It looks like I'll conduct the airshow off the port bow. Now put that thing back in your boot before it makes one of us throw up or Mongo marries it." I turned to Clark. "Do we need to call Dominic?"

He stared at the ceiling for a few seconds. "No, this one's on me." We shared a knowing nod, and he turned to Hunter. "How's it going in the Wild Kingdom?"

"It's more like Sea World, but it's all set up. There's been a change, though. Stinky has a cold, so I'll be borrowing a sea lion named Flipper. She's actually been trained to do exactly what we need. She went through the training in San Diego."

"Sea lions get colds?" Clark asked.

Hunter nodded. "Sure. They're mammals, like us, which means they have lungs and sinuses. If you ask me, Stinky's milking it just a little too long. I think he likes the attention. That's okay, though. Flipper is probably a better choice anyway."

I said, "What kind of sick person names a sea lion Flipper?"

He rolled his eyes. "What kind of sick minds come up with a plan like this one?"

"You make a good point." I noticed Anya making great effort to hide her laughter. "What's so funny?"

"I am sorry for laughing, but I was thinking what officers inside Kremlin would think if they knew this is how country who never loses war makes planning."

I said, "We're not exactly the Joint Chiefs of Staff, and this definitely isn't the Pentagon. I don't think this is how they do it up there, but it works for us. Besides, you're the one drawing on your insole."

"I promised to give heart and *sole* to America when I defected, so this is what I am doing."

A grumble of disapproval rolled through the library.

"That is funny American language joke, and all of you know it is. You should try to make Russian language joke if you think is so easy."

"At least you're putting your best foot forward," Singer said, laughing at his own joke far louder than anyone else.

I pinched my nose. "Stinky may have a cold, but it smells to me like he may have joined us anyway."

Clark said, "Okay, okay, that's enough. I'm going to put my *foot* down and get this under control."

Everyone had a good laugh at Anya's expense, and I believe it may have helped her feel a little more like a real member of the team.

Clark finally got control of the room. "It's time to check in with Skipper. Let's keep our fingers crossed that the ship is where we need her to be and that the weather is in our favor."

Skipper answered. "I was just about to call you. Please tell me you're ready to go."

Clark looked up, and everyone nodded. "Yeah, we're ready."

"Good, because our window is opening. The *Leonov* has been steaming north for almost eighteen hours, and if she holds to her pattern, she'll be turning south anytime now. That'll put her right where you need her to be tomorrow afternoon around fourteen hundred."

"How about the weather?" I said.

"It's not the best, but it'll have to do. The ship is slowly moving out to sea with every track, so if we wait any longer, she'll be too far offshore for the wind and current to get her into U.S. waters. In my opinion, it's now or never."

Clark folded his arms and sat on the edge of the desk. "Can anyone think of a reason we shouldn't go?"

I said, "I can come up with hundreds of reasons we shouldn't do it, but I say we go anyway."

A round of, "Me too," and "Let's do it," followed.

"Then, the decision's made," Clark said. "Weather and position updates at zero eight hundred tomorrow, feet wet at noon, and wheels up at thirteen hundred."

"Before you go, there's one more thing," Skipper said. "There's a Russian support ship steaming southwest of the Azores. We don't know if it's planning to rendezvous with the *Leonov*, but it's likely. It's probably the parts and divers they need to repair their port screw at sea, but there's no way to know for sure."

"How long will it take to get here?" Clark asked.

"They're in a hurry, so no more than three days."

Clark chewed on the inside of his jaw. "That means forty-eight hours from tomorrow afternoon. If we screw this up, we're not going to have time to regroup and try again. Failure isn't an option this time."

I lowered my chin and raised my eyebrows. "Is it ever?"

* * *

Sleep came, the sun rose, and Skipper declared the window open. "It's as good as it's going to get. She's heading south, and the surface wind is out of the southeast at twelve to fifteen knots."

Clark slapped the table with his palm. "It's go time. Hunter, if it weren't for the responsibility of handling the sea lion, you'd be the boat commander, but you're the only one who knows how to manage the animal. Who do you want at the helm?"

Hunter looked at his boat crew. "We need Singer on the gun just in case it gets hot. I need Mongo on the dive gear in case we have to splash."

Clark stared at Anya in her black cargo pants, tactical shirt tucked in tightly, and boots laced and tied like a corset. The only things that weren't black were her blonde ponytail, pale skin, and the tiny plastic red, white, and blue flag protruding from her pocket. He smiled and let out an almost unnoticeable nod. "Anya has the helm."

When the clock struck noon, Anya eased the throttles forward, leaving Bonaventure dock on her stern and her former Russian comrades twenty-five miles off the spearpoint of her bow.

Clark and I watched the Mark V disappear around the first bend in the North River, both of us hoping to see it round the same bend before the sun abandoned this side of the Earth again.

He slapped me on the back. "Let's get you to the airport, College Boy. You've got a date with a sixty-year-old girl and a couple hundred Russian sailors. It's going to be a big afternoon for you."

"I need to get a couple of things from the armory before we go. I'll meet you in the bus."

I had no idea why Clark insisted on driving me to the airport. Perhaps he felt better about sending his troops into battle face-to-face. I didn't need him to pat me on the butt on my way out of the dugout, but his demonstration of commitment to his team meant a great deal to all of us.

I wrestled my load into the back of the microbus and climbed in behind the wheel.

"What do you got back there?" he asked as we pulled from the driveway.

"Oh, just some party favors in case things get interesting."

He looked over his shoulder, curiosity burning a hole in his head.

When we reached the hangar, Cotton had the big door closed tightly, just as I'd asked him to do.

Clark scowled. "Why doesn't he have the Mustang out and ready to go?"

"It's ready to go," I said. "I just wanted to keep a few things under wraps."

We parked beside the hangar, and I pulled the pair of fifty-caliber ammo cans from the back of the bus, hefting them through the hangar door and onto the waiting cart.

Through his crooked smile, Clark said. "Under wraps, you say. I should've known."

With Cotton's help, we loaded the right wing with every fifty-caliber round it would hold.

"Are you sure it'll still fire?" I asked as Cotton closed the hatch over the old gun.

He wiped his hands on a greasy shop towel. "The solenoid clicks, and the firing pin cycles, but they ain't no way to know for sure 'til you get up there and squeeze off a few. I reckon you oughta open the hangar door first, though."

Clark pulled the latch and pressed the switch, sending the folding door slowly rising, flooding the hangar with the midday sun. The glistening metal of the sixty-year-old, battle-ready fighter sent beams of sunlight bouncing around the ceiling of the hangar like shooting stars. The long, elegant legs of the dark-haired Russian beauty graced the nose of the flying fighting machine, and the graceful script, "Katerina's Heart," made me long to relive the day Dr. Robert Richter told me of his love for Anya's mother and had opened a door for me into another world—a world I never imagined existed.

I followed the airplane into the sun as Cotton towed it onto the ramp.

He disconnected the tow bar and shook my hand. "I kinda feel like a crew chief in the Big War. You bring that pretty girl home to me, and don't get her shot up. You hear me?"

"You would've made a fine crew chief back then, but I sure am glad you waited sixty years to be mine. I'll see you in a few hours."

He whipped out a sharp salute, and I returned it the best I could.

Clark followed me onto the wing, and I climbed into the front seat. The straps of the parachute and seat harness were a spiderweb of nylon and buckles. When I finally had everything situated, buckled, and pulled snug, Clark slapped me on the shoulder. "You good?"

I looked over my shoulder and reached for his hand. "I'm good. I'll see you in a few hours. We'll make you proud."

"I know you will." He leaned in across the top of the cockpit, and for a minute, I thought he was going to kiss me on the head, but he stepped into the back seat and settled in like the old warrior he was.

He put on his headset and pulled the microphone to his lips. "My dad said the rest of my missions would be fought sitting down. I guess he was right."

Chapter 30
Fire in the Hole!

We blasted off with the sun almost directly overhead. The landing gear came up, and I stopped our climb at thirty-five hundred feet.

The new satellite communications systems the techs installed in our headsets were designed to give us comms with both Skipper and the boat crew, but so far, they hadn't proven themselves in a mission environment.

"Skipper, Chase, commo check."

Her voice appeared in my ears as if she were in the back seat. "You're loud and clear, Chase. How me?"

"I have you the same, Skipper. Have you established comms with the boat crew yet?"

"Affirmative. They're loud and clear as well, but you should give them a check from your end."

"Boat crew, boat crew, Chase . . . commo check."

Singer replied, "You're loud and clear, Chase."

"You're the same, Singer. Say position."

"We're standing off five miles, but we have radar contact and visual with the objective."

I keyed the mic. "Roger. We're airborne and should be on scene in less than ten."

"Did you say we?"

"He did," Clark said. "I couldn't let you guys have all the fun and leave me behind. Besides, Chase might need some help finding his way home."

Skipper fed us satellite positions for the *Leonov* as well as the Mark V, but a blind balloon pilot could've found them that day. The visibility was limited only by the curvature of the Earth, without a cloud in the sky. It was a perfect day for an airshow.

"Hey, College Boy. You might want to consider exercising that gun a little. God only knows the last time it was fired, and it'd be nice to know it'll go *bang* if we need it."

I raised the nose a few degrees above the horizon and added enough power to climb two thousand feet, then conducted a series of clearing turns to make sure there wasn't anyone around to report shots fired from a WWII fighter over the Atlantic. Satisfied that we were sufficiently alone, I pulled the throttle back and let our airspeed bleed off. At one hundred miles per hour, I pushed the nose over, extended the flaps and landing gear to keep our speed under control, and started a dive for the water. Risking a few fifty-caliber rounds skipping across the ocean like flat rocks on a pond didn't interest me. If the gun fired, I wanted to make sure my rounds hit nothing but water and the sandy bottom.

I peered through the gunsight, imagining what it must've been like for those young, inexperienced fighter pilots over the English Channel in 1944.

"Here comes the lead," I said as I wrapped my index finger around the trigger and sank it into the stick.

I expected to hear and feel the report of the machine gun, but . . . nothing. I released and pulled the trigger several more times with the same result. No holes appeared in the ocean below, and no belching fire came from the right wing.

Raising the nose, I added power and retracted the gear and flaps. "It looks like we loaded five hundred pounds of lead in the right wing for nothing."

"In that case, it's a good thing you brought me with you."

"What are you going to do, hang out the window and throw rocks at the Russians?"

He chuckled. "As much fun as that sounds, I think I've got a better idea."

"Let's hear it."

In the tone he always used when I was screwing up, he said, "Take a look at that switch on the lower left side of the panel—the one that's labeled 'weapons master.' Give that a flip and try again."

The subsequent dive toward the ocean held one distinct difference from the first—a three-second burst of fifty-cal machine gun fire roared from the right, leaving a patchwork of white foamy impact circles on the surface below.

Skipper's voice appeared in my headset. "If you're through playing with your guns, it's time to go to work. The boat crew is four and a half miles in trail of the objective and matching her speed, southbound."

The position data she was feeding to our onboard navigation system agreed and showed us nine miles north of the boat crew.

"Let's see if we can have some fun with these guys." I pushed the nose over and eased the throttle forward. As we accelerated toward the water, I pounded my fist against the canopy and yelled, "I feel the need! The need for—"

"Don't," Clark said. "That's too corny, even for you."

Fifty feet off the water, at just over three hundred miles per hour, *Katerina's Heart* roared through the sky like a dragon aching to spray her fiery breath on some unsuspecting foe. Hopefully the presence of the dragon would be enough and the fiery breath wouldn't be necessary.

I overflew the Mark V in a blur and made my first run down the port side of the *Viktor Leonov* like a rocket.

"Grit your teeth, Pretty Boy. We're going up."

I yanked the stick into my lap and shoved the throttle full forward. The nose shot upward like a rearing stallion—a Mustang stallion—and the ocean disappeared. I grunted and tightened every muscle in my body as the g-forces tried to shove me through my seat.

As our speed bled off and our altitude grew, I said, "You okay back there, old man?"

The grunt that came through my headset told me he was still conscious, but not very happy with me.

At the top of our arc, I performed a wingover and accelerated into a dive back toward the ship about a mile ahead of their bow. Leveling off, again at fifty feet above the water, I pointed my propeller and gunsight straight down the centerline of the Russian ship. As my speed increased through three hundred, I rolled right and broke to the east, showing the Russians my belly and drawing every eye away from their stern.

"How you doing back there, papaw? Don't you puke in my airplane."

There was another grunt, followed by, "How 'bout a little warning before you break like that again?"

I keyed the mic. "Okay, boat crew, I think I've got their attention. Do your thing."

"We're closing now, Chase. Flipper will be in the water in thirty seconds."

I didn't have time to check the position data. My eyes were focused outside the airplane, and my mind was planning my next pass. "If you've got any spare change in your pockets, you might want to watch for falling metal objects."

A mile east of the ship, I rolled the Mustang upside down and continue the inbound run. I don't know how far above the bow our heads were when we crossed the ship, but I'm pretty sure the deck crew could see us grinning.

"Flipper's wet," Hunter announced.

Clark replied, "Get out of there and report ready to blow."

I was running out of creative ideas for high-speed passes, so I put the ship off my tail and climbed away to the southeast. A series of barrel rolls and hammerhead stalls ate up ninety seconds, while hopefully still exciting enough to keep the crew's focus on me.

I glanced over my shoulder. "I'm running out of tricks. What should I do next?"

"I have the controls," he said.

"You have the controls."

While I was trying to guess what Clark was about to do with my airplane, Hunter announced, "Flipper's back on board. I'm ready to blow it on your mark."

"Give us a second to get turned around," I said. "I want to see it."

Clark whipped the Mustang around and started a head-on run, obviously intending to pass down their port side.

"Blow it!" I ordered.

Hunter said, "Fire in the hole!"

I stared intently down the side of the ship, expecting to see an explosion of water and spray from near the stern, but it didn't come.

I keyed up. "Did it blow on the starboard? I didn't see it from here." An interminable moment passed, so I yelled into the mic, "Report!"

Hunter said, "Fail! It didn't blow. We're coming about for a second approach. I'm going in the water with the back-up charge."

In spite of being completely fearless and competent beyond compare in the water, Hunter was about to attempt to do the nearly impossible: place an explosive charge on the rudder of a moving ship at sea within feet of a spinning propeller.

Through the gunsight in front of me, I saw the Mark V racing toward the stern of the ship, with Hunter poised on the rail, a diver propulsion vehicle cradled in his arms, and the explosive charges clipped to his vest.

I took a long, deep breath. "Clark, are you going to call this off?"

In his calm, measured tone, he asked, "Can Hunter pull it off?"

"If anybody can, it's him."

"Then the show must go on!"

I watched the throttle crash to its forward stops and felt the nose of the Mustang roll to the left. Clark performed a perfect barrel roll and crossed the ship directly above the navigation bridge. The face of Commander Krusevich loomed large against the glass as we roared by at two hundred fifty miles per hour.

I wondered if he had any idea what was about to happen to his ship . . . and his career.

Singer's voice came over the static. "Hunter's in the water!"

I acknowledged. "Do you have comms with him?"

"Negative comms. He's on his own."

Staring into the water in search of my partner was wasted effort, but that didn't stifle the overwhelming need to search for him. I forced myself to focus on the ship. The eighty-foot-long Mark V stood out like a sore thumb in the ship's wake, but if Clark and I were doing our job, no one on board would look back.

I checked my watch every five seconds expecting hours to have passed.

Clark positioned us southeast of the ship and on an intercepting collision course. He lowered the gear and flaps, slowing the airplane down to barely above stall speed. It felt like we were crawling toward the ship, but it kept growing larger and larger through the windscreen.

"Uh, what's your plan here? This leaves us a little vulnerable if they decide to start shooting."

"Not as vulnerable as Hunter dancing with that propeller down there," Clark said from the back seat.

As we approached the ship, he advanced the throttle and began to rock the wings as if saying, "Hey, guys, how ya doin' down there?"

Suddenly, the blast of spray I'd expected to see from the first charge came . . . and in grand fashion. The bow of the spy ship rolled violently to port, and the ship started an impossibly tight turn.

Clark and I were low, slow, and in no position to change either of those things quickly. I ached to grab the controls, pick up some speed, and send every fifty-caliber round we had through the glass of the navigation bridge, but instead, I dug my heels into the floor pan and scanned the surface north of the ship.

Our gig was up. Our diversion was now useless and dangerous, but the worst result of the explosion was the ship's aggressive, uncontrollable turn to port.

By the time the commander had issued the all-stop command, the ship would be facing north with Hunter still in the water—if he was alive—and the Mark V in plain sight less than five hundred meters away.

Our mission had immediately shifted from diversion to close air support, a mission the Mustang knew well, but neither Clark nor I was qualified to execute.

We accelerated through one hundred fifty miles per hour, and I'd waited as long as I could. "I have the control! Get eyes on Hunter. We've got to get him out of the water."

"You have the controls," Clark said, offering no resistance, and I continued letting the airspeed build.

When the needle passed two hundred, I yanked the stick, sending the Mustang in the tightest turn I'd ever flown, and rolled out, headed directly for the ship. I pulled the nose up and started a spiraling climb.

"I don't think they'll shoot straight up at us."

Clark said, "I hope you're right, but that's a wounded beast down there. Who knows what she'll do next?"

I divided my attention between the altimeter, airspeed indicator, and the water. Finding Hunter and keeping the boat crew alive was priority number one. Everything else could wait.

I had almost forgotten Skipper was listening in until she said, "Uh, you wanna let me in on what's happening down there?"

"No time, Skipper," I said. "If we survive, I promise to tell you all about it."

Clark said, "Anya's making S-turns looking for Hunter. That'll make her harder to hit, but not impossible."

I lowered the nose and leveled off a thousand feet above the ship, hoping the vantage point would give us a hint of where Hunter was, but the ocean looked the same in every direction.

I rolled the right wing over and stared directly onto the deck of the Russian ship. "Hey, Clark. I think they're through playing nice."

Sailors armed with AK-47 rifles poured from the interior of the ship. Counting wasn't possible, but it also wouldn't matter. It would only take one lucky gunman to ruin our day.

"We've gotta get down there!" Clark yelled.

I shoved the nose toward the ocean and maneuvered the Mustang out in front of the crippled ship. "I'm going to strafe bow to stern. Maybe that'll send them ducking for cover."

"Yeah, or maybe it'll get them shooting back at us."

"Either way, they won't be shooting at the team." I rolled the wings level, nose to nose with the ship a half-mile away, and started my gun run.

I mentally ran through Dave Floyd's checklist.

Weapons master . . . armed.

Target . . . identified.

Egress . . . straight out.

Airspeed, altitude, angle . . .

I suddenly heard Dave's voice in my head, reminding me, *Just like Lewis Grizzard said, 'Aim low, boys. They're ridin' Shetland ponies.' Your speed is going to make every shot long, so aim short and walk it in.*

I lowered my nose, aiming a few hundred feet in front of the bow, and wrapped my finger around the trigger. I blinked twice, refocused on the target, and instantly yanked the stick into my lap, sending us skyward away from our foe, and then straightened my finger, determined to do absolutely anything besides pulling that trigger.

Chapter 31
I Forgot to Mention

"What the hell are you doing!" Clark yelled from the back seat.

I leveled off and caught my breath. "Hunter's on the bow."

"What?"

"He's hanging onto the bow at the waterline."

Clark laughed out loud. "That's the safest place in the ocean right now. Nobody on that ship can shoot him there, but we've got to pick him up."

I keyed my mic. "Anya, Hunter is at the bow."

"My bow?" she asked.

"I'm afraid not."

"They will fire at us, Chase. We can fire back, yes?"

Clark said, "You'd better shoot back if you want to stay alive. Put Singer on that fifty, and get in there. You've got to get Hunter out of the water!"

The bow of the Mark V shot into the air as Anya applied full throttle and yanked the agile boat around the stern of the foundering Russian ship. She ran the boat inches from the ship's hull, accelerating as she cut through the water.

Singer stood poised behind the deck-mounted fifty-cal, daring the Russians to escalate the fight. Mongo was folded over the starboard rail with his massive arm forming a perfect hook to retrieve Hunter as they roared past.

"They're going to make it," Clark said, "but we have to cover their escape. Get us back out front, and we'll pin those bastards down as soon as they pluck Hunter out of the water."

I followed his orders, positioning us perfectly to cover the team. I strained to watch the scene unfolding at the waterline of the ship while keeping the Mustang under control and out of the water.

Just as Anya passed amidships, an explosion of rust, dirt, and corrosion blasted from the hawsehole near the bow of the ship, and the massive anchor plummeted toward the water . . . and toward my team.

Anya must've seen it the same instant I did. The boat made a ninety-degree break to port, the centrifugal force sending Mongo's feet up and over the rail.

"Dammit!" Clark growled. "Now we've got two men in the water."

Breaking off my second attempt at a gun run, I rolled the Mustang toward my team and couldn't believe my eyes.

Clark saw it at the same time. "Look at that kung fu-action grip on the big man!"

Mongo's three hundred pounds bounced across the surface of the water beside the Mark V, with one gargantuan paw clamped on the rail. Singer abandoned the fifty and ran to reinforce Mongo's grip. The anchor chain ceased its explosive descent, and Anya spun the boat back toward the bow of the ship looming overhead.

"She's turning back for Hunter. Get in position!" Clark demanded.

I rolled across the ship and accelerated hard to regain the angular advantage, but before I could get the screaming plane aligned for a third attempt, Clark yelled, "Hunter's in the boat!"

I sent up a silent thanks and kept rolling the airplane into position. Anya was accelerating away from the ship as Hunter and Singer pulled at the giant hanging on the rail.

A flash from the bow of the *Leonov* caught my eye, and I jerked my head up to see two dozen 7.62-millimeter Kalashnikov rifles pouring lead into the ocean behind my team.

"Send 'em to Hell, Chase!"

There would be no more abandoned gun runs. I crushed the trigger beneath my index finger and watched a wall of fifty-caliber rounds demolish the bow rail of the *Viktor Leonov*.

With the immediate threat temporarily neutralized, I made an aggressive turn, hoping to see the Mark V disappearing to the west. Instead, I saw it execute a punishing two-hundred-seventy-degree turn to the right and stop dead in the water.

They were still well within range of the Gatling gun on the *Leonov* if the Russian crew escalated the encounter, so I maneuvered to draw the potential fire away from my team. If the Mark V was damaged or disabled, there was nothing I could do except provide covering and suppressing fire until I ran out of bullets . . . which wouldn't be long.

I was looking back at the boat crew when Clark announced, "Gatling gun's alive!"

The massive AK-630, six-barreled, 30-millimeter rotary gun could shred my Mustang in seconds and sink the Mark V almost as quickly. My single fifty-cal with only a handful of rounds left in the wing was no match for that gun. I'd picked a fight I couldn't win, and the exits were closing fast.

I dived for the bow and the waterline. Putting a big chunk of that ship between the barrels of their Gatling gun and my airplane was my only hope for survival. The topside of the ship disappeared overhead as my propeller dug into the air only inches above the water. I prayed the Mustang and I could outmaneuver the gun and make an escape, but I was terrified for what my boat crew was about to encounter if they were truly dead in the water.

A blazing stream of 30-millimeter tracer rounds poured over the canopy, and I could almost feel the heat from the flaming red phosphorous as they came. Forcing myself to ignore the ribbon of death snaking through the sky above my head, I pulled the airplane as hard as I could in an effort to get astern of the ship. In my desperation to escape the stream of fire, I overcorrected, and the thundering impact of countless 30-millimeter rounds tore through the nose of my Mustang. I closed my eyes, preparing to hit the ocean at three hundred miles per hour.

The sketch on Anya's insole suddenly filled my mind's eye. I could see it as plainly as if I were holding it in my hand. The narrow alley directly behind the *Leonov*, where both visibility and fan of fire were limited, glowed like the Saint Simons Island Lighthouse in my mind, and I stuck *Katerina's Heart* in the only spot in the sky where that airplane-eating Gatling gun couldn't pour any more rounds into her.

The tracer rounds continued to illuminate the sky, but they were winding their way harmlessly into the Atlantic, beyond our wingtips, and the Mustang was still flying. Black smoke poured from the engine, but it was still making power.

Oil pressure . . . good . . . for now.

Hydraulic pressure . . . good.

Fuel pressure . . . good.

We weren't dead yet, and neither was the P-51.

I keyed my mic. "Boat crew, boat crew, Sitrep!"

A panting voice filled my ear. "We're two miles west of the fight. All hands on deck."

Clinging to the tops of the waves, I turned for home at full speed and slowly raised the nose. "I'm going to trade some of this airspeed for altitude and get us high enough to get a parachute to open."

Clark sighed. "Sounds like a good idea to me."

"Uh, boat crew. How about trying to keep up with us? We're going to be that big shiny P-51 Mustang trailing black smoke. If you've got room for two more on board, we may need to hitch a ride if this doesn't go well."

"Roger," Singer said. "We'll do our best."

I laid my head back against the headrest and felt the sickening feeling of a failed mission boiling in my gut. "Why didn't we think about the anchor?" I said. "They'll sit right there until the support ship arrives, and all of this will have been for naught."

"You can't win 'em all, Chase. We did our best. Now let's just focus on getting this thing home."

I watched the needle of the oil pressure gauge slowly fall with every passing minute. Soon there'd be no oil left in the engine, and just like Dave Floyd warned, that quarter-million-dollar engine would eat itself alive. The coastline came into view, and thoughts of the landing gear replaced my oil pressure concerns.

"Hey, Clark. I'm gonna put the gear down out here in case we need to shake it around."

"I've got my fingers and everything else crossed," he said.

I lowered the landing gear lever, and the floor pan beneath my feet shuddered as the wheels came out of their wells, but the safe-gear indicator never illuminated. I pecked on the tiny bulb, beg-ging it to glow, but it offered no reassurances. "I felt them come out of the wells, but I can't get a good light up here."

"Do you know how to do a wheel landing?" he asked.

"Sure, if there's actually a pair of wheels under us."

"Walk it in nice and easy. Feel for the runway with the main landing gear, but keep enough airspeed to keep flying and keep that tailwheel airborne. If you feel the gear collapse, get us back in the air. We can step out and ditch her in the ocean or slide her in. That's another bridge we can burn when we get there."

I took a long, sour breath, letting the procedure play out in my head. "Hey, Skipper. You still with us?"

"Yeah, Chase. I'm still here."

"Get Cotton on the phone, will you?"

"I'm way ahead of you. He and Earl are at the airport now with binoculars in hand."

"Okay, we'll be there in two minutes."

I flew the approach right on the numbers as Dave Floyd had taught me, but sliding Dr. Richter's beloved Mustang down the runway on her belly was a sickening thought.

A glance at the oil pressure gauge told me the engine would run long enough to go around.

Skipper's voice rang in my ears. "Cotton says the main gear is down, but he can't tell if they're locked."

We crossed the airport fence at a hundred miles per hour, and I felt for the runway with the left main gear. I felt like I was descending into the pits of Hell as I waited to feel the wheel to kiss the concrete. With the right wing still slightly high, the left main touched down.

"I think it's solid."

Clark whispered, "Me, too."

I eased the stick to the right, lowering the other wing, hoping against hope the right main gear would hold. We were rapidly running out of runway when the right tire chirped against the concrete.

"Land the tail now. Nice and easy," Clark said.

I pulled the power off and let the tail wheel settle to the ground. We made the last taxiway before running out of concrete and limped the Mustang to the ramp where Cotton stood, hands on hips and fury on his face.

"I thought I told you not to bring this thing back all shot up, Lieutenant."

My feet hit the ground. "Well, Sergeant, I've never been good at following orders, especially from a crew chief."

Penny and Maebelle ran across the tarmac and leapt into our arms.

Back at Bonaventure, the Mark V motored up to the dock as we pulled into the drive, and we all instinctually made our way to the gazebo, where Singer wasted no time thanking God for bringing all of us home in one piece.

After a group "Amen," I opened my eyes. "Why didn't we think about the anchor?"

Hunter smiled like the cat who ate the canary. "Oh, I guess I forgot to mention that I blew the anchor chain, too. That's what I was waiting for at the bow when you almost made a strafing run on me."

* * *

Twenty-four hours later, the breaking news banner scrolling across the television caught my attention, and I turned up the volume.

"This is an ABC News Special Report: ABC News has learned the U.S. Navy, Coast Guard, and Border Patrol are on the scene of a bizarre event unfolding at this hour. Early reports seem to indicate a Russian intelligence-gathering ship has run aground off the coast of Georgia, in an area known as Blackwater Shoals. A Pentagon spokesperson has told ABC News that both military and civilian intelligence services have been closely monitoring the ship's activities for several weeks, and report that the ship's actions presented no threats to the U.S. Stay tuned to your local ABC affiliate. We will keep you updated as details of this bizarre story unfold."

Penny muted the television and let out a muffled laugh. "Thank God for those military and civilian intelligence services who've been 'closely monitoring.'"

Clark reminded us, "We don't do this to get our pictures on the evening news."

Anya pulled the plastic flag from her pocket and waved it just below her chin. "We do this because we are Americans."

Chapter 32
You're a Pig

Penny emerged from the bathroom five minutes after I laid my head on the pillow. Women, in general, and Penny, in particular, are far more intelligent than me. They listen, learn, and store information in ways my simple mind could never comprehend. All men have weaknesses—those particular things we simply can't resist—and women are masters of identifying and exploiting those weaknesses. Penny Fulton was no exception.

She sauntered across the bedroom in the dim light of a small lamp on her nightstand. Hanging loosely from her shoulders was one of my pressed white dress shirts. She wore nothing else and chose not to make use of any of the buttons.

Weakness identified. Weakness exploited.

I was mesmerized. "It doesn't matter what you want, the answer is yes."

She leaned down and whispered, "I want to make you forget everything outside this room."

And she did.

An hour later, we lay wrapped in each other's arms, watching the blades of the ceiling fan cast wispy shadows across the room.

"I'm proud of everything you do, Chase Fulton, even when you scare me to death."

I kissed her gently. "I'm a lucky man."

"No," she said. "It's not luck. You have the things and the people, especially me, in your life because of what you are"—she laid her hand gently on my chest—"inside here."

I smiled because I didn't know what else to do.

She touched my chin with her fingertips. "Those men, and that woman downstairs, would follow you to the ends of the Earth and beyond because they know you'd never ask anything of them that you wouldn't demand of yourself, twofold."

I kissed her fingertips. "Those men, and Skipper, are some of the most fearless and capable people on the planet."

She lowered her chin. "You know I wasn't talking about Skipper."

"Don't you think it's a little weird to be talking about Anya after, you know, what we just did?"

She ignored the question. "Is she part of the team now?"

I considered the question. "She wants us to believe she's on the good guys' team now."

Penny shook her head. "That's not what I meant."

"I know, but it's not as simple as you think."

"Then, make it simple."

"What do you mean?" I asked.

"It doesn't have to be complicated. If you trust her and need her skill set, lay out the ground rules and put her on the payroll. If you don't, then pack her up and send her to Athens."

I ran my fingers through her perfectly unruly hair. "What if it's something in between those two?"

She stared at the fan again. "In that case, lay out the ground rules, give her a sat-phone, and send her to Athens, pending recall upon the demands of the service."

"Upon the demands of the service . . . I like it. Did you come up with that all by yourself?"

"Mostly. So, is that the plan? Something between the two?"

"As far as I'm concerned, it is. She has some skills we don't have, so there may be a time in the future when she's the best operator for a particular mission."

"What skills?"

"She understands the Russian mindset better than any of us ever could. She's the deadliest person I've ever seen with a knife in her hand. She can walk into a bar, sit down beside a man, and make him do anything she wants without causing a scene or firing a shot. Mongo doesn't have that particular skill."

"Speaking of Mongo," she said. "Anya seems to have him eating out of her hand."

"I've noticed," I said. "I hope she's not—"

"I don't think she's playing him. Mongo's not like the rest of you pigs."

"Pigs? I'm not a pig."

She pulled away and propped up on her elbows. "Yes, you are, and I can prove it if you'll be honest."

"Okay, then. Prove it."

"I will, but you have to be completely honest. Promise?"

"Sure. I promise. Let's hear it."

She grinned. "Okay, but remember, you asked for this. Do you remember the first time you saw her up close?"

"Anya?"

"Yes, Anya. Do you remember?"

"Oh, boy," I said. "You're right. I'm a pig."

"Oh, no. You're not getting off that easy. Tell me about it."

"You don't really want to hear that story."

"Oh, yes, I really do."

I closed my eyes, and she poked my ribs with her index finger. "I didn't say picture it. I said tell me about it."

"I wasn't picturing it."

"Yes, you were, because you're a pig. So, let's have it."

"Okay, the first time I saw her was in Elmont, New York, at the Belmont Stakes horserace in nineteen ninety-seven. She was on top of a water tower about a half-mile away—"

Penny held up a finger. "Nope. Not that time. I mean the first time you saw her close up. Like closer than six feet."

"No! I surrender! I'm not telling you that story. I'm smart enough to know this is a trap, and I'm not walking into it. You made your point. I'm a pig."

My mind flashed back to the shallow water off the beach in Saint Thomas, where Anya had trapped me facedown in the sand by lassoing my arms, sitting on my back, and shoving my snorkel full of sand and salt water. In the life-changing minutes following my entrapment, I'd shot off her little toe and kissed her for the first time.

Penny ran her fingers through my hair and smiled that irresistible smile that always left me defenseless. "Okay, I'll let you off the hook, but I have another question. Were you there the first time Mongo saw Anya up close?"

I replayed the scene in my mind when we pulled off the one and only successful prison break from the Black Dolphin, Russia's most notorious high-security prison.

"Yes, I was there," I said.

She leaned in, allowing her lips to brush against my ear. "Now, think about the difference between how Mongo reacted to her and how you reacted during that first up-close encounter."

I stared into my wife's perfect eyes. "He treated her like an innocent child and literally tore the world apart to save her life, with utter disregard for his own safety."

"Would he have done the same if she looked like a troll?"

I sighed. "Yes, he would've done the same, regardless of how she looked."

She slid her finger down the slope of my nose. "Would your first up-close reaction to her have been the same if she looked like a troll?"

I looked away.

"See? That's exactly what I mean. Mongo's not like the rest of you pigs. Sure, Anya's beautiful. Nobody would disagree. But Mongo looks beyond the exterior because that's what he wants the world to do for him. Everybody who sees him sees a giant who could tear down a building with his bare hands, but that's not what he really is. That's what he is on the outside. Maybe for the first time in both of their lives, they've found somebody who knows exactly how it feels to be trapped inside a shell that isn't who and what they really are."

"That's pretty insightful for a North Texas girl."

"Hey, I'm a lot more than just a pretty—"

I pulled her against my body. "Do you remember *our* first close-up encounter?"

She giggled. "Yeah, I was a little bit of a pig that night, wasn't I?"

"You certainly were, Mrs. Fulton. You certainly were."

* * *

I awoke the following morning completely alone with the sun beaming through the window. Whether it was the night with Penny or the action of the previous few days, my body apparently needed to sleep.

Coffee was in the pot when I made my way down to the kitchen, so I poured my first cup of the day and headed for the gallery. The door, of course, was standing open, and I caught myself wondering if I'd continue that tradition when Clark and Maebelle were four hundred miles away in Miami.

I decided I probably would not, and I reached for the screen door as I heard voices floating in from outside. I'm not proud of the eavesdropper that screen door had turned me into, but I stopped in my tracks when Penny said, "Can you forget about him?"

The next voice I heard definitely didn't belong to anyone raised west of Stalingrad.

"I cannot. He is reason I am now American."

"Maybe I'm not asking the right question," Penny said. "What I mean is, can you forget about how you once felt about him and how he once felt about you?"

"*Zabyvat'* is Russian word meaning *do not remember*. I cannot do this. I will always remember about what you are saying, but *Chuvstvovat'* is word meaning to feel same. I think this is what you mean, no?"

Penny didn't answer. I imagined her sitting in the rocking chair, looking into Anya's face, and trying to imagine the mind of a woman who could compartmentalize emotion and affection, and perhaps even hatred.

"Is for you to love him and for him to give to you everything. This is what makes him happy, and I am nothing in that. So, yes to your question."

I listened as Penny drank a long sip of her coffee.

Anya cleared her throat. "I can say to you something that will sound odd, okay?"

Penny chuckled. "Sure, what is it?"

"You have smile like you know secret you will never tell. Is smile all women all over world would love to have. How do you do this?"

"If I didn't know better, I'd think that was a compliment, but do you really want to know why I smile like this?"

"I do, yes."

Penny said, "My smile is because I don't have to keep any secrets. I don't have to lie about anything. *That* is the secret."

I'd like to say I felt bad about listening to their conversation, but as Penny said, I'm a pig. I made enough noise to alert them to my presence before I strolled onto the gallery.

"Good morning. I didn't mean to interrupt. I'll just head on down to the gazebo and let you two continue whatever's happening here."

Penny stood and wrapped her arms around me. "Good morning, sleepyhead. You're not interrupting. Anya was just teaching me some new Russian vocabulary."

"Is that so?"

The two women shared a knowing smile, and Anya stood. "Yes, is so, and now I think is time for me to go to Athens where I can watch baseball match and have chili dog every day."

* * *

While Anya packed what few things she owned and said her goodbyes to the team, I drove to the airport.

Inside the hangar, *Katerina's Heart*, the perfectly restored P-51D Mustang Dr. Richter loved so much, lay in pieces on the concrete floor. Her massive Merlin engine rested in defeat on an oil-stained wooden pallet, and the blades of the propeller that had drawn me through the air of battle with such grace and power sat wrapped in plastic sheets and bound together like shackled prisoners awaiting their fate.

The cowling that had been the canvas on which Katerina Burinkova's timeless beauty was captured lay near the back wall. The nose art depicting Anya's mother and Dr. Richter's only love was riddled with thirty-millimeter bullet holes and blackened by fire and smoke. I'd ridden the old warhorse back into battle, and she'd faithfully carried me home, though she wore the gaping wounds of combat. Valiant to the end, the warrior she was born to be still breathed and lingered just beneath her tattered skin.

I slowly shook my head. "It breaks my heart to see her like this."

Cotton Jackson pulled a rag from the back pocket of his coveralls and rolled his hands through it as if nothing else would heal the Mustang's wounds. "Yep. Mine, too. I ain't got no idea how she got you home. By all rights, that motor should've seized up and left you up a creek. It ain't nothin' short of a miracle."

"Can you fix it?"

He kicked at an imaginary pebble on the polished floor. "With enough money and time, I can fix anything. And this ain't no exception."

I nodded, a lump forming in my throat. "Do it. Put it back exactly like it was. With one exception. . . ."

* * *

Back at Bonaventure, Penny was frantically pulling drawers open and riffling through every nook she could get her fingers into.

"What are you looking for?"

She huffed. "I had two sets of keys made for Dr. Richter's house, and now I can't find either one."

I pointed toward the library. "You put them in the bowl on the corner of the desk in there."

She brushed past me, kissing me on the cheek as she went. "What would I do without you?"

The keys jingled as she pulled them from the bowl. "Hey, what's in that package on the desk? It's addressed to me."

"I don't know what you're talking about." I stepped into the room where she was holding up a brown packet.

"Oh, that was on the front porch when I came in a couple days ago. It's probably some estate documents or something."

She settled into the chair, peeled back the manila flap, and pulled out a stack of neatly bound papers with a business card clipped to the upper left side.

With every line she read, her eyes grew wider, and her expression more animated.

"Chase, you're never going to believe what this is."

I walked behind the desk and read across her shoulder.

Dear Mrs. Fulton:

I hope this letter finds you well. Having made numerous failed attempts at convincing your husband to accept monetary payment for the brave rescue of my granddaughter, I wish to offer the services detailed in this document as a comparatively minuscule token of my and my family's immeasurable gratitude. Without the efforts of the astonishing men and women of Mr. Fulton's team, the situation would have, undoubtedly, reached an unimaginably horrifying conclusion, leaving our family broken and forever empty without little Melanie's beautiful laughter to fill our hearts.

In brief:

I wish to personally represent your interest as your lawful agent in the negotiation of a motion picture production contract with Greater Century Studios for your screenplay, Of Lesser Men.

My firm represents talent including, but not limited to, musicians, actors, writers, and other artists whose contracts totaled over one billion dollars last year. We are the largest talent agency in the Southeast, and the fourth largest in the country.

As long as I serve as president and chief executive officer of this agency, you will be represented by some of the finest agents the industry has to offer at absolutely no cost to you.

With deepest gratitude,
Graham Lightner, CEO
The Lightner Talent Agency, Inc.

In disbelief, she thumbed through the contract behind the cover letter and leapt to her feet. "This is amazing, Chase! I've got a real agent!"

I didn't understand why having an agent was such a big deal to Penny or what an agent was supposed to do, but seeing her bouncing up and down in hysterical euphoria was worth more to me than any check Graham Lightner could've written, regardless of the number of zeros at the end.

She waved the letter over her head and danced around the library like a crazed ballerina until Mongo stepped through the door and froze. The look of astonished disbelief on his face made Penny's exuberance even more entertaining.

He stared at me, wide-eyed. "Congratulations, I guess . . . for whatever you're celebrating."

"Thank you, Mongo!" Penny danced out the door and down the hallway, screaming for Maebelle as she went.

Mongo watched her go, then turned back to me. "What was that?"

I shrugged. "I'm not really sure, but when she's that happy, I'm not going to question it."

"Smart man, boss. Hey, listen. I need to talk with you about something."

I motioned for him to have a seat. "Sure. Is everything okay?"

He stared down at his boot, his expression making him appear small inside his massive shell. "Uh, I'm not sure how to say this or ask it or whatever, but. . . ." He paused and swallowed hard.

Part of me wanted to watch him squirm and wait for him to eke out his confession about Anya and request to help her move, but I couldn't put him through the agony.

I leaned forward and kicked the toe of his boot with mine. "I think it's a great idea, Mongo."

Epilogue

In the weeks and months following the mission that left the Russian spy ship, the *Viktor Leonov*, grounded on Blackwater Shoals, almost everything at Bonaventure Plantation changed.

After changing every ounce of fluid, every belt, and practically anything else that could be changed aboard *Aegis*, Earl went back to St. Augustine with a few thousand bucks in her pocket. Her parting words through the window of her dually as she drove out of the yard were, "If you go and get yourself killed doin' something stupid, I'll come find you in the afterlife and kick your ass every day for all eternity. You hear me, Stud Muffin?"

Singer, God love him, spent ninety percent of every penny I paid him doing what he called "feeding the hungry."

"Everybody's hungry for something, Chase. And it's our job, as men with food, to feed them."

He taught Boy Scouts to shoot everything from slingshots to shotguns, and he became the leader of the choir at the First Baptist Church only three weeks after joining the congregation. He even spent three days out of every month at the Mepkin Abbey Monastery in Moncks Corner, South Carolina, with the Catholic Trappist monks. It was never clear to me what a Southern Baptist sniper did in a monastery full of monks of the Order of Cistercians, but it made me think of Mark Twain's *A Connecticut Yan-*

kee in King Arthur's Court. He lived modestly in the small house that had been built as a stable keeper's cottage at Bonaventure.

Maebelle and Clark moved to Miami, where they leased seven thousand square feet on South Beach and opened el Juez, the restaurant *Gourmet Magazine* called "The hottest mix of Cuban, Southern, and world cuisine, where diners get to be the Judge."

Clark liked to believe he played some role in the success of el Juez, but in reality, the days he spent with his father, away from the restaurant, learning the business of running covert operatives like me, were the most stress-free days of Maebelle's life in Miami. Of course, Charlie, the black lab and Maebelle's chief taste tester, made the decision to become a resident of South Beach as well. As much as Penny loved Charlie, the bond Maebelle and he formed in the kitchen at Bonaventure was too strong to break.

Anya finally learned there was no such thing as a baseball match and started calling them *games.* Her season tickets to watch the Georgia Bulldogs play every home game at Foley Field cost me less than dinner at el Juez. Although I'm quite sure he figured out she's gorgeous by anyone's standard, Mongo kept looking beyond the surface and discovering that beauty is far more than just skin deep. Although my conversations with Anya were rare, I spoke with Mongo almost daily. He reported buying a box of twelve dozen miniature plastic American flags because his girlfriend refused to leave home without one in her pocket.

Stone W. Hunter officially resigned his position as a special agent with the Naval Criminal Investigative Service and came to work full-time, at least as far as the IRS was concerned, for Bonaventure Plantation. As a tactical operations partner, Clark Johnson is irreplaceable, but if I could've designed and built the man I'd want by my side when the bullets started flying, that man was Hunter. We pushed each other and ourselves harder than most men could tolerate. We ran, lifted, swam, shot, and trained as if every day would begin with a call to battle, because in our minds, that was the reality of every tomorrow we faced.

Cotton Jackson commuted from New Smyrna Beach to Saint Marys almost every weekend in his Lake Amphibian to restore *Katerina's Heart*, my P-51 Mustang, back to the flawless condition she'd been before the fateful day when she, along with two scared pilots and four brave operators in a Mark V fast patrol boat, changed history.

After months of painstaking labor and countless thousands of dollars, Cotton declared the Mustang ready for her first test flight. It would be a momentous occasion, so everyone showed up for the unveiling. Anya stood beside Mongo with the springtime sun dancing in her long, blonde hair. Clark traded in his University of Alabama cap and T-shirt for a white Cuban hat and linen sport coat. Maebelle, of course, made appetizers for the occasion. Singer brought a pair of monks with him, which was a little weird. Earl showed up in yoga pants and a tank top . . . God help us all. Skipper and her Coast Guard boyfriend, Tony, took turns trying to sneak a peek under the huge sheet draped over the Mustang.

Cotton sat cross-legged on the tug we used to pull the airplane in and out of the hangar. I'll never know for sure if the beginnings of tears in his eyes were the result of pride in what he'd accomplished, or concern that I'd be disappointed. Pride made sense. Concern was wasted.

I held Penny's hand as we stood side by side, just in front of the left wing, as Hunter pulled the sheet in a flourish, unveiling Cotton's masterpiece, the perfectly restored 1944 North American P-51D Mustang. The museum-quality nose art shined in the midday sun and revealed the heart-stopping beauty of not a dark-haired Russian KGB agent, but a wild-haired North Texas girl with the perfect smile beneath the script "Penny's Secret."

I'd known my beautiful wife for what felt like a lifetime, but that was the first time I'd ever seen her truly speechless.

We flew *Penny's Secret* gently and cautiously throughout the afternoon, taking every member of the team, and even the monks, aloft for rides they'd never forget. Maebelle, my only living blood relative, was last to climb into the cockpit behind me. She and I concluded our flight in a low, slow pass over Oak Grove Cemetery, in a reverent salute to Judge Bernard Henry Huntsinger.

Back on the ground, Cotton immediately went to work checking every inch of the airplane as the rest of us celebrated with champagne and Maebelle's goodies. For a few hours, we almost forgot that we weren't just like everybody else in the world, until my phone rang and I pressed it to my ear.

Conversations hushed, and every eye focused on me.

"Yes, of course, Mr. President. We can be ready in twelve hours."

Author's Note

As often as possible, I use actual places and events in my novels. Occasionally, it becomes necessary to apply creative license to enhance the excitement in my stories. In this novel, I chose to creatively enhance or create scenarios and locations to suit the demands of the novel. After all, I'm a novelist, and by definition, a professional liar.

Although the *Viktor Leonov* actually exists and is an active *Vishnya*-class signals intelligence-gathering ship of the Russian Navy assigned to the Northern Fleet, I have greatly exaggerated her capabilities in this novel. In late 2019, the *Viktor Leonov* was observed by the U.S. Coast Guard and other U.S. government agencies operating in the vicinity of coastal South Carolina and Georgia as described in this novel; however, to my knowledge, there is no reason to believe she or any other Russian vessel has ever been engaged in the activities I describe, nor does such technology as I describe exist, as far as I know. Although the weapons systems I describe are accurate, the capabilities, crew complement, and tactics of the *Viktor Leonov* in this novel are completely the product of my imagination. But just because I made it up doesn't mean the Russians won't try it someday.

To my knowledge, Blackwater Shoals does not exist in the area described in this novel. There is no record of the pirate Blackbeard ever running any ships aground or conducting any act of piracy in the area described. To my knowledge, no ship named *Marguerite de las Estrellas* ever existed or fell victim to Blackbeard, although it is possible. He was, after all, a pirate, and that would've been a great name for a Spanish treasure galleon in 1715.

The Mark V fast patrol boat exists and is in use by U.S. Special Warfare operatives. Many of the descriptions of the Mark V in this novel are mechanically accurate; however, I have greatly exaggerated her capabilities, performance characteristics, and survivability in the conditions described. But I still want one.

The North American P-51D Mustang described in this novel exists and can be found in private collections, museums, and in airworthy condition across the country. The descriptions of her weapons systems are mechanically accurate; however, to my knowledge, there are no Mustangs remaining in use today that have serviceable fifty-caliber machine guns installed. All of the aerial maneuvers described in this novel are possible in the Mustang with a competent pilot at the controls, but the application of the aircraft as described is entirely the product of my imagination, extremely unlikely, and a violation of numerous existing laws. But it sure sounds like fun.

The U.S.S. *Tennessee*, an Ohio-class ballistic missile nuclear submarine, exists and is currently in service with the U.S. Navy, although the descriptions of interior equipment, compartments, capabilities, tactics, and crew complement are entirely the product of my imagination. To my knowledge, no American submarine crew has ever been infiltrated by operatives of the Russian government. Although women now routinely serve aboard American submarines, I chose to create the fictional crew of the *Tennessee* as all-male for dramatic and comedic purpose. Just imagine the chaos Anya Burinkova could cause on a submarine full of military-age men.

Believe it or not, the U.S. Navy-working dolphins and sea lions described in this novel actually exist, although their names and ranks are entirely fictional. What kind of sick person would name a sea lion Flipper?

I sincerely hope you enjoyed *The Forgotten Chase* . . . even if I did make it all up.

About the Author

Cap Daniels

Cap Daniels is a former sailing charter captain, scuba and sailing instructor, pilot, Air Force combat veteran, and civil servant of the U.S. Department of Defense. Raised far from the ocean in rural East Tennessee, his early infatuation with salt water was sparked by the fascinating, and sometimes true, sea stories told by his father, a retired Navy Chief Petty Officer. Those stories of adventure on the high seas sent Cap in search of adventure of his own, which eventually landed him on Florida's Gulf Coast where he spends as much time as possible on, in, and under the waters of the Emerald Coast.

With a headful of larger-than-life characters and their thrilling exploits, Cap pours his love of adventure and passion for the ocean onto the pages of The Chase Fulton Novels series.

Visit www.CapDaniels.com to join the mailing list to receive newsletter and release updates.

Connect with Cap Daniels
Facebook: www.Facebook.com/WriterCapDaniels
Instagram: https://www.instagram.com/authorcapdaniels/
BookBub: https://www.bookbub.com/profile/cap-daniels

Made in the USA
Monee, IL
09 March 2024

54762567R00157